# BLACK DAYLIGHT

A JACK WIDOW THRILLER

SCOTT BLADE

Black Lion Media

Copyright © 2018.

Scott Blade.

A Black Lion Media Publication.

All Rights Reserved.

Available in eBook, paperback, and hardback.

Kindle ASIN: B07G9R3XPD

Paperback ISBN-13: 978-1-955924-31-3

Hardback ISBN-13: 978-1-955924-30-6

(Original KDP ISBN-13: 978-1790843169)

Visit the author's website: ScottBlade.com.

This book is copyrighted and registered with the US Copyright Office under the original ISBN. All *new* and *alternate* editions are protected under this copyright.

The *Jack Widow* book series and *Black Daylight* are works of fiction produced from the author's imagination. Names, characters, places, and incidents either are the product of the author's imagination and/or are taken with permission from the source and/or are used fictitiously, and any resemblance to actual persons, living or dead, or fictitious characters, business establishments, events, or locales is entirely coincidental.

This series is not associated with/or represents any part of any other book or series.

For more information on copyright and permissions, visit ScottBlade.com.

This book is licensed for your personal enjoyment only. This book may not be resold or given away to other people. If you would like to share this book with another person, please purchase an additional copy for each person you share it with. If you're reading this book and did not purchase it, or it was not purchased for your use only, then please return it and purchase your own copy. Thank you for respecting the hard work of this author.

The publisher and/or author do not control and do not assume any responsibility for author or third-party websites or their content.

No part of this book may be reproduced, scanned, or distributed in any printed or electronic form without express written permission from the publisher. The scanning, uploading, and distribution of this book via the internet or any other means without the permission of the publisher is illegal and punishable by law. Please do not take part in or encourage piracy of copyrighted materials in violation of the author's rights. Purchase only authorized editions.

Published by Black Lion Media.

## ALSO BY SCOTT BLADE

<u>The Jack Widow Series</u>
Gone Forever
Winter Territory
A Reason to Kill
Without Measure
Once Quiet
Name Not Given
The Midnight Caller
Fire Watch
The Last Rainmaker
The Devil's Stop
Black Daylight
The Standoff
Foreign and Domestic
Patriot Lies
The Double Man
Nothing Left

1

Killing a loved one in cold blood was harder than they thought. It wasn't like shooting a pedestrian in the street or killing a stranger, or a nobody, stealing his wallet and driving off, unnoticed, unidentified, anonymous, unscathed.

It isn't like murder, even though it is murder. Killing a loved one squeezes a little more out of the words' cold-blooded' than other kinds of murder.

They knew that because they had felt it.

Killing her shouldn't have been like killing a dog either. But that's how they went about it.

They put her down in the same way that a vet kills an animal, carelessly, compassionless, sterile. They murdered her with no regard for her relation to them, without empathy, without remorse.

It was still hard, though.

At first, it had been different. At first, they had two problems with killing the girl.

One, the act itself, the "killing" part, not the concept, but the "how to do it" part of the whole thing. And second, the "getting away with it" part, which was the most important part.

What was the point of premeditated murder if they couldn't get away with it?

Premeditated murder without the "getting away with it" part was like calling their drug dealer and not knowing what they wanted to order, a problem that they never had.

Their problem had always been paying for the drugs, not deciding what to get.

In the end, they strangled the girl and dumped out the body in what they considered being the middle of nowhere, which was also everything around them. They lived in the middle of nowhere. Compared to other states, theirs was mostly ignored, except for one busy attraction, Mount Rushmore, but not this time of year—too cold.

Strangled and dumped like a dog. That's how it would be seen on a police report if it ever got seen on a police report. That's how it would be reported in a newspaper if it ever saw a newspaper. But that's not exactly how it went down.

What a police report or the newspapers wouldn't say is how hard it was to do, how much strength it took.

Loved one or not. Killing someone is hard enough for most people, especially their first time, and this had been their first time.

Strangling a loved one to death happens in only two ways.

The first is a crime of passion. It's done in the heat of the moment, like an explosion of emotion and rage and indignation and hate and love, all at once, all straight from the gut, like a volcano erupting or an earthquake rattling the ground below. There's little warning if any, but the results are the same—deadly and messy and unstoppable.

Killing a loved one comes from a place of love. They knew that. One of them did, anyway. That was a big part of their rationalization for the whole thing, but it wasn't rationalization. It was twisted backward logic.

They loved her.

They were doing this for her, in a way. That was the twisted logic, they told themselves. And they believed it.

They brainwashed themselves into rationalizing it this way, like a man on death row, confessing his sins to the chaplain, thinking it would make a difference, hoping it would make a difference, but knowing in his gut that the end was the same.

Convincing themselves to follow through with it was as much an act of desperation as the killing itself.

There was another thing, another question, they asked themselves over and over. It was the question that started the whole thing.

What was the girl going to do with all that money, anyway?

She had a large sum of money coming to her. But why? Why should she get it and not them? What had she ever done to deserve it?

That amount of money was enough to set them up for a lifetime. At least, that's what they thought.

The money was better off with them, and she was better off dead. She had nothing to live for, after all. No husband. No kids. No prospects for a husband.

All she had in her life was them and a little dog, and some plans to get out of there, to move on to some place, maybe college, she had mentioned.

That was a joke.

What college would take her? She was a reformed meth-head from South Dakota. And she was barely reformed. She was more like one foot out of the grave.

No, that money was better off with them.

The money was the ultimate reason, the motive for killing her. Without it, they would've never come up with the whole scheme.

Still, they told themselves it wasn't just about the money. They told themselves it was out of love.

How could they kill a loved one without love?

That was what they asked among themselves.

The whole business was like how people talk themselves into committing suicide. It calls for backward and sideways logic.

Initially, a person jokes about suicide, maybe months before, maybe years before he or she actually goes through with it. Maybe it comes up on impulse, at first. Maybe they're stoned or drunk during the inception of suicidal thoughts.

Unlike most thoughts, this one doesn't leave them.

It lingers within them like a weed in the grass.

After mulling it over, eventually, the weed grows and grows until they've brainwashed themselves into thinking that suicide is a good idea until they convince themselves it's the only choice they have left.

It's the only way out.

With someone contemplating suicide, there comes a line that once crossed; there's no turning back.

Suicide is premeditated murder. It gets planned and thought of and rationalized, until that plan that thought that rationalization becomes reality, and then someone dies.

The loved ones also twisted that old saying: *There's a thin line between love and hate*, to help rationalize it.

A thin line between love and hate.

That's where her murder took place. Somewhere between love and hate. Somewhere on that thin line.

The loved ones didn't go about killing her in that first crime-of-passion way.

They didn't get the urge to kill in a fit of rage. It was no accident. No one lost control and did the deed that way.

They planned it.

They fed themselves the delusion that it was out of love for weeks leading up to the act, but they killed her for money—plain and simple.

What other reason did they need?

They planned the whole thing out, as best as two people like them could plan it out.

When it was finally time, it made total sense to them. The way the plan was laid out, they could get away with it.

Why not?

Who was going to catch them?

People got away with murder all the time. Every day. They saw the news. They saw the true crime shows on TV. They had social media, saw the retweeted and reposted news stories.

Plus, they had grown up here, a big state with lots of rural, rugged, mountainous areas and pockets. They heard the stories. People died all the time where they lived.

Part of the beauty of their plan was that no one else knew about the money.

It wasn't insurance money. She had no life insurance—no pending lawsuit that would award a large payout upon a final court decision.

There was no inheritance coming her way.

If she had ever been found, there was nothing to tie the murder to them. They had no visible motive. There was nothing to gain by killing her. Nothing that anyone could see. No cops. Certainly not the county sheriff's department. They had that part locked down.

There was nothing on paper.

The money was untraceable because it wasn't coming

from a legal source. Therefore, no one could track it. No one could find it. No one even knew about it, except the three of them, and one of them was about to die.

That was the beauty of it all. It was all secret: untraceable, secret money, a payment that only she was expecting for her efforts, a payment that they planned to kill her for.

Kill her and take the money. Easy-peasy.

Even though they planned it out, they had to be smart about it—no question. They had watched cop shows. They had watched the forensic shows. They knew that to get away with murder, you must get rid of the body. That part was crucial. It was imperative. The whole plan depended on it.

No body. No evidence. No crime.

That was the second mistake they made.

The first mistake they made was they thought they could kill her sober, without drugs. They thought that staying sober was key in order to make sure every little detail was accounted for, and all loose ends were tied off—the right way.

Once they did one hit, or one bump, or shot up, or popped a pill, eventually they'd lose their sobriety, lose their senses, and they couldn't let that happen. That's how mistakes get made. Everything would be reduced, and for murder, they figured it best to keep all brain functions working optimally.

But that was mistake number one.

They stayed sober all day long, waiting for when the completion of the money transaction came, waiting for the funds to be in hand, waiting for the moment to strike.

It started that morning for her, but for them, it had started the day before because they couldn't sleep the whole night long. They had too much anxiety; too much rode on getting everything just right.

The whole procedure was delicate after all, not the

murder, but the part before, the part that the buyers needed before they would even hand over the money.

The buyers were an X-factor that they did not expect, and they worried about it. Only the girl had spoken with them. They knew from the conversations with the girl that the buyers were serious, dangerous people. They were not the kind of people to be trifled with. When they first met the buyers, that assumption was proven correct.

The buyers turned out to be two guys. They claimed to represent the actual buyer, who they knew nothing about, and neither did the girl.

The buyers never revealed their names, at least not their real names. That's how it came off because the names they gave were generic—John Smith and Joe Smith.

The fake names might've been more believable if the men had been white or American, but they were neither. That was clear.

Neither of the men was American, not in the born and raised sense of things.

The two men were both dark-skinned and appeared Arabic, and they had accents, but not the Middle Eastern Arabic kind that they had seen in movies or on TV. These guys had accents closer to British than anything else, but they weren't from India. That was obvious.

They were from somewhere in the Middle East, maybe Saudi Arabia, one of the loved ones figured, with no real evidence or reasoning behind it. It just sounded right to them.

The buyers wore clean, pressed suits and ties. The suits were expensive, tailored pieces. They were customized to give enormous leeway so they could provide the wearer with room to move and fight.

The suits were tactical, like something James Bond might wear.

One suit was brown and the other straight black. Both ties were black. Both were clip-ons because the United States Secret Service agents only wore clip-ons. In close-quarters combat, the clip-on tie keeps the wearer from being choked with his own tie.

The buyers came off like soldiers because their behavior seemed bellicose and militaristic.

The buyers were armed. They had shoulder rigs under their coats, presumably with special forces grade firearms holstered in them.

After they met, the buyers, the loved ones, and the girl all waited in a ventilated, abandoned tire garage on the side of a road that was nothing more than a lonely turnoff from another lonely road that spider-webbed somewhere between the town of Deadwood and a sleepy town called Reznor.

They were closer to Deadwood than Reznor.

The buyers and the girl had scheduled the whole procedure to take place at this location. It was an agreed spot. It was abandoned, concealed from the main roads, and well ventilated. Plus, it had ample space for all the medical equipment that would be needed for a successful transaction.

The buyers were good at their jobs. Their entire organization was good at what they did. So, they did more of the suggesting of the location than the girl did, but they let her think she had input.

Unbeknownst to the girl and her killers, the buyers had scouted the location out beforehand.

Of course they had. They were professionals. They oversaw this kind of transaction all the time. At least once a week, they were on the road, somewhere in America, or Canada, and sometimes even Mexico, doing what they do.

Sometimes they oversaw transactions, and sometimes they dealt with problems—all part of the job description.

The buyers had mapped it, scouted it, and even timed the ambulance response. They'd arrived a day earlier and called nine-one-one to a similar distance from Deadwood and waited. When the paramedics arrived, they clocked the arrival time as seventeen minutes, give or take ten seconds. It was a good arrival time, considering that they were so far out from Deadwood.

Beyond Deadwood's city limits was nothing but empty roads, thick forests, and quiet people who liked to be left alone.

Once outside the city, the ambulance could pick up speed. They could probably drive close to triple digits on the speedometer gauge for several minutes before reaching a curve in the road or seeing another car.

After the procedure was over, the buyers were reluctant to hand over the money at first. They sensed that the loved ones weren't the most trusting people to chaperone the girl, who would need immediate medical attention.

Something didn't feel right to them, but she had come with them. She had picked them to be her guardians after the procedure was over. She had vouched for them. And she had lived up to her part of the deal. In this business, a deal was a deal. They got what they came for. Now it was time to pay up.

The buyers paid and left instructions to call nine-one-one ten minutes after they left.

They packed up all their equipment. Watched as the medical crew drove away, waited five more minutes till the coast was clear, and they were left alone with the girl, still unconscious from the sedatives, and her chaperones.

The doctor had left a bottle of painkillers for the girl. The loved ones were going to keep that for themselves, naturally.

The buyers and the chaperones shook hands. Deal done,

and the buyers handed over the money. They didn't wait for it to be counted, and then they drove off in a Chevy Impala, with the product they came for in hand, safely stored away in the proper container.

The buyers told the chaperones to wait ten more minutes and then call the emergency services. They explained the ambulance would come and they would take her to the hospital.

The buyers explained no one would get in trouble. The chaperones had broken no laws. It was the buyers who would get into trouble if caught. They were the ones breaking laws.

The buyers also made it clear what would happen to the chaperones if they snitched if the buyers were caught. They made a threat in a "keep quiet or else" kind of conversation.

The buyers weren't joking around either. They made that clear, too—no need to show off their sidearms. The whole spectacle—the shoulder rigs, the firearms, the expensive car, the tailored suits, the crew, and a large amount of untraceable cash—said it all.

The chaperones knew that. They could see it. It was obvious even to a couple of rural meth-heads like them.

After the coast was clear, the buyers were long gone, and before they killed her, they had to decide on how to do it. But first, they did what any junkie would do; they reveled in the money.

It came in a medium-sized black duffle bag. They opened it, stared at it, stayed quiet, and stared some more. They couldn't bring themselves to count it, but they touched it. They moved it around and studied the stacks of cash. It was all big bills, easy enough to transport and easy enough to spend.

After the reality of being a step away kicked in, they

turned back to what they had to do. The money wasn't quite theirs yet. They had to kill the girl.

They were still on the fence about how to go about it.

There were many ways to do it.

The best way would've been to just open her up from her stitches right there, and let her bleed out. No one would've pinned it on them.

But they couldn't do it that way. The trail might lead the cops to the buyers, and the buyers had already told them what that would mean for them.

Before they strangled her, they got nervous again. They got cold feet. They got the jitters—brought on by the act of killing someone and because they had both been sober for twenty-four hours, and that was twice longer than they were used to.

Like any junkie, they didn't make it to their goal of sobriety until after the deed was done. So they blazed up right there.

The meth they had wasn't particularly good. It was low quality, bottom-of-the-barrel type stuff, but it did the trick. They could buy better-quality meth later. With the money they just got paid, they could keep themselves in the good stuff for years.

The decision to strangle her came because they convinced themselves it was the hardest to track back to them.

First instinct was to shoot her. They had come armed. One of them had a gun. He always had a gun, but the deliberations changed their minds. They decided. No guns. No bullets. No knives. They talked themselves out of using weapons completely.

Weapons have handles and retain fingerprints and hair follicles and dirt and grime—too much forensic evidence.

They didn't want to get caught. Obviously.

What good was a bunch of money if you get caught?

Can't spend it in prison. Although, one of them commented they could get meth in prison, probably. They started a short argument over the idea, which caused them to blaze up one more time. It was more of the bad meth. This led to more of the deliberations until they came back full circle to the original method of murder that they had already vaguely planned on.

They had to strangle her. That was the right way to do it.

And it would be easy enough. She couldn't fight back. She was too doped up.

Truth be told, they all were at this point. But she was seriously doped up even though they had done meth twice.

The stuff she was on took the cake. It was all medical-grade, high-quality stuff.

The buyer's medical crew sedated her with serious medications.

They remembered hearing words like Prednisone and Fentanyl and Alfentanil and Meperidine. None of which they understood, but then they heard words like Oxycodone and Diamorphine, and they knew those.

They didn't know which was used.

They didn't know what any of them were. They weren't doctors. They weren't college-educated. They weren't even high school educated. Not really. Both of them had dropped out.

All they knew was that the meds she had in her bloodstream knocked her out cold, and she wasn't getting back up soon.

She wouldn't fight back.

After they decided on the method of death, they discussed disposal.

They could kill her and dump her on the side of the road.

One of them suggested that right off, but the other one rejected the idea. It was too easy for her to be found that way. There had to be more to it.

Some effort was needed.

The other one suggested they should do more to conceal the body, like bury it or stuff her with rocks and send her over the edge of a boat into a lake. Maybe they could incinerate her in a giant oven or a kiln like the ones used in morgues.

"Whatever that oven's called," one of them had said.

After a while, after all the deliberating, after it became apparent to both of them they were stalling, they came to an agreement.

It was time.

First thing was first. They had to kill her.

As their highs wore off, which was due more to the severity of the situation than the quality or quantity of the meth in their systems, they almost couldn't do it.

The physically stronger of the two of them hesitated. Then he chickened out. The smaller one couldn't do it either.

In the end, they opened the duffle bag and stare at the money again, like a motivator. They could still turn back. The girl would never know.

The smaller one opened the duffle bag. Inside, they both stared again at the stacks of hundred-dollar bills, bound tight with currency bands. It was all unmarked, and all theirs if they wanted it, if they did what had to be done.

Finally, the smaller one pushed harder at the stronger one.

"Okay. Now. It's time," the smaller one said.

The stronger one nodded, and he did the killing.

First, he opened the painkillers intended for the girl and popped a couple. He stuffed the rest in his coat pocket, safe for later.

He walked over to the girl, pulled her off a cheap

hospital bed the crew provided for her. She hit her head on the way down on the corner of the table. That had been an accident. Blood seeped out of a large cut. At first, they thought she might die from that. They hoped, but she didn't.

It wasn't deep enough. It was superficial, at worst.

The stronger one ignored the cut. No reason to patch her up, and he climbed on top of her, straddled her for a long moment. He held his hands up above her face. They shook and trembled violently for a long moment. His nerves rattled like jittering stones. He felt a pounding in his head that came on slowly, but far away at first, like a distant runner on pavement.

He closed his eyes tight and reached his hands out, gripped them around her throat, and strangled her.

She did not resist. She never woke up. He strangled her until he thought she was dead.

Once her body seemed to go lifeless, deliberations were pointless. Deciding to dump the body was easy. It didn't matter.

They had a good idea of where to take her, and it wasn't a lake or a grave.

The-Ninety has a three hundred and forty-mile stretch of road that passes through the state. This stretch of road was notorious for harboring dead bodies.

They had watched a special on it one night, back when they were only joking about the idea of murder.

The special aired on KOTA, the ABC affiliate out of Rapid City, but that's not where they saw it. They had originally watched it on the internet. It popped up when they were searching Google, trying to get ideas about where to dump the body. It appeared right there in front of them, like an answer to a prayer.

Four months ago, the KOTA news team did a piece on I-Ninety called "Death Road."

They watched the whole thing, one of the few times that either of them had ever watched a complete news story while sober.

The special shocked them. It was an amazing piece. Incredibly, over the last thirty years, more than two hundred dead bodies had been discovered there.

Although it turned out for some of them, there had been logical explanations: hikers frozen to death, or hikers eaten by bears, or hikers eaten by wolves, and so on.

Not all of them were so easily explained. Many of them had been murdered and dumped and stripped of clothes, which the loved ones figured was to get rid of trace evidence.

Some murders seemed to be connected, some by the nudity of the bodies. Some were found rolled up in rugs, some stuffed in trunks, and others wrapped up in plastic.

The news team tried to play it up like they had uncovered the dumping ground of an unknown serial killer, a mysterious killer out there somewhere. He was prowling hitchhikers, runaways, and nobodies. He raped the women, killed them, and dumped the bodies.

That was how the media had reported it, sensationalized it.

None of it was true, though. Many of the dead had been drug-related murders or thefts gone wrong or many other scenarios, and they weren't all women, either. They had found plenty of dead men. None of it was the work of a mysterious serial killer.

The truth didn't stop their imaginations from running wild over the story.

It led them to wild ideas. It led them to many possibilities about how to go about the girl's disposal.

That same night they watched the online news video, they smoked some heavy crystal, better than what they had now, and they sat back and talked about it.

One of them said, "You know if you wanted to hide a body, just do it off the Ninety."

The next one said, "You can even go farther and drive off one of the country roads. There are hundreds of dead ends out there. Lots of unknown dirt roads."

"Empty roads with nothing on them."

The smaller one took a deep puff from the meth, inhaled, and smiled.

"Nobody would ever find the body."

"Who would you kill?"

When the answer came, it shocked the stronger one. He played it off as a joke. And it was a joke, at first, but then they started talking about money.

How could they make a bunch of money? If there was money to be made, then it might not be a joke.

This conversation went on like this for weeks and weeks until the answer fell in their lap like it had been dropped there by the gods themselves.

The idea came from the most unlikely place.

The soon-to-be victim gave them the idea.

It turned out that she had also been thinking of ways to make fast money. The route that she had contemplated was drastic.

She had been thinking of a way to make a lot of money—fast and tax-free.

One of the loved ones asked her if she was going to sell her body.

She replied, "In a manner of speaking—yes. Yes, I am."

That was the end. The motive was there. Part of the plan was there.

All they had to do was wait until the transaction was complete, like spiders in a web.

That's what they did.

The wait had ended moments ago, after the strong one strangled the girl to death. Now, they were on to the next step—hiding the body.

# 2

The corridor of I-Ninety, running through western South Dakota and straight on through the state, had millions of nooks and crannies and overgrown brush and thickets and woods and ditches to spare.

That was why it had been called Death Road in the news report. That's what made it so attractive to killers.

All of which had to be considered with the forecasted long winter ahead and the dregs of massive snowbanks already out there canvassing the ground.

There was another factor to consider. There was what the locals called "white quicksand," which referred to snow that got packed down tight and settled down into a pit like a sand trap or a naturally formed deadfall.

The packed snow appeared to be stable ground. Passersby walked along and saw just another patch of snow—no big deal. But once stepped on, a person would sink into the quicksand, like a block of concrete tossed into an ocean.

Some of them got lucky. If not that deep, the bottom was only a few feet or inches below. Easy enough to climb out.

Others weren't so lucky. Others got sucked down into the ungodly, cadaverous place that lay beneath.

Some of these pits went deep, like subterranean holes burrowed underground by some undiscovered life form.

Some pits sank down so deep they caused the victims to get stuck and slowly freeze to death or starve to death or die from hypothermia or suffer all three until death finally arrived.

It was a horrible way to die.

The victim can't call for help because their lungs nearly freeze over. The voice box freezes up. The blood runs cold and slows down through the veins, nearly to a trickle.

The heart decelerates to a single drumbeat.

The white quicksand pits that were especially dangerous were the ones filled with ice-cold water at the bottom. In which case, the victim had all the same dangers to face, only with the bonus of drowning or freezing faster or dying from hyperthermia faster, whichever came first.

White quicksand wasn't a common occurrence, but it was common enough to become a local urban legend.

Everybody knew about it. But neither of the loved ones ever saw it happen. They didn't know anyone it had happened to.

They believed it to be true. Like most urban legends, true or not, most people bought into it.

The loved ones hoped they could find such a patch of white quicksand to hide her dead body in. Maybe confuse any police later about how she died.

That would make it so much easier. If they could find something like that and dump the body in it, then maybe she would sink to the bottom. They wouldn't have to worry about her being found for months, not until the snow thawed out in the spring. Or maybe they would get lucky, and she would never be found.

Either way, it didn't matter because, by spring, they could be long gone with the money.

How far could you go on a hundred and fifty thousand dollars?

Their answer to that question was pretty far. At least it'd be the hell away from where they had lived their whole lives.

Realistically, one of the loved ones knew that finding white quicksand probably wasn't likely because it hadn't started snowing as heavily as it would in the coming weeks.

This year had a slow-starting winter.

The loved ones did what they did to her.

They stripped away her clothes as they had seen done on TV and rolled her up in something that would help in transporting the dead body. It was nothing special, just a rug they found lying around, already rolled up in the garage's corner.

They had seen it done this way in the movies and on the news special. It worked there, so why not for them?

When she was finally dead and rolled up, they took one last hit of some crushed pills, a backup to the meth.

After, they worked together to haul her body into the back of the car. Luckily, she weighed little, and she was short. Even rolled up, she fit snugly into the trunk.

The rug made it a little harder, but they managed.

They had to let some of the rug stick up and out, but they had tied her down with rope they already had. She wasn't going anywhere.

Even near the town of Deadwood, no one would stop them. It was a quiet, snowy night, and they were going to get away with murder.

After about ten minutes of loading up the dead body and

tying her down, they cranked up the old car, let the engine run.

The other thing to deal with was her little dog. They didn't want it. So, they stopped and pick it up. It should be with her.

They waited another ten minutes till the fan was on full blast and blowing hot air instead of cold.

They waited till the inside of the car was warm and toasty. Then they set off to the destination that the man had picked.

They drove to the dumping ground.

# 3

Everyone gets scared. Everyone feels fear. Panic. Distress. Terror. Everyone on planet Earth. Except for newborn babies.

Maybe.

Who knows?

When a newborn comes out, terror may be the first thing it feels. It could be the original sensation of all sensations. It could be the first reaction ever made by every person, like God, saying, "Remember your place, little one."

Either way, everyone gets scared in his or her life—no escaping it.

It's possible for a man to go his whole life without feeling shame. Maybe.

It's possible to go a lifetime and never feel remorse or grief or guilt. Certainly.

But fear?

No way.

Some people grow up to be fearless. That's true, but they're only like that until they're not or they're dead, whichever comes first.

Jack Widow was no exception to the rule.

There are no exceptions to the rule.

Walking down a snowy, empty country road in the middle of the night, in the middle of nowhere, courtesy of South Dakota, an eerie atmosphere surrounded him.

A thick fog rolled across the ground and wisped up beyond eye level. It thinned out as it rose toward the sky, but it was still just as unnerving. It felt unnatural, like he was on the set of a horror movie. And the scene being filmed called for limitless fog from immense, heavy fog machines, hidden behind the trees so they would stay out of the camera's lens.

Widow plodded in the snow. Some serious stubble grew on his face. No beard, not yet. But that was the path he was headed down.

He smelled of gas and cigarettes. One because he rode into the great state of South Dakota in a car whose occupants were chain-smokers. And two, because the chain-smokers had abandoned him at a roadside gas station that reeked of gasoline as if the pumping trucks were right there still pumping the underground tanks full.

He had been standing around, waiting for ten long minutes. He knew that the chain-smokers weren't coming back for him. They had sent him inside to get supplies of bottled waters and coffee for the road on him since they were kind enough to give him the ride.

But standing there at the empty coffee line, deciding if this gas station coffee was worth it or not, he looked up and catch the chain-smokers backing up out of the parking spot, turning, and bolting out of the lot. He watched them turn onto the interstate and drive off east.

They had abandoned him—not the first time. And certainly not the last.

Widow didn't harp on it. Instead, he gave himself the

green light on the coffee, paid for it at the counter, where he made small talk with the clerk. He asked him about the area, about the nearest places, about what lay ahead on Highway Sixteen.

It turned out that nothing lay ahead on the old highway for thirty miles.

Along the north side of the highway, Widow had seen several turnoffs with no signs, no indications of where they went.

The clerk told him they all connected to Interstate Ninety.

That was why he took one of them. First, he camped out, waiting around on the highway, but he wasn't having much luck there.

So why not try one of the lonely roads? Take it up to the interstate, which surely would've been busier.

That's where he was now — walking one of those country roads with no visible name posted on a sign.

The road had been empty so far. It was devoid of life. No houses. No businesses. Nothing, but there were some power lines that led north.

That's what he followed. Powerlines have to lead somewhere.

Trillions of stars draped across a calm sky above him, as they did every night. The only obstruction was the thin veil of snow clouds rolling across the sky, slow and looming. They didn't block out the starlight; they just added a misty veil below them.

The moon was out, not full, but a half-moon. Still, it shone bright and illuminating like a dying sun billion of miles on the horizon.

The road under Jack Widow's worn boots was white, but the night was black. It was black behind him. It was black in front of him. Most of what he saw directly in his path was the endless, dull gloom and the snowfall.

Looking up, he saw treetops, exposed high, just peeking out from over the dispersed, low fog. The leaves on the trees were gone, replaced by hanging snow.

He walked on for around twenty minutes when he felt a change. It wasn't a fast, snap-of-the-fingers kind of change. It wasn't suddenly. It had been gradual. As he walked the road, it had happened to him.

The farther he walked on, the more the atmosphere turned to darkness that carried a sensation of evil, like taking a wrong turn, and the road becomes a dead end.

The atmosphere consumed him. It was hard to avoid it. Hard not to be affected by it. It was all around, like being trapped in a snow globe and knowing that something wasn't right.

Something was off.

It reminded him of a painting that he had seen once. It hung on the wall of an admiral's office, way back a lifetime ago.

He couldn't remember the admiral—not one detail. He must've been a forgettable CO, like a person he had passed on the street once. No reason to remember someone from so long ago.

The painting was famous. It was the one with the flat earth and the old colonial maritime explorer ship, sails fully extended, the wind blew hard, surrounded by rough seas, white swells crashed into the sides of the ship; but up ahead on its current course was a drop-off, like a cliff that fell into space.

It was the end of the world, literally.

The winds carried the ship straight off the earth's edge.

The ship sailed right to it. No stopping it at this point. No turning back.

The captain and the crew were utterly unaware of their pending doom. Completely unaware.

That's how the ocean is. When you're floating in it, waiting to be rescued, maybe you can see nothing ahead of you—no way to gauge what's over the next wave. You're just stuck there, bobbing up and down. Stuck at the mercy of the ocean, the mercy of nature.

You're helpless. All you can do is tread water and hope for the best. Or you can let the fear get to you. Wait and die—only two choices.

At that moment, Widow felt that way down, deep in the pit of his stomach. He wasn't sure why.

He should've turned back. He should've gone back the other way, but Widow hated turning back. What was behind him was behind him.

Fear wasn't a feeling he was used to, but that's how he felt. It came from his primal brain.

The human brain has fear receptors lodged way in the back, set there from another time, a prehistoric time. One aspect of the brain that was never touched by evolution was the fear of death.

Back during the Stone Age, the fear receptors fired off, alerting ancient man to be fearful of predators. It's the original survival instinct. Fear warns people of danger.

Stay cautious. Stay vigilant. Stay alive.

Unlike those of the sailors on the ship, Widow's fear receptors were firing as they should've been.

He stepped one foot in front of the other, down a snowy two-lane road, underneath snow-covered trees. They loomed over the road like giant gatekeepers who had once been intimidating but were now frozen and dormant and still and lifeless.

In the distance, above the tree line, Widow saw the cold shadows of jagged mountain peaks. He didn't know what range they were from. He knew he was somewhere in South Dakota's Black Hills, but exactly where?

He had no idea.

The trees and the mountains faded in and out of clear view through the snowy night mist.

The mist seemed to make everything around him just out of focus. Nothing was in perfect focus, nothing beyond a range of twenty yards in front of his face.

As he walked, he thought he was utterly alone, but he wasn't.

Widow walked to the top of a short hill when something happened that broke the stillness.

Hard to measure the distance away at first, but he guessed that about fifty yards up ahead, and down the hill, he heard a swift clang sound, like metal on metal.

It echoed and bounced off the trees.

A fast second later, whatever it was, clanged again, and then a third time. All three clangs echoed in and out of the treetops and through the mist.

Widow's brain registered the sound instantly. It was a common, everyday sound, manmade and known by everyone who wasn't raised by wolves.

The clanging sound was a trunk lid or a pickup's rear metal toolbox being slammed shut.

Widow stopped and stood frozen, and tried to keep quiet. He looked ahead so he could pinpoint the exact spot where the sound originated.

The trunk lid didn't clang again.

Instead, he heard a car door squeak open on rusty hinges;

then he heard another almost a second later. Two people. Following the car doors opening, he heard rusty old springs stretch. Finally, two car doors slammed shut.

Hoping to get a ride, he called out, "Hey! Wait!"

No one called back to him. He wasn't sure if they heard him or not. He tried again with more bass in his voice.

"Hey! Wait!"

No answer.

"Wait!" he called out again.

Widow paused, waited for a response, but there was nothing.

An ignition switch sparked to life, and a motor sputtered, followed by a heavy foot gassing the vehicle, hard at first.

Warming up the engine, Widow figured.

He didn't want to lose the ride, so he moved. He jogged down the hill, letting gravity and momentum push him. He jogged hard, carelessly, through the snow. He hoped he could catch them before they took off.

It was the middle of the night, middle of nowhere, and he was no one's ideal stranger to come upon under these conditions. But it was cold out, and getting a firm no from two people was better than not having the option of asking.

So, he hustled down the hill, trekking through the snow on the ground, kicking up the wetness. Before long, he saw the brake lights flash on. They flashed bright and vivid and red, which contrasted with the utter darkness that surrounded him. The beams were magnified through the mist, increased by the mist's potency, as if the brake lights went from zero to a hundred. They were so bright that the light blinded Widow for a brief second. It felt like a cop was shining a crimson Maglite in his face.

Next, the brake lights reverted to rear taillights, and an engine rumbled hard once more from a heavy foot. And he heard the winding of a drive belt, and the whirring of fan blades, and the sputter of tires in snow.

He called out once more, a shot in the dark, he knew, but worth the shot anyway.

"Hey! Wait!"

Then he stopped.

The cold wind slapped across his face. He watched for a long, long second as the taillights faded into the night vapor, into the blackness, into the trees.

Widow's shoulders slumped in minor defeat. He pushed forward and walked on, reaching behind where the lights had once been. The red beams had left spots in his vision, telling him the vehicle's last known position. He wasn't sure of the distance because of the fog, but once he got to the spot where the car had been parked, he knew it.

The spots faded away.

Widow stopped in the tire tracks left behind from the vehicle. He stood in them and trivially wondered why they were parked out there. Maybe a pair of teenagers messing around? Hanging out? Drinking beer or smoking pot? Or making out?

He sniffed the air, smelled no lingering smells like weed or booze. Marijuana would've definitely stuck around. Booze probably would still be present, but he smelled neither.

Ahead in the mist, Widow saw nothing but dense trees and snow and more mist.

He ambled up to the shoulder of the two-lane road and started walking, following the direction of the car, when he suddenly heard something. He waited, listened. He heard familiar sounds, living sounds—sounds that he knew he had heard before. These were the kinds of sounds that could only be made by a living, breathing thing, like exhales or grunts.

It was low at first, faint as if someone was muffled with a hand over their mouth, or a rag stuffed in it.

Widow turned and stared left, swiveling his head, scanning as best he could through the fog to pinpoint the sound. He stayed still and focused.

He heard it again and again, and then it stopped.

He recognized that there was another sound, drowned behind it in about the same direction out in front of him, which seemed down and to the west.

The new sound wasn't grunting or breathing or any audible noises made from a mouth, not like the first sound. It was different. It was something else, something that could be made by branches in the wind. He listened closer. He let the ambient sounds from the woods around him waft over his ears.

He listened and heard it again. It sounded like pawing or digging or the shuffling of dirt, like an animal. It must've been a woodland creature digging or pawing at something or trying to claw its way out of a trap.

Widow heard the first sound again. It sounded more like whimpering than before, which reinforced his theory of a woodland critter caught in a trap.

What could it be? Not a rabbit. They don't make sounds. Not that he had ever heard before. Maybe it was a mountain lion or a big cat.

Did South Dakota have mountain lions?

He wasn't sure.

There were mountains not close, but not too far. They were maybe a day's walk, maybe less.

*It could've been a wolf*, he thought.

Would a wolf be out there? Probably as likely as a mountain lion.

For a split second, Widow thought about moving on, but

then he heard the living sound again. It was definitely whimpering. Something was in distress. Something needed help.

Widow wasn't the kind of guy to let wrong things go. Never had been. He didn't take a pass on anyone or anything that was in distress. Widow didn't look the other way. He never entertained the thought of letting something go, or driving past a car accident, or doing nothing if he saw someone being picked on, or mugged, or harassed.

Never ever.

Widow was the type of man who stepped in. He stepped up. When others backed down, he stood his ground.

In the SEALs, even his teammates had referred to him as fearless, a big statement from the kind of guys he knew in uniform. But he wasn't fearless. It was quite the opposite.

Widow felt fear like everybody else, even more than others. But Widow's instinct wasn't to shy away from fear. If he felt fear, he ran toward it, not away. He had no choice. He had been raised by a single mother, a sheriff of a small town, and a former Marine at that. She didn't allow him to step down. She didn't allow him to give up. Ever. It wasn't an option.

Widow walked with confidence for the same reason. He stood with confidence for the same reason. No shred of cowardice existed in him—no shred of turning away. He was incapable of turning tail. He was incapable of backing down.

In the Navy, he had been trained hard. In BUD/S, he had been trained hard. In the SEALs, he had been trained hard.

If captured, if tortured, if facing the prospect of a bullet to the back of the head or a long, slow death, the only thing that Widow could do was give up name and rank. Nothing else.

Of course, he wasn't perfect. And all the Navy training, all the SEAL training, all the NCIS training came after he was a man. But there was one time in his life that he had failed. Only once in his life had he ever run away from a problem instead of facing it head-on.

That was roughly two decades in the past. It was when he ran away from home. In an argument with his sheriff-mother, he learned she had lied to him about his father.

He learned his father hadn't died in a war, as he had been told his whole life, as she had lied to him his whole life. He learned his father was some sort of Army hero who wandered through his small town in Mississippi.

The man had been a drifter—an Army vet out of the Army. Just some guy who came in impregnated his mother and washed out again like the rolling tide.

Where was he now?

Widow had no idea.

The guy was a drifter, a ghost in the wind which might explain Widow's drive to do the same. After Widow's mother was shot and murdered, he returned home for the first time in sixteen years. After he dealt with the people responsible, as he often did, he decided not to re-up with his NCIS unit. He moved on. Suddenly, like his unknown father, Widow knew he would be without destiny. He was fated to be without fate. He was a man who walked with chance and luck alone.

Widow stood tall and called out in case the whimpering was coming from somebody's lost pet or, if his worst fear was true, that it was whimpering coming from a human.

"Hello?" he called out.

No response.

"Anyone there?"

No answer.

"Hello?"

He heard nothing.

"Say something?"

And suddenly, the whimpering started up again. It wasn't far away. The sound was within a stone's throw.

Widow took a glance ahead at the road. He could keep going, but he didn't. Instead, he stepped off the road, four, five paces, and stopped at the edge of a ditch, barely stepping down into it and possibly falling over.

He looked down and saw the bottom. It was deep for a ditch. Maybe three or four feet. Hard to tell because it was full of snow.

Widow heard the whimpering again. It got louder, followed by the pawing, also getting louder, more pronounced.

He knelt closer to the edge of the ditch and took a better look at the bottom. The snow was wet. The mist rolled into the ditch like it was funneled through it. It looked like a stream of pure vapor.

Widow paused and listened.

The whimpering continued with the pawing in a steady stream of desperation.

The whimpering sounded almost human, full of sadness and emotion.

Widow dropped one foot down into the ditch. His boot sank down in the snow. It was cold and damp, not wet, like stepping into a hole filled with water, but he could tell his boots would be soggy from it, but not that bad.

He pulled his other foot in. The snow covered the tops of his boots, stopping at the hem of his jeans.

"Hello?" he called out again.

He was answered by more whimpering, more pawing, and the wind.

He stared along the ditch and walked, stomping his boots down with big, heavy steps so that the animal would know his presence in case it was something bigger than a bear cub.

Widow repeated the process for thirty feet more and stopped. He came to find a dog.

He was certain what it was from about ten feet away when he heard faint jingling coming from a license dangling from its collar.

"Hey there," he said.

He reached a friendly hand out so the dog could see that he meant no danger to it.

"Easy. Easy."

Widow stepped closer.

The dog didn't seem to mind. No barking. No growling. No signs of aggression toward Widow. The dog was friendly.

A quick peek at the license told Widow nothing, because there was no address on it. No name. No owner listed. It was just an imprint of a paw, like a cheap thing bought on the internet, a trinket.

The dog was not big but not small. He was somewhere between small and medium, maybe twenty-five or thirty pounds. He was a mutt. Widow didn't recognize the breed, but recognized shades of a couple of breeds.

The dog had floppy ears and an expressive face—big eyes.

He looked well-fed and cared for and loved. For being down in a ditch, in the snow, out in the middle of a country road, he was still clean. Widow figured he was an inside dog. That was about as obvious as the snow.

The thing didn't belong way out here.

Widow wondered if this was what the driver and passenger of the car had done that felt wrong. He wondered if they brought this poor animal all the way out here, and flung him out the car, and drove off as if to say "good riddance" to the animal.

The dog's coat was mostly black with random patches of

white. He had thick hair, not long, but not short. It was midrange length.

"Easy, boy," Widow said, not sure if he even was a boy.

The dog was frantic. He continued to whimper and paw at something in front of him. He didn't pay attention to Widow. He kept his back to him, pawing away. He continued to whimper. Nothing was going to deter him from whatever he was trying to get at.

Widow had served with the Navy for sixteen years, and much of those years were with the US Navy SEALs. So Widow knew exactly what relentless determination looked like. This dog was relentlessly determined. He would die before anyone could pull him off whatever he was getting at.

The first thought that came to Widow's head was that he was after a bone. Like that old saying, "a dog with a bone."

Widow came up behind him at slow speed because he still was having trouble seeing where he was stepping. As he got just behind the dog, he saw that the animal was pawing at a large, rolled-up rug. The dog pawed at it so hard it that if he had been a large wild cat or a bear, he'd be mauling it. There would be threads everywhere.

What made him so determined to get inside the rug?

Widow stepped up next to him, stopped, and knelt beside him. The dog was panting and wheezing. Suddenly the dog stopped pawing for a moment and stared up at Widow, desperation in his eyes.

"What's wrong, boy?"

Widow reached out and patted the dog's head and petted his fur. He was cold and damp. He sniffed Widow for a second, just a few snorts, and stopped as if his nose had downloaded all the information that he needed to determine if Widow was friend or foe. He must've determined friend or neutral because he didn't bark or fidget or scurry or make any other sign of aggression or fear toward Widow. The dog went straight back to mauling the rug.

Widow turned to the rug. He studied it. His eyes squinted and tried to focus in the dim starlight.

He realized the rug wasn't rolled up in a perfect cylindrical pipe shape. It was odd and angular and humped in strange, unnatural places.

It was rolled completely wrong.

The rug appeared to be Oriental or some kind of knockoff. It was rolled up tight and thick. The length of the roll was about six feet.

Widow stood back up and gazed over it. He paused, trying to see the whole thing, lengthwise.

Getting a bird' s-eye view of it, he knew why the dog was pawing at it so fiercely. For a split second, he felt stupid that he hadn't seen it before. At the very least, he thought his instincts would've set off the alarm bells in his head. But they hadn't.

He gasped at what he saw.

There was an odd shape in the rug, like the bulging from the recent dinner in the belly of a huge snake. But giant snakes don't just eat their dinner, not actually. They swallow their dinner. Often, they swallow their dinner while it's still alive.

The bulge in the rolled-up rug was human-shaped.

4

Snow fell all around Widow in an eerie calm as he stared at the horror in front of him and thought about the snake. The snow landed in his hair and on the stubble on his face that had slowly been growing into a beard over the course of the last five days. He hadn't shaved in that time—no desire to.

He had stayed on a horizontal line across a flattened map of the United States, traveling from west to east. The line had been straight across the northern middle of the country. He had gone from Portland to Idaho, where he spent two nights with a girl who claimed to be a schoolteacher. She was nice. He would've stayed longer, but one day she was headed off to class and took him for a coffee first with a quick breakfast at a quaint roadside diner.

After his third cup of coffee and before her second, but after they'd both finished their scrambled eggs and buttered toast, she laid it on him. The usual. She said she had a life there, and she was sure he had a way of life that didn't fit hers and so on and so forth—nothing that Widow hadn't heard before at this stage of life. Even before he started his path of wandering around with no particular destination in mind, he had encountered the same excuses all over the world from local women who wanted to pick up a sailor but wanted nothing serious.

He had no illusions about it. He held her or any of them no ill will. It is what it is. He smiled at her, let her give her speech without interruption. That was the best thing to do in that situation. An hour ago, he'd been in an embrace with a woman he hardly knew, having a good time, feeling the usual, instinctual feelings of intimacy. He asked himself the usual questions. Not voluntarily, but all involuntarily.

Does she want more with me than this? Is there a future here? Should I stick around and find a job?

Widow's mind posed these questions to him. It didn't mean that he wanted those things, but it didn't mean that he didn't want them either. Maybe sticking around wasn't so bad —for the right woman.

The school teacher looked at a Mickey Mouse watch she wore on her wrist. It had a brown leather band that appeared worn, as if she had the watch since childhood.

She looked back at him and told him she had to go. School started in a half hour. He nodded, thanked her, and said goodbye.

No big deal.

Widow stuck around for another hour after she had gone. Then he left and went on his way east, stopping again here and there.

Now, he stood over what looked like a disposed of, dead body rolled up tight in a rug out in the middle of nowhere, South Dakota, and he had witnessed the disposers just taking off. He wasn't sure if they had seen him in the rearview or not. He doubted it because of the low visibility in the mist and snow, but maybe the car he had seen was equipped with rear-facing cameras. Perhaps they had night-vision capabilities.

Was that an option on today's cars? He didn't know. Maybe. Anything was possible.

Widow licked his lips. Another involuntary action. He tasted slivers of icy snow.

In the foreground, ahead of him, an owl hooted from high in a tree. The hoots continued randomly with no discernable pattern.

The wind blew and chilled his hands, which were now out of his pockets. He reached down and poked at the rug with medium pressure—no response. He switched to quick, hard jabs, hard like punches, more like swift prods. He used enough force and pressure to wake up a sleeping Marine. Experience told him that was the way to do it.

No response.

Widow moved up the length of the rug bulge to where the midsection of a human rolled up in a rug would be. He pounded with one heavy fist like a judge's gavel in a court that was out of order.

Once. Twice. Three times. Nothing happened. No movement. No response.

Widow called out at the same time.

"Hello?"

No answer.

"Hello?"

No response.

"Hello?"

Again, no reaction.

"Hey?"

No result. Nothing.

Widow stopped pounding and scrambled to one end of the rug and reached in through the circular opening at the end. He felt around. Loose threads brushed his fingers. He strained to reach in until he found something that he knew.

He continued to feel around, pinching it, poking it until he realized it was the tip of something.

It was cold and soft like soft paper. He pinched it again. There was something smooth and hard on it, like the glass screen on a phone.

Widow moved his hand farther to the other side. He felt around until he found something else. His fingers swiped across a texture that he knew well. Everyone does. It was something that he had felt recently, on a woman back in California. That was the last time he had felt it.

It felt smooth and bony and cold. It was the skin on the heel of a foot. The smooth, harder surface that he had felt was a toenail.

He jumped back and pressed his hand on the rolled-up rug. Quickly, he hoisted himself back on his feet.

He called out again, instinctively, like a cop who was first to arrive on the scene of a car wreck, the driver an unconscious woman stuck inside.

"Ma'am?"

No answer.

Widow scrambled back around the sniveling dog until he reached the opposite end of the rug, where the woman's head should be. He dropped to his knees, let them crash into the snow and the dampness and the fog. This time he found the wet bottom of the ditch. Wetness slogged through the denim of his jeans. His knees were hit with wet coldness. Shivers shot up his legs and spine.

"Ma'am?"

He poked at the end of the rug.

No answer.

He reached in with one hand and felt around, traced the threads and texture with his fingers. The threading was coarse and tightly knit, at first, until he found thinner, looser threads.

After a few seconds of tracing his fingers through them, Widow realized it wasn't threads from the rug.

It was human hair. It was long and soft and felt as though it had product in it, some kind of hairspray or gel. It was a woman's hair; he figured.

Carefully, he ran his fingers through the strands of human hair until he found the woman's head. He looked for warmth, body heat, to see if she was still there—still alive. But his fingers were cold. He thought maybe he felt something, but he couldn't be sure.

The hair was long, curly, and damp, almost wet. It was wetter than the snow in the ditch. The wetness was thicker than water, more sticky.

It was blood. He knew it. Being a former NCIS agent, he had investigated plenty of murders. That was how most investigations started. He had been introduced to a dead body, usually a fellow sailor or a Marine or sometimes a civilian. Then he had been briefed on the investigation, the mission. He had been given his orders. And he had been sent in undercover to investigate.

Widow found the woman's head and palmed it for a moment. He called out to her.

"Ma'am?"

No response.

He sent his fingers down to her mouth and nose. He let them sit there for a long second, trying to feel her breath as if he was gauging wind speed.

Widow paused and waited.

Nothing.

He pushed and tried to get down to her neck so he could feel for a pulse, but he couldn't force his hand down that far. The rug was wrapped too tightly.

Widow kept that hand where it was. Using the other, he

felt around the top of the rug, searching for her outline, searching for the lip of the rug so he could try to loosen it. He patted the sides. He patted the top.

After several attempts, he finally found it.

On the very end toward him, about a foot down, the rug was rolled up and sealed with duct tape.

He was about to peel the tape away when he felt something with the hand inside the rug's opening. On the palm of his hand, over the woman's mouth, he felt a wisp of air. It was faint and frail and ephemeral. But it was there.

"Hold on!" he shouted.

Widow pulled his hand out fast and felt around in the dark for as much of the duct tape as he could find. Once he got both hands on it, he started ripping and tearing and shredding. Violently, he ripped, jerking his arms back and forth like he was jerking the chain on a lawnmower in a competition to see who could start his mower the fastest.

Stunned, the dog jumped back and then retreated for a few seconds. Then it moved alongside the rug and got next to Widow. It joined him. It pawed and ripped simultaneously as if it knew what he was doing, as if it sensed that he was there to help.

Widow cleaved and pulled and tore through the duct tape as if his own life depended on it.

The duct tape was already dense, but it was layered as if someone had used half a roll, which he could only guess meant that the other half had been used on the other end.

"Hold on!" he called out to the woman inside the rug.

He continued to tear globs of duct tape off the rug. It unraveled and tore and came off one strand at a time.

He heard a mumble from inside the rug. It was the woman breathing.

Widow felt a surge of energy from hearing that sign of life. He tore and ripped faster. The duct tape came off in big globs. The tape had been wrapped around tightly and unplanned, as if it had been a last-minute thought or done in a hurry.

"Almost got it!" he said.

Ten more seconds went by. He felt light snow drift onto his lips and nose and forehead.

"Hang on," he told her.

After a long, arduous effort, the last shred of duct tape ripped into pieces, and he stopped.

His arms burned from the exertion and the speed. There was no time to rest.

Widow pulled and unfurled the top of the rug until he could lift the woman's head up and out. It felt like an eternity before he got results. Even without the duct tape, the rug was still thick and heavy.

He shifted the weight and grabbed the woman's head and shoulders, and slid her head up and out. He stopped pulling and reversed course and peeled the rug down instead and finally got it all down to her shoulders.

The woman in the rug was topless. Her breasts came out and were bare in night and mist.

Widow turned and gently twisted her to pull her head up to an angle comfortable for her.

He plopped himself back down on the heels of his boots, getting as comfortable as he could. Then he rested her head down on his lap and caressed her hair like a parent comforting a dying child.

He touched her face, caressing in both hands. His hands were cold, but probably felt like warm oven mitts on her freezing cheeks.

Carefully, slowly, he turned her head from side to side,

looking for wounds, making sure that her neck had not been broken or sprained. It seemed okay so far.

Widow sped up the twisting of her head, slightly. He tried shaking her face as well. He was trying to get a cough or a gasp or any sign of consciousness out of her.

Nothing happened. Nothing from the woman, anyway, but the dog did something.

At first, he stood behind Widow, staring over his forearm, but then he saw Widow shaking her face, and he scooted closer, got up on his hind legs, and pawed at Widow's forearm.

Widow stopped and looked at him.

The dog scooted in closer, ears down, as if he wasn't fully trusting of Widow. He climbed over the top of Widow's arm and licked the woman's face. It was out of recognition and concern and love.

He was her dog.

Widow needed to get the woman completely free. He needed to unravel her legs and the rest of her body, but he didn't want to set her head down on the snow. The last thing he wanted to do was have her drown or catch cold while he got busy trying to free her feet and the rest of her.

Plus, it's better to keep a person's head up when unconscious.

So, he reached up fast and took off his coat. He balled it up and lifted her head and set it down gently on the balled-up jacket.

The chill South Dakota air struck him hard. It blasted him with quick, short gusts of snowy wind.

After the woman's head was safe, Widow moved down and out of the way. He reached his hand in and touched her neck, two fingers, and pressed down. He waited a beat, counting to himself, and registered her pulse. It was there, but it was weak, not as weak as her breathing, but not far off.

She was fading away. She was dying.

In the low moonlight, Widow could see what he thought was killing her. She had a vicious wound on the top left side of her head, just above her ear. She had been hit hard with something blunt, or she had hit something in a fall.

Blood was caked and wet and matted in her hair.

Widow squinted to see the rest of her body that was exposed. He searched for any other signs of injury or struggle. Not looking for forensic evidence, but searching for any visible reasons he shouldn't lift her or move her.

He didn't get past her neck and collarbone when he found that the head wound might not have been what had almost killed her.

She had been strangled, not to death, but nearly. There were bruises on her neck, big ones, brutal-looking. They were thin across the throat and the center of the neck, but thick on the sides, like the palms of two meaty hands.

His guess was she had been ambushed. Probably attacked with a baseball bat or some other blunt object, or she had been pushed down hard and hit her head. He was going with the blunt object theory just because that was a more effective way to knock someone out, especially if her attacker planned to strangle her.

Hit once, from the looks of it. Then her attacker strangled her two-handed while she lay on the ground, unconscious.

Widow traced the bruises with his eyes, down her collarbone, then over her chest.

The bruises were purple and dark across her chest and on her breasts. The top of her abdomen, just under her solar plexus, followed suit with more purple and dark bruising.

Widow studied the bruises for a moment. The best he could figure was they were made by a pair of knees.

Her attacker had hit her with a bat and then hopped on top of her, straddled her. He used his weight to pin her to the ground while he strangled her. Not that it would've been necessary. Widow saw patterns of effectiveness, and patterns of downright amateurs. Like the attacker knew what he was doing, but had killed no one before. Or maybe he was stoned out of his mind.

Why didn't he kill her?

That was all he could see of her body. The rest of her stomach and the lower half were still wrapped up in the rug.

Widow hopped up to his feet and scrambled down the rest of her and stopped at the bottom of the rug where her feet should've been.

He took one quick glance back up to her head.

The dog stayed where he was. He continued to lick the woman's face and neck. He stopped every few seconds and pawed at her shoulder lightly with one paw.

As the dog moved, this was the first time that Widow noticed another sound coming from him. It was a tag clinking back and forth on the dog's collar.

Widow dumped his knees down in the snow again and ripped and clawed and pulled at the duct tape securing her feet just as he had before, only this time he had a better idea of where the seams were.

It took him about five minutes to get it all loose. That end had been pulled tighter than the top, as if her attacker had started at the top, where he was sloppy, and then gotten better once he got to her feet. Maybe he found his rhythm by the time he could no longer see her face. That was plausible.

In Widow's experience, most killers were sloppy. Most were first-timers. By definition, first-timers are virgins. And like all virgins, they're inexperienced and scared and nervous and in a rush.

This guy got a little more confident after he got the head wrapped, Widow guessed.

Widow continued to rip and shred and pull at the duct tape until he finally unraveled her lower half. Then he jerked the rug back and down and got her completely free of it.

He stopped, looked up, and stared.

The girl in the rug was young, not a kid, but a young woman, somewhere in her mid to late twenties.

She was white and pale, as if she hadn't seen the sunlight in six months. Which was probably a combination of living in South Dakota and being at death's door because her skin was more than just pale; it was turning Maya or light blue.

She was completely naked without the rug.

Widow looked her up and down, searching for more injuries. He could see that she was so close to death that her skin and knees and body parts didn't shiver in the cold temperature like they should have—not one bit.

Her body lacked the natural capacity to care anymore to keep her warm. It must've been burning up all the resources it had left just to keep her breathing.

Widow took a quick glance over her body once more, in case there was evidence that he might need to see. It was automatic. He hadn't meant to look her over again. He just wanted to make sure that there was nothing else—nothing that might be helpful for the police to catch whoever did this to her.

He couldn't prove it, but he would've bet money that she had been raped. She had wounds and bruises that coincided with those on the rape victims that he had seen before.

Plus, why else would her attacker attack her and pin her down and nearly strangle her to death?

One quick theory that automatically went through

Widow's brain was that, probably, the attacker hadn't intended to kill her. He probably attacked her with the bat. It put her down but didn't knock her out like the guy saw in the movies. So, with no other option, he strangled her until she passed out. Then he raped her.

That seemed to make complete sense to Widow.

Why the guy wrapped her up like this and discarded her way out here, still alive, made little sense. The best Widow could figure was after the deed was done. The guy just figured she was so close to death that she'd probably just die on her own, which she would have if Widow hadn't come along.

Still, the whole thing was mostly sloppy.

Just then, clouds shifted overhead, and the snowfall thinned, all of it like it was smoothly coordinated by the weather, and the night became a little brighter.

Widow could see a little better in the dark now. And he saw something that he hadn't noticed before.

Down along the woman's navel and waistline was a double layer of field dressing or hospital dressing, maybe. It was the color of flesh, which was why he hadn't noticed it before.

It was wrapped tightly around her stomach. He squinted in the dim light and saw dark bloodstains on the right side of her abdomen. The stains were fairly recent. The blood had kept some color, and there was no smell.

The dressing had been administered within twenty-four hours.

Widow stared at it. He didn't know what to make of it.

Why would her attacker wrap her up in bandages and then rape her or try to kill her?

It made little sense.

He reached down and brushed across the bandage with

his fingertips. He refrained from applying any pressure. He didn't want to hurt her.

Tracing along the bandages, he guesstimated where a wound might be. After several slow attempts to find a sign of anything, he found it.

The right side of her stomach, inches southwest of her navel. He found a straight, diagonal line of medical staples. Gently, he traced his fingers over them, followed them all the way up and all the way down.

It was a closed incision. Someone had performed surgery on her recently.

The incision was professionally done. The staples were spaced out correctly, and the design of the scar would be straight.

This had been done by a professional surgeon.

Now Widow was confused because if she had major surgery recently, she would've been in a hospital bed, which meant that her attacker had abducted her from a hospital.

That would be hard to do. Not impossible. But hard.

If her attacker had done this to her, why? What was the purpose of opening her up? Why close her back up again if he was just going to kill her?

If she had been abducted before the surgery and the staples, why place the staples completely straight, wrap her up with so much care and then hit her with a bat and attempt to strangle her?

Why dump her way out here? Why the rug?

He didn't get it.

5

There was no time to dwell on the *why*. So Widow took off his Henley and draped it over the young woman to cover up as much of her naked, pale body as he could. He did so while averting his eyes to the shadows around her curves, trying to avoid seeing more than was gentlemanly or more than was necessary.

He had to look in order to find any wounds that needed his attention or evidence that might help the cops pinpoint who might've been responsible for this. But that was all.

Luckily, Widow was a tall man, six feet four inches from the bottom of his bare heels to the hairs on his head. And he had been born with long baby gorilla arms that grew into long adult gorilla arms, a fact that didn't always make him the most aesthetically pleasing man in the world but came in handy right then because it gave his Henley more fabric to cover up the woman.

The long-sleeved pullover swallowed her up like she was wearing a casual dress that was two sizes too big for her.

After Widow wrapped her up in the pullover, he doubled

her warmth and coverage with his peacoat and a warm winter beanie, both black. He'd purchased them before heading through Wyoming from an outlet mall that was going out of business.

They were both fashionable, pricey—normally. But because of the poor economy in the local region of Wyoming that he was in, an outlet mall was a thing of luxury. The local population couldn't support it. The mall closing was bad for the workers, bad for the companies, but good for a passerby on the cheap, good for the woman he'd found nearly dead.

The cold temperature might've helped to preserve her life at first, but now it was slowing her heartbeat and slowing her breathing and slowing her vital organs and functions.

Once she was wrapped up as tight as she could be wrapped up—and after Widow was out of clothes to spare, his jeans and boots wouldn't help her—he lifted her up and held her close to him like a groom and bride, or a monster and his victim, depending on a person's point of view.

Widow lifted her and carried her up and out of the ditch. They went back down the path he had come and onto the quiet, wintry road.

Her head kept falling back, hanging off his arm.

With a quick elbow up, he boosted her head back up and into a more comfortable position. He had to repeat this process often.

Before they left the scene behind completely, Widow turned and looked one last time. He stared at all of it, the rug, the ditch, the tire tracks left by the car, and the dog. He found not one stitch of her clothing or a wallet or purse or anything.

He saw no indication of the other one. Maybe it was there in the dark. Maybe not.

At the icy road, Widow didn't stop or pause or hesitate or

dawdle around. No time to waste. He set one foot in front of the other and headed toward the taillights, because one thing he hated was turning back.

6

The snow gusted in squally and patchy patterns but was still soft and almost quietening. The ground was cold and wet and slick in places, but the road was basically straight after the thirty-minute mark.

Widow calculated that the last stretch of it had led him uphill and up in elevation, which was a godsend in a small way because the farther he hiked and scrambled up in elevation, the more that the wind forced the snowfall to pile up into the ditch. It made his feet close to the pavement beneath the snow for a time until finally he could feel it.

The ditch turned out to be useful because after it wound around for a period; it looped back closer until it ran parallel to the road, allowing Widow to maintain a better sense of direction. When in doubt, he followed the ditch.

The ditch wasn't the only thing that helped guide the way ahead. Widow also had the tire tracks left by the car with the squeaky doors and trunk lid. He walked in the tracks for a long time. He traced them until the snow had melted down or been blown away, not leaving enough for the tracks to stay visible in the dark.

Eventually, the tire tracks from the car with the timeworn squeaks blended in with tracks from other vehicles. He had seen no other vehicles, but maybe he had passed merging roads that were entirely undetectable for him in the dark and the gloom.

Despite the dark and fog and cold, Widow carried her, shirtless and for a long time. And then he carried her longer.

At first, he tried to count the seconds and minutes in his head, but after he got to seventy minutes, he stopped counting—no point. It was a nice way to distract him from how the peaceful cold weather had turned freezing and harsh and dangerous, and not because the temperatures had dropped anymore. It was only because he was bare-skinned and vulnerable to the elements.

Counting the seconds and the minutes worked to keep his mind focused on the one simple task of moving on, but when he hit the hour mark, it turned deadly for him to continue. He realized that at minute six-one because the unknowing of how much farther, how much longer he could go, turned against him. It sucked the motivation from him, and Widow wasn't the kind of man who gave up.

So he regrouped. Re-threaded. Re-strategized in his head about how to proceed. And his brain had shut down the timer.

The nerve endings in Widow's skin tingled, and his teeth rattled, and his cheeks chilled, and his arms hurt, and his legs ached.

But he never stopped to put her down, not once.

The only thing he did was pause periodically to check and see if she was still breathing.

He watched each time until he saw little plumes of chilled breath puff out from her open mouth.

Once he stopped and touched her face, running his hand over it to feel her skin and feel her breath.

Her nose was wet. Her skin was icy. Her cheeks were cold. Her ears were stony.

To counter the cold, he rubbed one hand across her face in big, fast motions like he was warming up his own hands over a fire. Then he leaned her face back into him and continued on.

He felt her breathing on him. It chilled his chest, but he was grateful for it.

The girl's left hand and arm folded over her breasts. Her right arm hung freely out in front of him. It swung from side to side as he marched up the road.

Her knees were slung over his other forearm. Her feet and legs hung out of the peacoat and Henley and swayed back and forth, loose like wind chimes on a still day.

Widow stopped once because he was worried about her feet getting frostbite. So, he set her down gently and pulled his boots off, took off his socks, and slid them over her feet. He pulled the ends up all the way to her knees. He rolled them tight at the top to keep them from falling off.

He put his boots back on and lifted her up, and continued on.

Occasionally, Widow braced her body up, using his elbow and his upper body strength, one-handed, so he could reach down with his other hand and rub her feet and toes over his socks. He did this to keep her feet from getting anywhere close to frostbite, which was a concern because the gusts of wind and the prolonged exposure to the cold made it a possibility.

In the US Navy, Widow had been trained to hump heavy gear uphill, downhill, over hills, across vast deserts, up mountains, and through heavy snow—all of it heavy gear—all of it vital.

The SEAL instructors hammered him always to consider

every piece of gear to be lifesaving, to be absolutely necessary. Without the gear, he was to consider the mission a failure.

If he dropped or abandoned any shred of gear, even as small as a toothbrush, from his rucksack, then the instructors considered it mission failure, and his life was forfeited.

Everything they gave him counted.

Never leave a man behind went farther for SEALs than for any other military unit that he knew of. In his experience, it was: *never leave a man behind or his toothbrush.*

Widow learned many tools of the warfare trade in the SEALs. He learned to hold his breath for long periods of time. He learned to free dive to great depths — no oxygen tank. No fins. No divers down there at the ready to save his life should he fail—no second chances.

As soon as the Navy saw he could accomplish a deep free dive, they made it worse. They added things. First, they added a weight belt, loaded with lead plates, making it hard for him to swim up, and easy for him to sink.

Over time, they added another belt, and then they added weighted gauntlets and more weighted ankle bracelets.

Finally, Widow could swim with all that weight and to a great depth. Then they doubled it all.

Widow learned to free dive while hauling heavy equipment down to the bottom of deep training-pools and then back up. And over again. And over again.

Once he perfected that, they moved him to ocean water.

Out of all that training that he had endured, none of it helped him as much as one external factor right there at that moment.

The one external thing that helped him the most, carrying the girl to safety, was that little dog.

The whole time Widow carried the girl, that dog was right

there, alongside them, the whole way. He never stopped unless Widow paused.

That little dog was huffing and puffing the whole way.

Widow told himself that if that dog wasn't giving up, then neither was he.

7

CARRYING the hundred-pound woman for three or four or five miles was exhausting.

Widow was getting close to collapsing, and she was getting closer to death, and the dog was getting closer to giving up.

He could feel it.

Everything that had been aching was now growing numb every second that Widow carried on. He felt like the tinman running out of oil. He wasn't sure how much longer he could go.

Before he gave up, something happened. The dog started barking loud like there was something up ahead in the mist.

The animal jolted to attention, full of alertness. It barked a moment longer, and then it took off running. Within seconds, the dog disappeared around a bend in the road and into the darkness.

Widow swallowed and slowed, and stopped in his tracks. He stared forward and listened.

He heard its bark grow weaker and weaker, like it was getting farther and farther away. Then it stopped growing weaker and stayed the same level of pitch, the same level of sound like it had stopped at something and was barking at it.

Maybe it was barking for Widow to follow.

He picked up the pace and continued forward. He felt adrenaline returning and energy hitting his limbs once again. A second rush of determination overpowered him, and he was walking, standing taller, standing straighter. He marched through the fog and around the bend, into the same darkness as the little dog. He stayed the course until he came out from under a swallow of trees and stepped into bright, artificial lights.

He stopped there for a moment, allowing the light to bathe over him like a Black Hawk helicopter coming to pick him up after a deadly mission.

It was quite a welcoming sight.

*A sight for sore eyes*, he thought.

A steady stream of highway lights posted high on poles lit up the road ahead as the little country road that he had walked on expanded into a two-lane highway, complete with highway signs and a grassy median cut in the center of the road.

Another fifty yards ahead and the two-lane section of highway T-boned into a four-lane highway that went in two opposite directions. One direction of highway disappeared southwest in virtually the opposite direction that he had come — the other direction curved north like the trajectory of a curveball.

Just beyond the curveball was a two-story building that looked more like a compound than a storefront.

The establishment must've been built from the time of the first regional settlers, with much of it being restored or updated over the years, like a historical landmark that the county was proud of. The construction was three-quarters brick, laid with the utmost care, and the rest was solid wood. The roof was high and steep, like the attic was a cone hat.

Behind it was an old barn, no animals. That was clear because the thing looked to have been boarded up a long time ago.

Cemented into the ground on a slab was a brick sign. It read: *Overly's Haberdashery & Motor Bar*.

The words Haberdashery and Motor threw Widow for a loop.

A haberdashery, as far as Widow knew, was an old Western store that doubled as a shop that sold sewing supplies like buttons and zippers and acted as a men's outfitters.

The Motor part, he had no idea. He knew the Bar part.

The old haberdashery had been maintained over the century, kept up, probably by the county, and now it was a bar.

A stagecoach from the nineteenth century stood out front with no horses attached and no wheels on it. It was mounted up in place by a pair of big cement slabs underneath the front and rear wheel wells. The bottom foundation was a combination of the two slabs, and intricate metal bars and wiring bolted into the bottom of the wagon.

It was a gimmick, like having a furniture store in the middle of nowhere with the world's largest rocking chair out in front, or the tallest footstool.

Widow wondered if tourists actually came out of their way to take photos with it.

For sure, it attracted passersby from the highway. People driving from out of the west on their way east probably saw it and made an impulse stop to take photos with the kids. Maybe to take a pic inside and purchase overpriced keepsakes, meant to imitate far cheaper items made nearly two hundred years ago.

The newest feature to the outside of the haberdashery was the parking lot. That was obvious.

Handicap signs were posted up on two parking spaces closest to the entrance. A wheelchair ramp zigzagged off to the side of a front porch.

Looking over the front of the building, Widow saw why it was called Motor Bar.

Out front, along the walkway near the entrance, eight motorcycles were parked in a neat row. There was a special canopy set up on poles that covered that row of the parking lot.

Overly's was a roadside museum by day and a biker bar by night.

The bikes were all the same basic colors and all the same basic models. All were Harley Davidsons.

From the looks of them, the riders had been at the bar for a while. The bikes were all cold and lifeless, and the tires were caked in snow, but there were no tracks behind any of them.

The rest of the lot was snowed over. One set of fresh tracks caught Widow's eye.

The tracks appeared to have either pulled into the lot from the highway or from the snowy country road that he had walked in on.

It was hard to tell, but his suspicions couldn't help but wonder if the vehicle he had seen out in the dark had been there, right in front of him.

The people from inside the car could've been in the bar right then. That would've made them the dumbest people, probably in the whole state. But it wouldn't have surprised Widow. In his professional history, he had encountered a lot of dumb criminals.

Besides the eight motorcycles, he saw four parked cars and two parked pickup trucks.

He couldn't tell which of them had left the tire tracks in the snow because the tracks had filled in by the time they led to the cluster of parked vehicles.

Any of them could've left them behind.

The only thing that Widow could rule out was the motorcycles and the pickup trucks, because the taillights he had seen were closer to the ground than the rear lights for the two trucks in the parking lot. But any of the cars could've been the taillights that he saw because all four cars were old enough to have doors on squeaky hinges or a trunk that wouldn't close properly.

In fact, it was entirely possible that none of the cars made the tracks. And it was possible that none of the cars were the taillights that he had seen.

Beyond the haberdashery, Widow could see a bubble of lights over the trees like there was a town there.

Town or not, Widow was going to stop here. He was nearly drained from the exertion of carrying the girl. No way was he going to go down the road. His body couldn't go any farther.

He trekked up through the snow and stepped past two of the cars and over a parking lot divider. He passed the eight parked Harley Davidsons, and the handicapped parking spaces and the wheelchair ramp. He trudged farther through more snow and made his way to the front porch. He carried the girl up the stairs and stopped at a set of huge, double oak doors.

A sign scrawled in sloppy handwriting on a piece of torn cardboard from the lip of a cardboard box was duct-taped to the left door.

It read: *Doorbell busted. Knock. Hard.*

And stated nothing else.

Widow gathered this meant that the entrance was locked

after dark for protection of the staff, or it meant that it was to warn them of cops, like an alarm system. Unlike a normal bar, cops couldn't just walk through these front doors like a normal customer. They had to knock and wait for permission to enter, giving the bartender time to warn the patrons and to hide whatever needed hiding.

Widow also noticed a plaque next to the right side of the doors that indicated he was on camera.

He looked up and saw a security camera bolted to the top corner of the porch's ceiling.

Widow stared up at the camera and called out.

"Hello!"

No answer.

"Somebody! I need help!"

No response.

With a quick one-two motion, he bent down and jolted back up so he could adjust the girl's body in his arms. He wanted to get a grip on her with one arm so he could free up the other one. He used his free hand to try the doorknob. Nothing. He readjusted and tried the other one. Nothing.

The snow picked up behind him. The wind picked up. Both combined to drop the temperature five degrees, just like that in an instant. And both forces sped up like it was the beginning of a snowstorm.

The sudden temperature drop made Widow's body shiver vehemently. He had to get in.

He didn't give up. He doubled his efforts and banged on the door with his free fist, hard like a battering ram. The sound was loud enough to be heard deep inside the haberdashery. He knew it. Then he realized no one would hear him if there was loud music.

He leaned forward as best he could and listened, but heard nothing.

He had to repurpose his hand and grip once again to brace the girl's body in his arms.

After he still heard nothing, he decided it was time to go all the way.

In a burst of violent movement, Widow sprang back, knees bent, with the girl clung close to his chest, and his adrenaline pumping through his veins like a rush of drugs. He reared back on one foot and came up hard with the other. He landed a solid kick right below the doorknob and the lock.

Widow prayed the deadbolt was unlocked, which he figured it was because the door was on an electronic lock so that it could be unlocked by someone on the other end of that camera by a buzzer. A deadbolt system with the electronic buzzer would've taken forever to open every time someone came to the door. Plus, it would've been overkill for a bar.

He was right. The electronic lock was only for the doorknob's internal lock.

The lock busted. And the door burst open. One big wave of power and force and pressure and Widow was in.

Wood splintered around the lock. Half of the metal ripped out of the doorframe.

Behind Widow, the night was dark. Cold fog rolled on the ground, whipping past him and rolling into the haberdashery's foyer. The wind gusted in and chilled his back.

Inside the bar, the front door opened right up to one enormous space. On the left was a small gift shop with buttons in cases and zippers and old sewing knickknacks—the daytime side of the business. The rest of the place was one huge open room with tables, chairs, stools, some armchairs by a fireplace, and a long horseshoe bar that started on the far wall and thrust out like a stage to the center of the room.

There were fourteen people inside. Three at the bar, two sat on the armchairs at the fireplace, one bartender, and eight bikers around a single pool table and a dartboard. They had two games going on at once.

Widow saw pitchers of beer on three tables they shared.

Everyone in the bar turned and stared at him like it was right on cue.

At that moment, Widow realized he must've looked like a monster returned from the grave. His shirt was off. His vascular system was working overtime, exposing his veins like they were all going to pop. He stood tall and weather-beaten by the snow. His hair was wet and slicked back. And there was a naked, dying girl laid out in his arms.

The looks on the faces of the patrons in the bar were nothing short of utter shock, which quickly turned into sheer horror.

8

The people in the haberdashery bar ranged from middle-aged white locals to older white locals and the eight bikers, who were mostly older than Widow.

The bikers were a part of a motorcycle club, sporting the patches and attire. They wore leather vests, jackets, and blue jeans. Except because they had differing facial features and shapes and sizes, they could've been interchangeable. But they weren't.

The bikers stopped and stared at Widow, but said nothing. They weren't that surprised as they had been around the block, and they had seen things.

The bar's regular locals were a different story.

The two sitting in the armchairs were old men. One had a harmonica in his hand, like he was showing it off, and the other was playing around on his phone. They looked like Widow had interrupted them from what they thought was a deep philosophical conversation. Maybe it had been about music.

The three at the bar were all middle-aged women. They were drinking and sharing an evening together. Perhaps after work. Perhaps they were having a regular get-together, like a weekly custom, established long, long ago, and kept up with. What else were they going to do?

The bartender was the youngest of everyone in the bar. He was a guy of average height, but a stocky build. He had faded tattoos showing on folded arms.

Everyone stared at Widow in shock and dismay, like he was holding a gun, which he wasn't, but the bartender had one. He reached down in a fast, fluid movement behind the register and came up with a pump-action shotgun. It was a time-tested store-bought thing like from a local sporting goods store. Nothing special. But a shotgun blast was a shotgun blast. It was bad news, no matter what brand or year the model was from. It was bad for whoever was on the business end of it.

Right then, that was Widow.

Widow paused a beat, tried to let his brain settle. Hauling the half-dead woman through the cold and elements for more than an hour had taken more out of him than energy and muscle fibers and breath. It drained his mind to the point of only focusing on the simple things, as if the brain had been the place where his body tapped into the rest of the energy needed to carry on. Now it was tapped out.

Nobody spoke.

Widow looked up at the bartender and then past him and froze, because he saw exactly what they were seeing.

On the counter, behind several half-empty whiskey bottles, was an old, black-and-white TV monitor, about a ten-inch screen on it. On the screen, Widow saw himself exactly as the patrons in the bar had seen him.

On the TV monitor were four split-screens. Each showed the view coming from security cameras. One was footage from outside. Widow saw emptiness and the parking lot beyond the front porch. On the inside left of the feed, he saw the shattered lock and busted front door.

The other three screens were of the interior of the bar. All three were different angles of the inside.

He saw himself in each of them—big and intimidating, holding a half-naked, half-dead girl.

The picture quality was good enough to show that his hair and face and shoulders were covered in snow. And his skin had turned ghostly white.

To the patrons in the bar, he looked like the abominable snowman coming out of the Black Hills to kill.

Breaking his thought process, the bartender crunched the shotgun. It was a statement more than a necessary action. Widow knew that instantly, because the weapon had already been ready to fire. The second that the bartender cycled the crunch completely, a perfectly good slug ejected out of the mouth and flew and bounced and rolled across the bar top.

A shotgun crunch is one of the most powerful sounds invented by man. No one confuses the crunch of a shotgun for anything other than the crunch of a shotgun. That's why the bartender pumped it.

He wanted the whole room to know that he had the weapon, that he was ready to shoot Widow, and that he was in charge.

It worked too.

Widow thought he could hear his heartbeat above the silence filling the room. The bartender still said nothing. No one else spoke.

The silence carried on for another long moment until Widow made the first move. He opened his mouth to speak, hoping to clear the air, but standing there, still, had caused the cold in his blood to catch up to him. He shivered, and then he was out of breath.

He hadn't noticed it before, but there was a jukebox in the foreground to the far left of the room. It had either been silent before he busted through the door, or it was dormant on a timer because suddenly the thing kick-started to life.

The jukebox wasn't one of those new electronic ones. It was an old push-button machine with actual vinyl records in it. He could see them through a glass dome on the top of the machine.

The jukebox jumped to life, filling the room with loud mechanical sounds. He heard scratching and bumping and motorized whirring noises.

After a few seconds, the automated sounds subsided, replaced by music. An old song started playing. It was "Don't Fear the Reaper," which was ironic or appropriate or both.

Finally, the bartender said, "Who the hell are ya?"

Widow slowly stepped into the room, keeping the girl up in his arms. He passed the jukebox halfway to the bar and walked down a couple more steps that were marked with neon orange tape for safety.

Widow stopped on a soft shag rug in the center of the room. He looked like he was going to speak again, but didn't. Instead, he unintentionally dumped down onto his knees, hard. Even on the shag rug, he felt the hard flooring beneath.

He said, "Help."

After that, Widow's arms moved against his will. They slowly laid the girl down on the rug. He cradled her head and let it lay on his open palm, making sure not to injure her.

Once she was safer, Widow lay down next to her, kept one hand under her head, and passed out.

9

Alaska Rower started up a year-old Ford Taurus, black with law enforcement lights packed into the front grille and packed into the rear brake lights. They were all blue, no red lights.

The plate on the car was only in the rear. The state of North Dakota, where she had borrowed the car from a police motor pool, did not yet require front plates, unlike the state she was stationed in. The plate was government-issued and issued with government designations, alerting the cops and the state troopers that the vehicle was law enforcement classification. It did not show whether the driver was FBI.

A Glock was nestled tight into a holster on her left hip. Driving with it was uncomfortable the first month of working for the FBI. One of her trainers had hammered it into her to keep it there. Better to wear it and know where it is in a pinch versus the alternative.

In the front cup holder, she had a Starbucks black coffee in a Starbucks-branded paper cup. Grande, not a tall like she usually got. She saw a long day ahead of her, about a five-hour drive, going the speed limits. Therefore, the grande was the right choice to go with.

Special Agent Rower worked out of the Minneapolis field office but was spending time in Bismarck, North Dakota, working a case that she had literally wrapped up the day before when her SAC, Special Agent in Charge, called her late in the night. He had told her to get her ass down to South Dakota. Someplace she'd never heard of.

The FBI field office in Minneapolis was assigned to watch over both of the Dakotas—North and South. They had satellite offices in both states, and there were closer agents. But Rower had seniority and experience, and she had worked a case in the same field as the one that was happening in South Dakota.

She spent a lot of time in one of the Dakotas or the other. Both big states. Both small populations compared to other states. Both large interiors with long spaces to drive through in order to get from one lowly populated place to another.

This time she was driving to the Black Hills, about three hundred miles south.

Her SAC told her to be there in the morning. She had wished that she was in Minneapolis because that was a distance of one thousand plus miles, which meant she could fly to Rapid City and rent a car from there because the drive would've been eight hours nonstop.

Instead, her luck had plopped her into Bismarck. And her luck made it to where she was just finishing up one thing. So, she was free for another.

She'd slept four hours in a motel room after she clicked off the call. Now she was up and showered and dressed and in the vehicle.

After stopping at Starbucks, she pulled into a gas station, filled up the Taurus's tank. She was the only person in the gas station other than the clerk behind the register and behind bulletproof glass. Or at least that's what a sign posted inside the window had read.

Automatically, she wondered if her Glock 22 would shoot through the glass. A .40 caliber weapon. A nine-millimeter parabellum round. And the likelihood of a major oil and gas company spending the extra expense on bulletproof, reinforced glass to protect a minimum wage employee at three o'clock in the morning seemed highly unlikely. And not because she didn't think that the extra security was needed. It was only because she was skeptical of a major corporation taking all those steps and spending the money.

Rower was skeptical by nature. That was one aspect of her character that made her a good agent.

After she pumped her gas, she paid the clerk at the window with a gas card, FBI-issued, naturally. She did not shoot him.

Rower paid at the glass because she hated paying at the machines. It seemed too robotic, too impersonal. She liked to take every opportunity to interact with people over life's easy solutions.

She figured the card swiper on the pump was best used if she needed to be in and out in a hurry. And what was the hurry?

She didn't even know the details of why she was going to Reznor. She guessed that if it had been a life-or-death situation, her SAC would've given her more details.

Rower wore black jeans and a black button-down top tucked into the jeans. She wore a warm bomber jacket, also black and simple. There were no girly design features. It was just a straightforward winter bomber jacket, which she considered a part of her comfortable clothes.

This time of year, North Dakota was too cold to be

dressing like an FBI agent every second of every day. Because of the early November cold, gusts were blowing down south off the Canadian Rockies.

The weather was cold out, so she also wore a thick wool scarf for good measure.

Just then, as Rower slipped the gas card back into her wallet, revealing her badge to the clerk, her phone rang in her pants pocket.

She turned, slipped the wallet into her inner jacket pocket, and took out her phone.

She checked the caller's name and phone number first. It was her SAC.

She clicked the button and answered.

"Hello."

"Are you on your way?" he asked. She could hear grogginess in his voice as if he had been fast asleep only minutes before.

"Yes, sir. I'm gassing up now."

"Get there as fast as you can."

"So, what's going on? You didn't tell me much earlier."

"The sheriff's office down in Lawrence County phoned the office earlier. Told us they had something of interest. But I was just called by the local sheriff. He was woken up by a deputy and didn't sound too happy about it."

"What did he say?"

"They found a guy. A strange guy," he said and paused a beat like it was for dramatic effect.

"They found a guy? What's so strange about him?"

"This guy walked into a bar down there four hours ago carrying a half-dead, naked woman. She's unconscious. The staff at the bar says he walked in with no shirt, no jacket on. They said he looked like something terrible had come out of the forest. He carried her and then dropped and blacked out."

"That sounds exaggerated."

"I agree."

"So some guy carries a half-dead woman into a bar? What's that got to do with us?"

"They said she looked like she had been strangled."

"So?"

"So, the bar is on Interstate Ninety, which makes it our jurisdiction if we want it."

"Pardon me, but I'd like more of a reason than a non-murder, possibly on the interstate to validate driving five hours in the middle of the night."

Her SAC was quiet for a beat. And she knew he wasn't telling her everything. He seemed to relish whatever he wasn't telling her, which was a part of his personality. Often, Rower thought he must've wanted to be an actor in a previous life.

He said, "I'm glad you ask. Because the other thing that puts this on our radar is that the girl just had major surgery. I don't know the timeframe, but recent."

Another dramatic pause.

Rower popped open the Taurus driver's side door and sat down, kept her feet out on the concrete, and waited.

Her SAC said, "Rower, her kidney was extracted."

"What?"

"Yep."

"Where?"

"From her body."

"I know that. What geographical location?"

"That I don't know. That's why you're going."

"Who's the girl?"

"The sheriff will have all the details that you need."

Rower paused a beat and asked, "You think it's them?"

"I don't know. But I sure hope so. I hope the girl can give you some answers."

"Thanks, John."

She called him by his first name instead of sir or boss or chief or Bukowski, which was his last name and the normal way she addressed him.

Bukowski said, "Don't thank me. I didn't take the girl's kidney. This guy did. I suppose."

"Or he's another carrier."

"Possibly. The whole thing sounds strange."

"Did the sheriff give you a name?"

"Not yet. He's not met the guy yet."

"Why not?"

"It's the middle of the night."

*You woke me up*, she thought.

"He's got a big rural county. I don't think he lives anywhere near where they got the guy. But don't worry. He'll meet you in Reznor in the morning."

"Okay," she said.

"Call me tomorrow when you have details," Bukowski said, and he clicked off the call with no goodbye.

Rower tossed the phone into the empty cup holder and slid her legs into the footwell and shut the door.

She started the engine, gassed the car, and drove off.

## 10

Gypsy moths slammed into a dull yellow bulb plugged into a bare white ceiling over Widow's head. He stared and squinted and blinked and came to, but he stayed where he was.

He didn't sit up. He didn't move. He assumed he was in a local hospital bed since he'd walked into a haberdashery biker bar complex and passed out from exhaustion.

Widow figured the bartender had called the sheriff or the police, or whatever they had there. The ambulance was called for the girl and probably Widow too.

The first thing he wanted to do was recon his current situation without making big movements because he felt he wasn't alone. He could feel someone else in the room.

Widow had learned from experience to trust his first instincts. It's the cognitive mind that you must doubt because afterthoughts and doubt and calculating the gray areas always came right after the first instinct has already accessed the situation. It is when the mind makes you question things after you first see them, where hesitation is born.

Widow stared at the ceiling until it came into normal

focus. Casually, slowly, he looked left, looked right. He looked above him, then down toward his feet. He was lying down on a bed small enough to be a hospital in a place with no budget. But the bed felt more like the bed in a mental hospital than it did a hospital room. It reminded him of the small cots they had back in boot camp, the kind with metal springs and a metal frame. And never provided a good night's sleep for any sailor, ever. But that was one advantage sailors had over the rest of the armed forces; they could sleep anywhere.

Considering sailors sleep at sea for months and months on end, dealing with crashing waves, the ship rocking violently, sudden swells, and surging storms that magnified it all by a hundred, all of this while always maintaining ready alertness that enemy states could fire on their vessel and sink it at any moment, they learn to sleep anywhere under any conditions. No problem.

Widow was no different. He could sleep on boulders. He could sleep on a bed of nails and wake up rested with a crick in his neck and still be ready to go.

Above him, he saw nothing but a bare white tiled ceiling, too high to reach and too dirty to be a major hospital that passes annual state inspections. He saw a wall made of big cement blocks, painted a dull gray.

Widow turned his head slowly and slightly to the left until he was sure no one was watching, and then he turned on his side.

There was nothing to see but another wall, nothing special, nothing different, just another brick wall with the same cement blocks and the same dull gray paint.

His head backtracked and turned to the right. There were no hospital machines or staff or anything else that could be found in a normal hospital room.

Instead, there was an empty, narrow space, and then there

was another wall with a door hole cut out of it. But there was no regular door plugged into the hole where a door should be.

Instead, there was a door made of thick iron bars. It hung on rusty hinges, painted over in black.

*Refurbished cell bars*, Widow thought.

The bars, the hinges, everything, but the rust on the hinges was painted black to hide the ailing quality of the iron.

This was no hospital. This was a jail cell. This was the last place Widow wanted to be. This was the first place he always seemed to end up.

He couldn't help but crack a smile. His life had been a good one. His life's luck had been all over the map in terms of good and bad.

He chuckled. Not to himself so much.

He had no reason to remain quiet.

He sat up as well. He was lying on a jail cot, not a boot camp cot, not much difference.

He was all alone. No cellmate. No bunk cots. No neighbors either.

The cell wasn't meant to be shared. It was exclusive and narrow and barebones. All it had was the cot, a steel panel with a crudely reflective surface, like the surface of a butter knife, screwed to the wall above a metal sink with metal knobs. The panel replaced a regular mirror. No glass, so there would be no glass shards if broken.

The faucet knobs were push-down-and-hold for water only. No turn-on-and-leave-running. American jails were barebones and designed to be run as cheap as possible.

There was a toilet next to the unpolished sink. It was also metal, with no lid and no visible tank. The tank was embedded into the wall so prisoners couldn't get to it and sabotage the pipes or dig tunnels or hide contraband in the tank.

Widow was wrapped up in extra blankets, more than the standard single blanket, a single sheet he had seen in most jails. Probably because when he had been taken into custody, his body temperature had dropped below normal.

Can't have him die from hypothermia before the local cops charge him for whatever it was they thought he did.

*How generous*, Widow thought.

He swung his feet out and planted them on a concrete floor and stood up off the bed.

He was fully clothed, not shirtless as they had found him. He wore his own boots. His own jeans. But not his Henley or his jacket. Someone had dressed him in someone else's white thermal shirt. It was tight but fit in the chest and stomach. The sleeves were a different story. They reached halfway down to his forearms and stopped dead. That was it. They had no more fabric to give.

Widow couldn't believe he'd slept through someone arresting him, if he was under arrest, and dressing him too. He must've been pushed to his max carrying a half-dead girl for miles and miles in the coldness of a November South Dakota night.

Widow walked through the narrow cell to the bars and grabbed them. He pushed forward and pressed his face between two bars, right in the center.

He tried to look out.

Beyond the bars was a long, narrow hallway that jetted to the right.

The hall was shady, not dark, but not well lit either, as if the lights were dimmed to help the occupants sleep, which made no sense because his cell was lit up. Then again, maybe they couldn't control the lights in his cell. Or maybe they didn't know what to do because they got little overnight visitors.

Widow saw faint lights coming from down the hallway at the very end. The light came from around a corner.

There were two other cells to the left and none on the right, just another block wall, same dull gray as his cell.

The two cells were empty. The bars were all closed and locked, but there were no sounds of breathing or snoring or movement, and, unlike his cell, they were dark.

Widow waited for a beat and listened.

Beyond the corner, he could hear faint mumbling like a radio chatter, or maybe a television set turned down low.

No reason to stay quiet. He called out.

"Hello?"

No answer.

He called out again, louder this time. He put bass in behind his voice, a cop trick.

"HELLO! ANYONE THERE?"

His voice *boomed* in the silence and the natural acoustics from the barren cement block walls.

The last word echoed for a moment. All the words carried to the outer rooms; he knew that. Whoever was there heard him just fine, unless they wore sound-canceling gun muffs.

Widow waited.

Then he heard someone. They didn't answer him back. Instead, he heard an office chair's roller wheels on tile, just the one set. He heard shoes shuffling and footsteps and the floorboards squeaking.

After listening to the footsteps get closer, a man turned the corner. Widow saw his face first, because it was at eye level. The guy was big, tall like Widow, but had a different body type, about as different as he could.

The guy was tall, but had short legs and a long, thick torso, like a former bodybuilder. His shoulders were wide, his chest round like an oil drum. He had a gut, nothing considered overweight, but there was some early bulge developing.

He'd probably played football in college or high school.

The policeman was younger than Widow, but over the threshold of thirty, barely. He wore a brown police uniform and a department coat that looked warm. His hair was brown, darker than his uniform, but lighter than his coat.

A .38 Police Special was strapped into a hip holster on a scuffed-up leather belt—brown, not black. It didn't match his shoes, grave violation of the United States Navy uniform code. It was probably a violation of the South Dakota Sheriffs' uniform section of a manual that the guy probably never read, or read ten years in the past so that he could pass his police test, but has since used the manual as kindling for a campfire.

The guy's face was flat and clean-shaven, as if he'd just done the act five minutes ago. He smelled of cheap aftershave, bought in a green bottle at a drugstore, probably jammed into a clearance bin.

The scent wafted down the corridor, announcing his approach only a second after he turned the corner. It didn't smell bad, just overpowering.

The guy held a hot cup of coffee, full and black, and steaming and just poured.

He said, "Mister. You awake."

He said it as a statement, an out-loud observation of the obvious, not a question.

Widow stayed quiet.

"Want some coffee?"

Widow nodded like an automatic, pre-programmed response. His body answered without his consent.

The policeman stopped short of the bars and held the coffee in his view, taunting him with it.

The guy's eyes were big—large pupils. He fidgeted with the cuff of one of his sleeves like a nervous habit.

He said, "Step back. Middle of the cell."

Widow stepped back, one long back-step.

The policeman set the coffee on the middle, chest-high rung of the bars. It was set horizontal and flat on the top, but it was thin, so he braced the mug against the cross-section of the nearest vertical bar. After it was stable, the policeman retreated into the hallway. Took him two extra back-steps to cover the same distance as Widow had.

Widow noticed dark circles under the policeman's eyes, like he hadn't slept in a long while.

*The night shift*, Widow thought. He had done it many times himself, lost quite a lot of sleep because it messes up your days.

"Go ahead. Take it."

Widow stepped forward and took it.

He sniffed it before deciding on drinking it. He was curious if the policeman's gesture was authentic or a trap. A cup of coffee offered from a cop as a peace offering wasn't crossing the line of entrapment, but it could be a gateway breadcrumb.

"It's not poisoned."

Widow nodded and took a pull from it. He was right. It wasn't poisoned. It was far worse than that. It was delicious, which was not what Widow was expecting from coffee brewed in a middle-of-nowhere police station. Maybe one of his only prejudices was coffee. The best coffees in the world were brewed right at home, with love. That was his opinion. The closer coffee was to being brewed in the family kitchen, the closer it was to perfection. Thus, why coffee brewed in greasy spoons or family roadside diners was the best. And coffee brewed in the company break room was the worst, with coffee brewed in a nowhere police station being somewhere in the middle, but closer to the bad side than the good.

Even though Widow wasn't aware of the time or how long he had been unconscious, he knew that he had passed out from exhaustion. Carrying a naked, one-hundred-ten-pound woman over miles of snow and for a little over an hour would do that to a man.

Being passed out for longer than twenty minutes was often the result of medical issues. A doctor in Quantico told him that once after he'd knocked out a guy sparring practice that got out of hand.

Years later, Widow blacked out in the field. But off duty, from a head injury, all his fault from an accident involving not wearing a helmet on a motorcycle.

That story became exaggerated by his teammates. It was a basic story.

Widow was in New Zealand, some half undercover mission and half babysitting gig. Technically, they weren't supposed to be there.

The mission itself turned out to be a waste of tax dollars, but not a waste of time for Widow, personally.

On shore-leave, Widow had a brief affair with a woman he had met there. It went on for a couple of weekends—no big deal. But it turned out that the woman was going through a divorce, but technically still married. The husband found out. He'd been stalking her. One night, the husband and three of his friends tried to fight Widow. They ambushed him and took four broken ribs, two broken noses, five broken fingers, and one fractured skull for the ambush. It was a hefty price for them.

One guy got lucky. He had hit Widow in the head with a pipe or a wrench. Widow couldn't remember which.

After Widow took them all down, the head injury got

him. He blacked out for nearly an hour and woke up in a CIA safe house. One of his guys was a medic. He told Widow that being blacked out from a head injury was always unwanted. Twenty minutes of blackout time differed little from four hours. None of it was good.

He lived.

The policeman asked, "You got a name, sir?"

"You got a name?"

"I asked you first."

"You're the cop. Aren't you supposed to identify yourself?"

The policeman stood still and folded his arms across his chest. But only for a moment. Then he fidgeted with the sleeve of his cuff again.

Widow stayed quiet.

The cop stretched his index finger out, right hand, and tapped it on a nameplate tacked over his left breast shirt pocket.

Widow didn't look.

"My name's Rousey. I'm a sheriff's deputy."

"Deputy? Where's the sheriff?"

"Probably home in bed. Or at his station."

"This isn't his station?"

"He's the county sheriff. Sheriffs are for counties. We're in Reznor."

"Reznor?"

"It's the name of the town. The one you're in right now."

"Never heard of it."

Rousey said, "Lawrence is the county. It's big. The sheriff's station is in Deadwood. This is my post."

"You alone here?"

"No, there are other deputies, but I'm the main one here."

"And where's this?"

Rousey shifted his weight away from his gun hip, folded his arms again, stared at Widow like he was a lunatic.

"Reznor. I done told you that."

Widow stayed quiet.

"You escape a mental institution or something?"

"You think that?"

"You busted into Overly's carrying a naked girl."

Widow just looked at him.

Rousey said, "You tried to murder that girl. Now you don't know where you are?"

Murder?

Widow paused a beat and said, "I didn't kill anyone. I didn't try to kill anyone."

"We got witnesses saying different."

"What witnesses?"

"The people that saw you."

"What people?"

"From the bar. Don't you remember? They all saw you."

"They saw me?"

"They saw you."

"They saw me do what, exactly?"

"They saw you attempt to kill that woman."

"No one saw me kill anyone."

"Attempt to kill."

"No. No way. No one is saying that."

Rousey stared at Widow, hard.

He said, "They saw you carry that girl inside. They saw you, a big guy, with your shirt off, your coat off. Out in the cold like that. Carrying a half-dead girl."

"They saw nothing."

"We got you on camera kicking the door down. I saw nothing like it before. Looked like a horror movie. So, I ask you, have you escaped from a mental hospital?"

"I didn't attempt to kill anybody. I didn't kill anyone. I found that girl."

"That's not what the witnesses say."

"No one is saying that."

"They saw you carry her in. Saw you with no top on."

"If I attempted to kill her, why would I wrap her up in my clothes and carry her into a bar?"

Rousey said nothing.

Widow said, "I found her—side of the road. And I carried her to the bar. Trying to get her medical attention. I was trying to save her life."

"You found her?"

"That's what I said."

"Where?"

"Where's she now? Is she okay?"

"Why?"

"Is she going to make it?"

"Why? Wanna know if you're facing murder one?"

"Is she safe?"

Rousey was quiet for a second. Widow could see him working out calculations on his face, which amplified the bags under his eyes because he cocked his head up while thinking.

A giant carrying a near-dead woman with intentions of saving her life sounded unbelievable, but it made more sense than a giant carrying his victim into a bar and passing out in front of witnesses.

"I don't know."

"Where is she?"

"She was medevacked to the hospital in Deadwood. The sheriff will meet with her first, and then he'll be here to talk to you."

"Thought you said he was at home?"

"I lied. He won't stay home when something like this happens in his county. Not when we got an attempted murder and the culprit behind bars. No, you'll be a top priority."

"I didn't try to kill anyone. I told you I rescued her. Why else would I bring her into the haberdashery?"

They'd already gone over this, but Widow felt the endless cycle of round-and-round they go over his version of what happened.

"I don't know. That's what I'm trying to understand."

Widow was quiet for a beat, and then he lifted his free hand to his face, stared at his fingertips. Rousey watched Widow's face. He saw a realization come over it.

Widow asked, "You take my fingerprints?"

"Why? You worried we gonna find out something that you don't want us to find out about you? You wanted somewhere?"

Widow shook his head.

"Am I under arrest?"

"What's it look like?"

"You didn't read me my rights?"

He said nothing.

"Can you fingerprint a man without reading him his rights?"

Rousey said nothing to that.

Cops aren't supposed to fingerprint someone without reading them their rights, but they do it all the time. Miranda rights are supposed to be read to a suspect when an arrest is made. But it's often not done that way. Real-life doesn't work like it does in the movies.

Who's going to challenge the police department over it?

It usually comes down to your word against the cops. Easy enough for them to lie about it.

In Widow's experience of being arrested in the civilian

world, sometimes what they do is offer you early release on lesser charges, but first, you've got to sign a piece of paper saying that you were read your rights at the time of the arrest.

Not like the movies, but then again, almost nothing in life was.

"If I'm under arrest, I'd like my lawyer now."

Rousey shouted at him.

"You don't get a lawyer!"

The shout *boomed* and echoed like Widow's voice had earlier.

Rousey stopped and dropped his arms down straight.

He paused. They both did.

Rousey looked like he wanted to say he was sorry for the outburst, but he said nothing.

Widow ignored it. He figured the guy was high-strung being out here by himself, forced to deal with a potentially attempted murder suspect, especially one that looked like him.

"Constitution says I do," Widow said calmly.

"Don't worry if it comes to that; you'll have time to speak to an attorney."

"What about my phone call?"

"No phone call."

"I get a phone call. Everyone gets a phone call."

"You're not under arrest."

Widow stared at Rousey for a second and then looked around the cell. Made it big and obvious. He stared at the bars, at the walls, at the metal toilet and sink and crude steel-surfaced mirror, and then back at Rousey.

"You're not under arrest yet. Right now, you're being detained."

"Detained? Like a suspect?"

"A person of interest. That means no, I didn't fingerprint you because you've been accused of nothing. No charges. Not yet. The sheriff will make that determination when he gets here."

"Okay."

Silence.

Widow drank more of the coffee and thought maybe the coffee, combined with the late shift, and the boredom was making Rousey a little agitated.

"Thanks for the coffee."

"Don't mention it. Might be the last decent thing you get for a long, long time. If the sheriff decides it so."

"Not the sheriff."

Rousey cleared his throat, big and obvious. It echoed in the narrow corridor, not as loud as his outburst, but close.

"Pardon?"

"The courts decide. Don't they?"

"Right, the courts."

Widow took another pull from the coffee.

Rousey asked, "Gonna tell me your name?"

"You already know it. Don't you?"

"Didn't fingerprint you! I told you that!"

"You took my passport. You took my ATM card. Both were in my pockets."

Rouse thought for a second, like he wasn't sure if he should relay the information, but he nodded anyway.

"I just wanted to see if you knew your own name."

"Why wouldn't I?"

"You don't know where you are?"

"South Dakota. The Black Hills. Someplace called Reznor."

"I told you that."

"And I remembered it."

"You're not high?"

"High?"

"You know, doped up? High?"

"I'm high on coffee."

"There're no drugs in your system?"

"Only the most powerful drug known to man."

Rousey's eyes lit up, revealing his pupils.

Widow held the coffee cup up into view and said, "Caffeine."

"You're not on anything else?"

"Like what?"

"Meth?"

"Why would I be on meth?"

"It's a thing here. You didn't smoke any?"

"I never smoke anything, except Cubans whenever I was in Havana. That's the only place to get them, you see."

"Havana, Georgia? Is that where you're from?"

"That's Savannah."

"What?"

"Savannah, Georgia, not Havana."

"That's where you from?"

"No. Sad to say, I've never been there. I'm talking about Havana, Cuba."

"Where's that?"

Widow looked at him, not meaning to be judgmental, but how does he not know about Havana, Cuba?

Widow guessed that maybe that was just the lack of education in his upbringing, combined with the fact that the guy probably never left the state, combined with his obvious insomnia affecting his daily life.

Widow knew the signs. Being out at sea during Operation Freedom, where they had to watch out for the Iranians more than anyone else, or sneaking through the mountains in Afghanistan at night, hoping they didn't run into the Taliban for long stretches; Widow had seen the effects of insomnia on SEALs in his unit. Hell, he had experienced them firsthand.

He gave Rousey the benefit of the doubt.

"It's in Cuba?"

"You Cuban? Don't they have drugs?"

"What's with you and drugs?"

Rousey straightened up like a wolf on a lonely road with a pair of headlights barreling down on him suddenly.

"Don't get hostile. I'm just asking questions here. I'm interested in what you know, your state of mind."

"My state of mind is normal."

"You didn't know where you were before I told you. That's weird. Don't you think?"

"No. Not really. Middle of the night. I never been here before. Why would I know where I am? Doesn't mean I'm high on drugs."

Silence for a moment.

Rousey said, "You should know where you are? How could you not?"

Widow shrugged and said, "Lots of reasons someone might not know exactly where they are. People get lost every day. Doesn't mean they are criminals."

He nodded.

"What's your name?"

"What's it say on my passport?"

"Do you not know what it says?"

Widow stayed quiet. This conversation was going nowhere.

Rousey repeated, "What's your name?"

"You've talked to me. Does it seem like I'm mentally

incompetent? Like I really don't know my own name? Why do you keep asking me that?"

"I have to ask. I need to tell the sheriff my professional assessment."

Widow smiled at the phrase professional assessment from a rural deputy. No way did this sheriff care about his professional assessment. Widow figured the guy just wanted to make himself look as good as possible for the sheriff.

Widow shrugged and answered.

"Name's Jack Widow. I'm innocent of whatever it is you think I did."

Widow stopped and thought about it. He pictured it. What he must've looked like. The image of somebody like him carrying a half-dead woman into a strange place, around people who've probably known each other their whole lives. Then he thought about how he would feel about it.

So, he could understand how it looked to Rousey and the people at the bar. He knew he was innocent. But they didn't.

Rousey asked, "You didn't abduct this woman. Try to kill her?"

"I haven't tried to kill anybody. I told you that. But you need to have them do a rape kit on her. Someone assaulted her, and someone tried to kill her."

"So why not tell me how it went down? What did you do?"

Widow shook his head, eyes closed. His face didn't show frustration. He wasn't surprised at all by the deputy's tactics.

Repeat the crime to them. Over and over. See if they admit to it. See if they make a mistake. These tactics were taught in Detective work 101, right after it was taught that any confession learned this way would be meaningless because a terrified innocent person was just as likely to confess as a guilty person.

Widow saw this was going nowhere. He would just have

to answer the same questions when the sheriff got there. So, he took a last pull from the coffee, tilted it all the way until he was sure it was empty. He handed the empty mug back through the bars to Rousey, who waited again for Widow to take a step back before he came forward to get it.

"Just place it on the bars."

He didn't want to get within reach of Widow, a valid precaution.

Widow wasn't restrained. He could have exploded fast, and shot his arm through the bars, grabbed Rousey by the shirt collar, and jerked back and slammed the deputy violently into the other side of the bars. Could have put him into a temporary coma with two slams of equal power, equal calculation. He could have killed Rousey with three slams.

But Rousey was staying clear, which made Widow suspect he might've been carrying the cell's key in his pocket. Like he was staying back in case Widow tried to get at the key.

Even if he wasn't carrying the cell key, he carried that .38 Special.

If Widow had been an escaped mental patient, like Rousey claimed to suspect, then Widow might've tried to go for the gun. Might get it. Then he'd just shoot Rousey. Escape or not.

Why would a mental patient care?

Widow said, "You know what? If you won't give me my phone call, then I'm just going to wait for the sheriff."

Rousey stared back at him.

Widow said, "I don't want to have to repeat myself endlessly. And talking to you won't get me out of here."

"You're not getting out."

Widow nodded.

"When's he get here?"

"Like I said, he'll get here when he gets here," Rousey said and paused a beat. Then he repeated, "Where is here?"

"Reznor. You told me, remember?"

He paused a beat and said, "The city of Cheyenne Crossing."

Silence.

Widow asked, "Anyone live here?"

"There's people here."

"How many?"

"Enough."

"They let you police the people here?"

"What's that supposed to mean?"

"Never mind. Got any food?"

"There's a twenty-four-hour diner. Right across the interstate."

Interstate? It wasn't a highway like Widow had thought. It was an interstate. That was good. It meant he could get a ride a lot faster once he was out of here.

"What time is it now?"

Rousey looked at his watch and stayed silent for a moment, debating on whether to tell him the time.

"Early."

"How early?"

"Too early for the sheriff to show up."

Widow nodded and asked, "You gonna buy me some food?"

Rousey thought and said, "Sure. We're required by law to provide food for overnight stays. And technically, you've been here overnight."

"Am I gonna be here another night?"

"Told you. That's up to the sheriff. But my guess is yes. My guess is you'll be behind bars for the rest of your life."

Widow ignored that.

"Can I see a menu?"

"No menu. You get a burger and fries. That's it."

"This early in the morning?"

Rousey shrugged.

"It's too early for breakfast."

*Too early for breakfast? Must be between four and six a.m.,* Widow thought.

"And coffee?"

"You just had a coffee."

"I could use another. I like coffee."

"I don't care. Have what you want. I won't order you any. You can have what I made here."

"Fine by me. Do I get a choice of cheese?"

"You want cheese?"

Widow nodded.

"Sorry, no cheese."

He took the coffee mug off the bars, one fast swipe, and turned and marched out of sight.

Widow returned to the cot and kicked off his boots.

That's when he noticed the deputy had taken them off before, because his socks were missing.

He found them balled up under the cot.

Widow kicked the boots under the cot with the socks, and then he lay back down. He rested his head on one open palm like it was an airplane pillow, then he stared at the ceiling.

He had a lot of questions. He lay there and fell back asleep—no reason to be until his food arrived. He let the questions fill his head and counted each one like an insomniac counts sheep.

Who's the girl in the rug?

Who was in the car he saw?

Was it a car or a truck?

Why was she left alive?

Did her attacker intend to leave her alive?

What about the dog?

Will she live?

He answered the last question out loud, just before dozing back to sleep.

"I hope so."

11

Widow returned to sleep. He returned to the same dream. He didn't stay asleep long enough to consider it sleep, more like a nap.

His eyes rolled open slowly, like being awakened by smelling salts. Which he wasn't. It was all automatic. His brain had enough sleep.

He stayed lying on the cot, stared straight up at the gypsy moths. This went on for most of an hour more before Rousey returned to the cell. He brought a takeout box with a hamburger in it with a side of fries. No cheese. No utensils. No condiments. No napkins.

Widow didn't complain. He took it and thanked him and ate it.

It was good. He wouldn't say it was the best meal ever, but certainly comparable to the mess deck on a battle carrier.

After Widow finished eating it, he heard a desk phone ring from the other room, which he assumed to be the station's office.

Widow set the empty takeout box next to the bars on the

inside of the cell. He returned to the cot and dumped himself down on it, then scooted to the edge.

He sat with his feet on the concrete floor and his hands on top of his knees. He tried to listen. He heard nothing but a single voice repeating "Yes, sir" over and over.

Then, he heard someone drop the telephone down into its cradle, loud like a mic drop.

There was silence for nearly a minute, and then Widow heard shuffling, breathing, and pacing. It all sounded a little like someone's nerves, like someone trying to figure out what to do next.

Widow heard Rousey talking to himself; at least, that was what it sounded like. The strange thing was that he was whispering. It was loud enough to carry down the hall but whispered like someone's parents fighting in the other room, trying to keep the volume down but doing a poor job of it because they were so heated.

The whispering turned into more than whispering, more than quiet arguing. The level rose, but Widow still couldn't make out the words.

He was wrong about Rousey talking to himself. He knew that because another voice, a female, came to the forefront of the whispering.

Rousey wasn't alone. A woman was there with him. They were arguing like a married couple. But they still tried to keep the volume down. They must not have wanted Widow to hear what they were saying.

After a couple of minutes, Widow heard footsteps. Two people came around the corner and down the hall from the office.

One was Rousey. He brought a young female with him.

The girl was about twenty-one or twenty-two or twenty-three years old and not a day older. She had short blonde hair, like a boy's haircut. It was fresh, as if it had been cut earlier in the day.

She had a welt under one of her eyes, like a punch to the face would cause—not a hard, heavy fist to the face, but more like a hard slap or backhand. Widow knew the mark well. He had seen plenty of domestic dispute violence. Often a backhand was used. Backhands hurt and stung and got the job done, usually leaving minimal damage behind.

The girl clung close to Rousey, not touching him or holding onto him, more like when someone hugs a wall in an apartment building because one neighbor is walking a big dog down the corridor.

She stared at Widow and stayed close behind Rousey like she was seeing a rabid animal in a cage.

The girl wore blue jeans and a short black leather jacket and a low-cut top underneath that displayed everything but the kitchen sink. She was rail-thin and had pale skin, which multiplied the mark on her face to look like it required medical attention.

She kept playing with her hair. She pinched the tips in her fingers and fiddled with it nonstop until she stopped and moved to rub her forearms.

*She got some nerves*, Widow thought.

He stared back at her. Her face looked familiar, like he had seen her before and recently, but the face he had seen wasn't so disheveled.

She was an attractive young woman; only she looked like she had been trying to destroy her natural good looks by living a hard life.

Widow took one look at her, and he could see that she was a party girl type. She probably drank a lot, probably smoked a lot, and she definitely did drugs. He knew it. He had seen it before. The Navy was like any other branch of the military.

There were a lot of downtimes and a lot of waiting around and a lot of boredom.

Boredom leads to daydreaming, leads to reckless drinking, smoking, and eventually drugs. Normally, it was weed, not so harmful. Most sailors with a habit of smoking weed were discrete about it. They did it on their shore leave, recreationally, in foreign countries, and they left it there.

Sometimes, they let things get out of hand, and they got busted. Sometimes, they got into some heavy bad habits and situations. And sometimes, they faced a nasty court marshal and stiff sentences, and there was always dishonorable discharge.

Widow had seen guys fall down the drug hole, and he had seen the women they partied with. Usually, sailors fell into the trap by falling for local girls, not always the case, but it was so much the norm that it was almost cliché.

The girl standing in front of him, fiddling with her hair, scratching her forearm, and hiding behind Rousey, had that look, like one of the party girls from overseas.

She wasn't quite a junkie, but Junkie Town was somewhere on the road she was living her life on. No question.

Her eyes were glazed. The skin on her arms was red in places, places with exposed veins. Her demeanor was a little fidgety, a little fretful, even a little frightened like a church mouse.

Her teeth showed early signs of a meth user, not the junkyard that can be found in a meth-head's mouth, but the early signs were there.

That's when Widow realized that Rousey's suspicions of him being high on meth weren't without merit. They were in South Dakota, near the Black Hills. People here were probably bored, probably looking for an escape, especially in the long snowstorm-filled winters.

Meth was likely a big problem out here, a problem that Rousey had to face every day.

Sometimes, living the nomadic life, Widow had become oblivious to the problems of others. There are so many battles to be fought in the homeland. He had fought his battles overseas for years. Now, he lived his life in peacetime.

The SEALs have many mottos and no official mottos.

One motto he remembered was in Latin.

Si vis pacem, para bellum.

It means: *If you want peace, prepare for war.*

Widow stared at the girl, stared at her problems. They were right there for anyone to see.

Her makeup was messed up. It ran everywhere as if she had been crying.

The mascara was black and big and obvious.

Rousey escorted her up the cell bars. He walked like he was taking her up a wedding aisle. She looked like he was taking her to be sacrificed to the monster.

They stopped a good ten feet out in front of Widow's cell. Rousey stepped to the side and reached out, pointed at Widow.

"Recognize him?"

The girl leaned out from behind him and stared at Widow. She looked him up and down and side to side.

After a long moment, she reset back to hiding half behind Rousey. She whispered something that Widow couldn't hear.

Rousey slipped a retractable baton out of his belt. Then he whipped it in a fast flick of his wrist, and it extended all the way out to full length. He showed Widow the business end like a clear threat.

Rousey clanked the baton against the bars and barked an order at Widow.

"Stand up."

Widow got the feeling that the whole act with the baton was a show for the girl. He doubted it intimidated him. Rousey didn't seem that stupid.

Widow could have stayed where he was. What was Rousey going to do? But he didn't want to rock the boat any more than he already had. He wanted to get out as soon as possible. Pissing off the one cop he'd met so far wouldn't do him any favors.

Widow stood up.

"Approach the bars."

Widow stayed quiet, but he did as he was instructed, and he approached the bars, slowly.

Rousey stepped up closer to the bars and shifted to his left, exposing the girl.

She trembled a bit. She kept her eyes down, stared either at the bars or Widow's legs. He couldn't tell which.

Rousey said, "Go on. Get a good look at him."

The girl shuffled back a little farther from where she was.

At the bars, Rousey kept the baton in view.

The girl stepped up and forward and stopped within six feet of Widow.

She looked up at him, a quick glance. She moved closer to Rousey and leaned up to him.

She whispered something to him.

Rousey said, "Extend your arms. Give us a look at your tattoos."

Widow's brow furrowed unintentionally. He could feel them.

What the hell was this?

Widow did as he was told. He rolled up both sleeves of the borrowed thermal, one after the other. They were already half up, anyway. He got them to the elbows with ease and then rolled them over. They were tight on his biceps. Tight enough for him to feel like he was getting his blood pressure checked.

Widow stepped to the bars and stuck his arms out toward them through the bars on the door. The whole thing made him uncomfortable, vulnerable. He felt weak. The fear of Rousey smashing his arms with that baton weighed heavily in the back of his brain.

Rousey looked at the girl and asked, "So?"

She was quiet.

"Have you seen him before? This, the guy?"

The girl looked Widow over again.

"You can get closer. He can't do anything."

The girl looked at Rousey, reluctantly, and stepped forward, inched closer to the bars, closer to Widow's hands, until she was as close as she was going to get.

"Can I see the bottom of the tattoos?" she whispered.

Rousey said, "Tell him."

"Twist your arms up. Show me the other side of the tattoos."

The tattoos on Widow's arms were American flags infused with Navy SEAL tridents. Not much to figure out.

But he did as she asked. She stared at his arms more, at the sleeve tattoos again. Slowly, her eyes panned up to his arms, over his biceps, up to his shoulders, where she paused and stared over his chest. Finally, she moved up his neck and then to his face.

Widow felt like he was on auction, like cattle, or like a slave in ancient Rome. The girl was a buyer, here to pick out a slave to carry her around in a lectica, the ancient Roman box comprising a golden throne, curtains, and long pipes resembling the ones on a casket for the slaves to lift like pallbearers and carry one rich prick from one place to another.

Widow pictured this for a moment, pictured that when he

turned old, she would promote him to be the guy who fans her with a giant leaf until arthritis in his knuckles and hands kicks in. Once he could no longer work, she would just have him put to death—no big deal to her.

"Recognize him? Is it him?" Rousey asked again.

Suddenly, Widow knew what Rousey was up to. And he knew who the girl was. He knew how he had recognized her face.

She was the half-dead girl's younger sister. Had to be.

Rousey was trying to get her to say Widow was the guy in the car.

Maybe she had known who her sister was hanging out with. One guy in the car might've been whoever she had been hanging out with. And whoever she had been hanging out with might've had sleeve tattoos, and was probably a big guy like Widow.

She was there to identify him, like in a police lineup.

The girl stayed quiet.

Rousey said, "Is it him or not?"

"No."

"Are you sure?"

Silence.

"Yes."

"Yes, what?"

Silence.

Rousey asked, "Yes, you're sure it's not him? Or yes, it is him?"

The half-dead girl's sister looked at Widow again. This time, she stared into his eyes. He could see the fear in hers.

She said, "Maybe."

"Maybe? It either is or isn't. Which is it?"

She stared at Widow again.

"I think so."

Widow said, "Whoever you're trying to get her to say I am, I'm not. I've never been here before."

"Quiet!" Rousey barked.

"Take a good look. Be sure. Is it him or not?"

The half-dead girl's sister stared hard at Widow and then at his sleeve tattoos again.

She said, "It's him."

## 12

Widow didn't know what to say, so he said nothing. This girl had never seen him before. He knew that. She had no clue who he was. He had never been there before, never to Reznor. Never met her sister.

The two things he knew were that he wasn't who she thought he was, and whoever they were trying to say he was must've had something to do with her sister. Maybe she had seen the attacker?

Widow stayed on the cot for the rest of the early morning hours.

By nine a.m., the town of Reznor was in as full a swing as it was going to get. He could hear street sounds of daily life echoing into the stationhouse.

Outside, daily commuters went to wherever they worked. Pedestrians walked the sidewalks. The little town was as alive as it was going to get.

It was the daily grind at its peak.

Widow smelled another round of fresh coffee brewing from down the corridor. It was followed by more voices talking.

Widow stood up off the cot and stretched.

He walked over to the sink. They had taken his toothbrush, which he had bought a couple of days earlier, in a gas station in Denver. It was new. He hated wasting a new toothbrush.

*Better get that back*, he thought.

The cell had no toothpaste, anyway. Which was a downer because he felt his breath was hot and bad from the burger and coffee he had eaten and drunk hours before.

Widow ran the water out of the metal sink and doused his face. Then he wet his hair enough to dampen it. He slicked it back and stared into the crude mirror. He leaned in close, trying to see his teeth. He took one index finger, wet it, and ran it over the teeth. He did his best to brush them with the motion of a brush and the cold water from the faucet.

He hoped it would do the trick. It was better than nothing.

After that, he returned to the cot, stopped in the middle of the room, and stared at the bars.

Thirty-five minutes and several muffled conversations later, three men came shuffling down the corridor. All three looked like local cops. Two were carrying mugs of coffee. And the third, Rousey, carried two cups. His wrist twitched slightly, like he was nervous, and Widow figured why.

The front guy was over sixty years old. He was clean-shaven with wispy silver hair. He had a cowboy hat in hand, not on his head. He wore a winter coat and button-down shirt underneath. He was the sheriff, Widow presumed. He had to be, judging by the way he walked out in front and the way the other two men followed behind him like a military scouting party with a clear chain of command.

The second man was another deputy, older than Rousey, but ten years younger than the sheriff. He wore no coat. He had a standard deputy uniform. Tan pants. Tan shirt. He had a badge tacked above his breast pocket, the same as Rousey.

Rousey trailed in the back of the other two, the lesser man on the totem pole.

The man in the front carried something in his hand. He whipped it against the back of his other hand like a riding glove. It was Widow's passport.

As the three men barreled down the hall toward Widow, the frontman whipped open the passport and held it up to his face like he had never looked at it before, which was a lie. It was a natural facade that cops and authority figures did all over the world. You get arrested for something, stuffed into an interrogation room, left for a while to stew in your own thoughts and doubts. The waiting causes you to hesitate and disbelieve yourself, especially if you know you are lying.

Cops call it simmering.

Widow had not been simmering because he had not lied. He had nothing to hide. They were wasting their own time more than his.

For Widow, there was nowhere in particular to go, and all the time in the world to get there. Not a problem.

The man in front glanced at Widow's passport and made a couple of steps ahead of the others and stopped.

He reached into his coat pocket with the closed passport in hand and thumbed out a small pair of reading glasses. Cheap probably bought off the rack at a drugstore.

He slipped the glasses on and stared at the passport.

He said Widow's name out loud in long stretches, as if he was taking roll call for prisoners on death row or something, like an announcement.

"Jack Widow," he called out.

The frontman took another short step forward and then

paced to the left and back to the right. He continued to read from the passport.

"American. Born November 9, in Mississippi."

He held down the passport and stared over it at Widow.

He said, "You're a long way from home, Mr. Widow."

When Widow said nothing, the frontman flipped back through the passport as if he was trying to create the illusion that a cartoon was drawn on it, and he was watching a hundred stick figure drawings move with each flip of the page.

At the end of the flip, he lowered the passport again and stared at Widow.

"Looks like you get around," he said.

Widow shrugged and stayed quiet.

"My name's Charles Shostrom. I'm the sheriff for Lawrence county here in the Mount Rushmore state. You've been caught in a peculiar situation, Mr. Widow."

Widow stayed quiet.

"Got anything to say for yourself?"

"When can I get out?"

The second deputy said, "You're not going anywhere."

Shostrom said, "This's Deputy Roberts, and that's Rousey."

Widow nodded.

"Rousey, hand me the coffee."

Rousey stepped up and held out the mug he was holding. Shostrom folded Widow's passport closed and dropped it into his cowboy hat, turned upside down like a drop bucket. Then he twisted at the hips and took the spare coffee.

Widow wasn't sure if he was going to offer it to him, or if he was teasing him with it like they knew he was an addict already.

Shostrom did the latter. He offered Widow nothing.

Shostrom took a pull from the mug, a long slow pull as if he was over-enjoying it like it was too much for him.

"Mr. Widow, you got a long story to tell?"

"Depends on what story I'm tellin'."

"You got one for me about why you're here?"

"I've got the truth if that's what you're asking."

"The truth?"

"That's what I said."

Shostrom shook his head and made a tsk-tsk noise.

Widow stayed quiet.

"Widow, I'd hoped you'd just make this easy on yourself."

Widow spoke, but the sheriff raised his coffee mug and shushed him.

Widow frowned and waited. What else could he do?

Shostrom said, "Rousey?"

"Yes, Sheriff."

"Get the chair."

Rousey nodded and turned and walked back down the hall. Widow half expected the guy to salute Shostrom, like a sailor recruit jumping to salute a superior officer.

After a minute and a half, Widow heard loud scraping noises coming from down the hall from the office. Finally, Rousey returned, carrying a plain foldable metal chair pulled out of a stack of metal chairs.

He walked it down the hall, unfolded it, and set it down behind Shostrom, just outside the bars. He gave it a quick wipe-down as if it was covered in dust, or it was meant for the king, or both.

Shostrom sat down and crossed his legs. He flipped the cowboy hat right side up, and the passport fell out onto his lap. He placed his cowboy hat on the end of his knee, hung it there. He took a pull of the coffee and set the mug on the floor. Then he thumbed open the passport again.

He leveled his reading glasses onto the bridge of his nose and stared at the passport.

Rousey leaned against a wall, and Roberts stayed standing. Neither spoke.

"You've been to a lot of places, Mr. Widow."

"That a crime?"

"No. No crime. Not yet."

"What is this?"

"This is a simple inquiry."

"Don't I get a lawyer?"

"In due time. Right now, you're not being charged with anything."

"I still have the right to remain silent?"

"You do. You always have that right. But silence is as good as a confession."

"What?"

"Silence is as good as a confession. At least in these parts. A man done something wrong, often he takes advantage of the law, thinking that saying nothing is the same as proving innocence."

Widow stared at Shostrom and then focused on the bars. He was headed nowhere, but sitting behind bars was literally going nowhere. And Widow would rather be back on his way, going nowhere, over rotting there, behind bars and going nowhere.

So he spoke.

"What do you want to know?"

Widow stayed standing. He towered over Shostrom. Which must've bothered the sheriff because he said, "Sit down."

"On what?" Widow asked.

"Bring another chair."

Rousey didn't wait for Roberts to offer to do the grunt

work. He knew the sheriff was speaking to him. So he hopped to action and repeated the same idiotic nod, followed by a scurry back down the hall.

Widow heard the same metal clanging sounds and the same footsteps.

Rousey returned with another foldable metal chair, same as the one he'd gotten for Shostrom. It was from the same stack.

"How do you want me to give it to him?" he asked Shostrom.

"Slide it through the bars."

Rousey stepped past Shostrom, who didn't get up, didn't budge from his seated position.

Rousey shoved the chair through the bars. It barely fit, but it fit. Widow wondered if this was intended when they bought the chairs.

Widow took the chair and carted it through. He unfolded it and plopped it down on the cell floor. He rocked it to make sure it was sturdy; then he dumped his butt down on it.

It was hard and cold, like a foldable metal chair was meant to be.

Widow looked at Shostrom and gave him a fake smile.

Shostrom said, "Okay, Widow talk."

"What do you want to know?"

"You know what I want to know. Who are you? Who's the girl? Why did you bring her here?"

"You know who I am."

"I know your name, but who are you? Why do you travel so much? What's with all the stamps?"

"I was in the Navy."

"They stamp your passport when you go to a new country?"

"They do. Of course, they do."

Shostrom looked back at Roberts.

"That true?"

Roberts nodded.

Widow looked at both men and then zeroed in on Roberts.

"You serve?"

"Four years on the Franklin."

"Four years, one ship?"

"That's right, and then all over a bit. You?"

Widow said, "A little of here. A little of there."

"I was an E4."

"Petty officer."

Roberts nodded and asked, "And you?"

"Commander."

"Terminal?"

"It was my last rank."

Roberts said nothing to that.

Shostrom said, "Commander? So, you were some hot shit in the Navy. Big deal. Get to what I want to know."

"I was walking along a road."

"Which road?"

"I don't know. Just a road. It was the middle of the night."

"Last night?"

"Of course."

Roberts asked, "Why were you walking a road at night?"

"How else am I supposed to get down it?"

Shostrom asked, "Why were you on that road? At night?"

"I got gas-stationed on the Sixteen."

"Gas-stationed?" Roberts asked.

"Sixteen?" Rousey asked.

"Highway Sixteen."

Roberts said, "Old Highway Sixteen."

"Gas-stationed means someone told me to run inside a gas station for something, and then they drove off."

Shostrom asked, "Someone ditched you at a gas station?"

"Yes."

"Why?"

Widow shrugged and said, "Not sure why. It happens sometimes. They didn't like the company, or they didn't like me, or they had planned to do it, or they did it all the time to people, for kicks. Who knows?"

"They didn't give you any inclination that they were going to do it?"

"Sure. I kinda knew the moment they asked me to grab some food for the road."

Rousey asked, "Your friends ditched you?"

"They weren't my friends."

"I don't get it."

Shostrom said, "Mr. Widow here is a drifter."

"You hitchhike?"

Widow nodded.

"That makes you look more suspicious," Shostrom said.

"It ain't a crime."

"No crime. But..."

"Suspicious. I get that."

Shostrom nodded and asked Widow to continue.

Widow did. He told him the whole story. He was abandoned at a gas station on the Sixteen and tired of waiting for a car to appear. The clerk at the station pointed him east on the Sixteen, but Widow didn't like the stillness of it, so he took the road less traveled, which was a country road that led north. The clerk told him eventually it'd run into Interstate Ninety but warned him it could be twenty miles or better. The clerk also told him that there were little communities sprinkled along the way.

But the icing on the cake was the Black Hills National Forest. That was home to Mt. Rushmore and Crazy Horse Memorial, two monuments Widow had never seen, and figured it best to do it while he was so close.

Rousey interrupted.

"You thought it was a good idea to wander into the Black Hills before nightfall, on foot?"

Roberts added, "In wintertime?"

"It's not winter. Not yet. And why not?"

"It's stupid," Roberts said.

Widow shrugged.

"Not to me. To me, it's life. We all gotta go somewhere."

Shostrom said, "But why would you go down a dark country road leading into the Black Hills? It's clearly a thick forest."

Widow said, "I saw power lines. And there was a road. Roads lead to places."

Shostrom said, "Not out here they don't, not always. But go on then."

Widow told the sheriff about the car lights, the dog, and the girl.

Finally, Shostrom asked, "That it? That's the whole story?"

"What more do you want?"

Shostrom looked over at Rousey, who nodded.

"That's all he told me."

"What about Kylie?"

"She says it's him."

Widow looked dumbfounded, but figured that Kylie was the name of the younger, drug-addicted-looking sister of the half-dead girl.

"She positive?"

Rousey stayed quiet.

Shostrom said, "Rousey, she positive?"

"I guess. She said yes."

Shostrom said, "Mr. Widow, it seems we got a witness that places you as a person of interest at the very least. I'm hoping you can give me a reason to discard her statement?"

"I didn't kill anyone or try to kill anyone. I told you. I found her. There was someone else there."

"Forgetting about what Kylie claimed for a moment. Can you tell us a license plate?"

This gesture told Widow that Shostrom was entirely convinced by any testimony that Kylie gave. She must've been known as a junkie, he figured.

"No plate. Too dark. Too far away."

"What can you tell us?"

"I can tell you that you're looking for an older model car. A sedan, probably. And you're looking for two people."

"Two people?"

"I heard two car doors."

"That could've been the driver opening the back door?"

"It wasn't. It was the passenger side door. It closed at about the same time as the driver's side door. There were two people, Sheriff."

"Okay. Anything else?"

"I'm sure you can get me on security camera footage from the gas station I was ditched at. The car that left me was a 2015 or better Nissan. White paint. A white couple drove it. Chris and Christy Smith are the names they gave me."

"Chris and Christy?"

Widow shrugged and said, "Probably fake. Happens."

"What was the gas station?"

"I told you it was off the Sixteen, right off a service ramp. It was a Conoco station. It's a truck stop too. That should help."

"What was the name of the road you found her on?"

"No name on it."

"It had no name?"

Widow said, "I'm sure it has a name. But I didn't see one posted anywhere. Told you. It was a country road. Country roads are rural and often nameless by nature."

Shostrom nodded and asked, "That it? That the whole story?"

"That's all I know of. Check the Conoco. They'll have me on tape in the store a little after sundown. Probably fifteen or twenty minutes. Plus, the clerk will probably remember me."

Shostrom kept the passport in his hand and picked up his cowboy hat. He stood up off the chair. Rousey stepped forward like a manservant and took the chair, refolded it, and stepped back to the wall. He held the chair under his arm.

Shostrom looked at Widow.

"I'll call over to the Conoco."

Widow grabbed the bars and looked out.

"What about the girl?"

"She's in the hospital in Deadwood."

"She gonna pull through?"

"I don't know."

Shostrom walked away.

Widow stopped him and asked, "What's her name, Sheriff?"

He turned back and said, "Her name is Lainey Olsen."

## 13

The two men had ditched the stolen Chevy Impala way back in Rapid City. Well, they didn't ditch it so much as their contact, a guy on the payroll, had met them with a cold storage biological supply van, older than the Chevy, but three times the price because of the equipment onboard had ditched it for them.

The contact hadn't been the one to steal it, not in the sense of scouting a parking lot and implementing the use of a jimmy to pop the lock and using hot wiring to get the engine running.

Instead, he stole the vehicle in the sense that the owner no longer needed it, as he was dead and buried out in the Black Hills.

The contact chalked it up to an occupational hazard. He had a business to run. Sometimes that business called for unsavory things, like murder. If he ended up with a new vehicle out of it, what was he supposed to do? Turn it over to the cops?

So, he'd have his guys clean it through a subsidiary in Rapid City, make the VIN number legal, put new plates on it.

The contact had a good arrangement with the subsidiary in Rapid City. Cost him an arm and a leg, but it was worth it to have new, clean vehicles at his disposal—all part of the care package that he charged the buyers. They paid too. They paid good, straight cash-money. They would probably pay in gold if he asked.

The biological transport van wasn't stolen. It was a state-of-the-art transport vehicle owned by the company the buyers worked for.

After picking it up from the contact, the buyers drove all night, occasionally stopping for gas and once for a sit-down meal where they stayed in the van and ate in the parking lot of an all-night McDonald's.

The driver yawned and snapped to attention when his partner reminded him that Exit Fifty-One C was coming up in ten miles. They drove on Interstate Ninety, heading east for nearly thirteen hours straight.

One man, the driver, was tired, close to exhausted. The passenger was not. He was the kind of guy who could sleep in a moving vehicle. He could sleep anywhere, a byproduct of years in his country's special forces. He slept on aircraft, Hummers, out in the desert, pretty much anywhere—no problem.

The driver was not so lucky. He couldn't sleep like that. He was more alert, which had been his byproduct of a similar background.

Some guys were blessed with the ability to sleep anywhere, and some were not.

The passenger said, "Want me to take over?"

The driver shrugged.

"What for? We're almost out of there now."

The passenger shrugged and turned and looked down at

his phone. He was following along on Google Maps, watching the little arrow move with them.

The driver said, "Why don't you just look out the window at the road ahead?"

"I'm just making sure we're headed the right way."

"We're headed the right way. We've done this drive before."

"Not from South Dakota."

"We've gone to Wyoming, which is on the other side of South Dakota."

"I enjoy staring at the map."

"Whatever."

The driver continued for another ten miles, almost exactly, until he saw the sign for Exit Fifty-One C. Then he took it.

The white panel van with the company logo on the side slowed and yawed and merged with the traffic on West Washington Boulevard. The local time was one hour ahead of Rapid City. They were now in Chicago and the central time zone. Even though it was only an hour difference, they saw the difference.

The early morning traffic in Chicago was brutal. They had caught the tail end of it, going almost into the early lunch traffic. It took them another thirty minutes to traverse the terrain, driving through the edge of downtown, passing it, and leaving it behind them.

They made their way to a service drive, hidden off an industrial thoroughfare that connected hundreds of roads in Chicago's industrial center.

From the gate, the driver was recognized by the guards, but he had to show his ID badge, anyway. Rules were rules.

The guards wore black uniforms and carried Glock 19s in hip holsters. There were double AR-15s fastened behind the wall, side by side. They were held in place by a simple metal twist knob. There was no lock-and-key system in place.

If the need ever arose for them to use the assault rifles, a key and lock wouldn't make any sense. At night, when the station was closed, the AR-15s were taken inside and locked up in the guard barracks, which comprised two rooms. One was the office where they kept their records and employee schedules. The other was a locker room with a metal mesh weapon lockbox embedded into one wall.

The driver nodded at the guard, who took his information with a quick scan of his ID. And then the guard said a pleasant, "Good morning" with a smile.

They were waved through the gates.

The driver moved the van past the guard station and into a large facility made up of three buildings and a single parking lot. The largest building was the size of a small airplane hangar and the same shape as one.

This was the storage warehouse.

Outside of it were huge metal boxes and various mechanical equipment. All of it was locked behind a high fence with a padlock on the only gate.

The equipment was mostly for cooling, freezing temperature controls. The rest of it provided power for the warehouse.

The next largest building was also a warehouse, but this one was for dry goods that didn't need to be temperature controlled.

The third building was an office building.

The warehouse was the only building to have two more guards posted outside. Both were armed with AR-15s and Glocks in hip holsters. They wore the same black uniforms as the guards in the gate station.

Standing outside the warehouse was a guy who wasn't a guard.

The driver pulled up the van and parked near the warehouse. He left the keys in and the ignition on and the engine running.

He and the passenger both got out.

The man standing there was six foot one, with fair hair and big blue eyes. His corneas were white like a blank sheet of paper. He was clean-shaven and well-dressed. He wore a black business suit, no tie.

The man was good-looking, like a celebrity or actor. He was in his early forties but could pass for thirties.

It was hard for anyone to believe it, but the man was actually retired SAS, the British Special Forces. These guys weren't the kind to mess around with.

He no longer worked in SAS, but he was still in the special forces business. But now it was at the corporate level, the money level.

He waited for the driver to approach to speak.

"Any problems?"

The driver said, "Not so far."

The man asked, "You paid the donor? No problem?"

"Our team did the extraction."

"Which doctor?"

"Burke."

"He flew in from LA?"

"They got another wildfire out there. Evacuated his community. He needed the work and can't work with business closed. So, he flew out. But the crew was out of Denver."

"He lose anything in the fire?"

"Don't think he's hit by it other than the evacuation. Which is just a precaution."

The man nodded.

The van passenger said, "Don't worry. Everything was by the book."

The driver frowned and looked down, only for a second.

The man asked, "What?"

"Nothing."

"What? Tell me?"

"It's the donor."

"What about him?"

The van passenger said, "It's a woman."

"Okay. What about her?"

"She was unconscious when they arrived with her."

"Unconscious?"

"Yeah, drugged up."

"Who's 'they'?"

"Two people with her."

"What two people?"

The driver shrugged.

The van passenger said, "We checked them out. They're legit."

"How?"

"They had proof of relationship and consent."

"Proof of consent?"

The driver said, "They had video of the donor. She consented to the procedure."

"So why was she drugged up?"

"We have the video," the van passenger said.

"Let me see."

The van passenger took out his phone and went to his text messages. He pulled up a text from the phone number of one of the two people with the donor. He handed it over to the former SAS guy.

He took the phone and pressed play, watched the video.

It was a woman, young and pretty. She was on camera in a selfie video. She confessed to giving consent to go through with the procedure. That was the first part of the video. The second was what she planned to do with the money.

"She appears to be stoned in this video. Is this how she was?"

"No. I told you she was already unconscious."

"Who did you meet with?"

The driver told the SAS guy who they ended up meeting with at the extraction site. He told the SAS guy about the verification of identities. He told the SAS guy about the relationship between the three of them. And he told him they wired the money to them. All of it went off without a hitch.

The SAS guy asked, "Did they call nine-one-one for her?"

"We told them to wait ten minutes after we were all packed up and drove away."

The van passenger said, "As we always do."

The SAS guy nodded and asked, "Did they seem trustworthy?"

The van passenger nodded eagerly. But the driver said nothing.

The SAS guy looked at him and waited.

The van driver said, "They were sketchy, but I don't foresee a problem. The girl gave consent. You saw it in the video. They definitely needed the money."

The SAS guy said, "They all need the money."

He turned away from the two men for a moment, walked over to the van. He rubbed his chin like he was thinking.

Then he spoke again.

"Okay. Take the merchandise inside. You know where to store it."

He was talking to the van passenger. That was clear.

The SAS guy placed a hand on the van driver's shoulder, holding him there like he was waiting for the passenger to get the merchandise and take it inside, which he was.

The van passenger went to the side of the van and unlocked the door with a separate extra key. Then he slid it open. He vanished inside the back for a moment until he came out with essentially a cooler. Only not a cooler for beer. This one was all metal and hard plastic. It smoked as it came out of a freezing cold temperature, like it had been packed in dry ice.

It was a medical cooler, marked *BioWaste* on the side in black block letters.

The top of the cooler had a combination lock embedded into it. Once it was closed, the combination was known only by a technician at the warehouse.

The tech with the combination was nowhere in sight. He would arrive within an hour to open the cooler and inspect the incoming stock.

The van passenger took the medical cooler and disappeared into the warehouse.

The SAS guy turned back to the van driver and said, "We don't take chances like this."

"I know. I'm sorry. I thought under the circumstances; it was okay."

"It is. But this donor better keep her shit together. No blowback."

"I got it."

"I want you to monitor it."

"How?" The van driver paused a beat and then added, "Need me to drive back there?"

"The contact in Rapid City."

The van driver nodded.

The SAS guy asked, "You trust him?"

"Yeah. He's been reliable."

"Call him. Have him check in on this donor and her two friends. Make sure there're no complications."

"Got it."

"Do it now."

The van driver hopped to it and pulled out his phone. He called the contact in Rapid City, who had just finished breakfast in his own house. He had finished lacing up his shoes and was about to head out the front door when the phone rang.

"Yo."

"It's me."

"I know. What's up? Problem with the van? You make it?"

"We made it. No problem."

"So, what's up?"

"We need something else from you."

"Okay."

"The donor may cause us problems."

"You need me to take care of him?"

"It's a woman. And no. Nothing that extreme. Not yet. We need you to check in on her and two others. Her associates. I'll text you their names."

"What you want me to do? Call them?"

"Don't call them. I need you to drive out there. Go to the nearest hospital and check for her. She'll be in recovery somewhere. She had major surgery last night."

The contact in Rapid City paused a beat and then asked, "Where was the surgery done?"

"Deadwood."

"Twenty miles up the road. I'll send one of my guys."

"No! You go!"

"Okay. Okay. Fine. I'll go check it out today."

"You go check it out now!"

The contact stayed quiet. He didn't like being talked to this way. He wasn't used to it. Guys who talked to him that way didn't normally get away with it. Normally, he ended up with their car.

But he said nothing about it. The money was good, and he needed it. His main business of late was peddling opioids on the bored rural population around Rapid City. This time of year, coming up on the middle of winter, business was booming. People were bored. Their incomes faded away like the colors of leaves on the trees. He didn't need the money from these guys, but the money was good, too good to pass up.

So, he told them what they wanted to hear. He agreed to go check out the donor, personally, today.

Five minutes later, he was off the phone and texting one of his guys who lived toward Deadwood to check it out for him.

14

By ten in the morning, Rower drove right past the turn for the Reznor sheriff's station. She drove past it by a good hundred yards when she got turned around at a barely maintained train yard. It was more of a ghost train yard than a working one.

She saw zero signs of life.

The yard had a chain-link fence wrapped around it that had been standing since the early eighties. The fence had too many broken links to count. There were child-sized holes all over the place.

Rower saw the rail. It came in from the west and went out to the east. The rail had been decommissioned long ago—no doubt about it. What remained were bent-up metal and missing rail blocks. Both directions, west and east, were barricaded by large metal, angled constructs that looked like Czech hedgehogs, a device used by the Germans in WWII. They were antitank obstacles that were extremely heavy. The Germans dropped them into the sand at Normandy Beach by the thousands to stop the Allied Forces from driving tanks up onto the beach.

There were still trains in the yard, prehistoric ones.

Some were rusted, and the rest were a different age of rusted, as if they were the first trains to come off the factory floor, the great-great-grandfathers of the modern train.

At first, she didn't know why the trains and the yard were still there until she saw a small two-story building off to the side with a sign posted out front with kid-friendly blocks of letters on it with little cartoon trains. The place had been turned into a train museum for kids.

She noticed a lot of the trains were covered in colorful graffiti, which was meant as a way of spicing up the colors for the children.

*Weird*, she thought. But then she imagined a family clan living out here, maybe losing their business because of staggering economic changes. Maybe someone in the family was a train lover, and they somehow bought up the trains and the yard and turned it into this. It was kind of neat.

Rower looked away from the trains and glanced down at her phone. Google Maps was giving her issues. It told her to continue straight for another ten miles, but she knew she was close.

She backtracked, and within a minute, Maps recalibrated and told her where to turn. She arrived at the station just as Sheriff Shostrom was stepping outside for a smoke.

She knew it was him because even though she had never been to Reznor before. She never heard of it; she had met with Shostrom before, naturally. She was the designated agent over the region that his county was in.

Shostrom was a short man, about five-foot-six. Standing next to his two deputies, that she couldn't identify, Shostrom looked even smaller.

Rower parked in the only other parking spot left open and got out.

"Henry, how are you?"

Shostrom never got the chance to light the cigarette. He kept it in his hand with a metal Zippo. He stepped forward off the front step of the station and greeted her halfway.

He nodded at her and offered a hand to shake, which she took.

"Special Agent Alaska, good to see you again."

"Good to see you. You don't need to call me: *Special Agent*. Just Alaska is fine."

A small breach of protocol, she knew, but the rural cops appreciated it. It gave her the advantage of trust. That was a price she was willing to pay for the potential verbal reprimand she might get if she ever got caught by her SAC.

Trust among rural cops was very important. For Rower, two of the three gunfights she had ever been in were out in less populated areas. People who lived out here were more likely to carry a lot more firearms than people living in urban areas in her region of the country, at least. Not to say that suspects in Rapid City or Minneapolis didn't carry guns and didn't shoot at her. But people out here collected guns, and they fired them a lot. Hard to fire a gun in a city without being noticed. Easy to fire guns out here. No one would even know in some areas.

So, for Rower, trust with local cops was essential.

"Alaska, these are my boys, Rousey and Roberts."

Rower shook their hands, didn't bother to memorize their names because they wore nameplates. She could look when she needed to.

Rower asked, "The guy inside?"

"He is."

Shostrom lit his cigarette and puffed on it, blowing the smoke away from her.

"He say anything?"

"He says he's not guilty."

"Who is he?"

Shostrom reached into his pocket and handed her the passport.

She flipped it open, noticed the many travel stamps, and read the name.

"Widow?"

"That's what it says."

She closed the passport but didn't return it. She kept it in her hand.

"What's his story?"

Shostrom told her the whole story—beginning to end. All of what Widow claimed happened last night, all of what they knew happened from the eyewitnesses and the security camera footage at Overly's.

She said, "Did you pull the gas station cameras? Check with the night clerk?"

"I called the gas station. The night clerk claims he remembers him."

"He sure?"

"He described him exactly."

"And?"

"And they are sending the footage to back up the story."

"Was the woman with him?"

"Not according to the clerk. And the clerk backed up his story about being ditched. No woman. No car. And Widow wandered off alone and down a dark road, just as he claims."

Rower nodded and turned and went back to the car. She opened the back door and took out a thin briefcase. She closed the car door and walked back to them.

"I'm gonna go see him."

"You don't want to visit the victim first?" Rousey asked.

She looked at him.

"The victim awake yet?"

Shostrom said, "Nope. Comatose."

"Then what's she gonna tell me?"

Shostrom smirked and took another drag off his cigarette. He was about to discard it when Rower put her hand up.

"No. You stay out here. Finish your smoke. I wanna talk with him alone."

Roberts said, "I should go with you, ma'am."

"For what?"

Roberts looked at Rousey, a quick side glance, then he looked at Shostrom, who puffed the cigarette and shrugged at him.

"He's dangerous."

"How do you know that?" Rower asked.

"He tried to kill that girl."

"Innocent until proven guilty."

Roberts asked, "How do you know who's dangerous then? If you go around seeing all suspects as innocent civilians?"

"I said innocent until proven guilty. I see everyone as dangerous. At all times. No exceptions."

Roberts looked her up and down. Not slowly, but not fast either. It was slow enough for her to note it.

Rower was in her late thirties, divorced, no kids, and she liked to drink more than the Bureau's recommended amount in a week. She only drank off duty, of course, which was most nights these days.

Rower didn't drink wine or mixers like a rookie agent. She drank whiskey, neat—the same brand. The same year it was barreled, if she could find it.

Despite the drinking, Rower ate moderately healthy. She didn't go to the gym, unless she was back in Minneapolis in her two-bedroom apartment, with one empty guest room and no pets. She had five fake floor plants that she had named. She called them all Debbie, which was the name of a calf she had growing up on a dairy farm.

With no motivation to seek new gyms every night that she spent on the job, on the road in motels, she did push-ups when she woke up, before coffee. She did the same number of push-ups before bed. Three days a week, she did sit-ups in the morning and before bed. And four days a week, she jumped rope.

She carried a jump rope in her briefcase.

Rower was proud of her fitness, but she hated guys on the job, making comments, or looking too long.

Roberts had done this.

She noticed, and she put him on notice with a look. He saw the look but didn't register it. She knew he didn't. Men who registered the cold look returned it with a shamed-expression, knowing they had been busted.

Roberts didn't express this to her.

But she said nothing to him about it because of trust.

It may come down to a gunfight with her life on the line, and Roberts might be the extra gun with the extra bullet to make the difference.

Trust.

## 15

Rower went in alone to the Reznor sheriff's station. The layout was easy enough—a simple bullpen that doubled as the entrance. There were three desks laid out, two back to back, and one facing the entrance like a reception area. There was a phone on every desk, but only two computers—one at reception and another on the farthest desk.

*Interesting,* Rower thought. She had seen a lot of small sheriff stations. This one wasn't that bad for the town it served.

Around the corner, through a door entryway, she saw a hallway with three cell doors.

She walked down and found the man called Jack Widow in the last one. He was standing a foot behind the bars, staring at her and waiting.

She walked to the center of the hall and stayed standing a good ten feet back. And then she looked Widow up and down, not blatant and rude like Roberts had done to her, but more like sizing him up, like most good cops did.

He recognized the movement.

Then she did something he wasn't expecting. She looked him in the eyes and walked right up to the bars.

She said, "Mr. Widow?"

Widow nodded. He noticed his passport in her hand.

She reached into her inner jacket pocket, popping her jacket open. He saw her hip holster and the exposed part of a Glock 22. She pulled out a faded black leather billfold. She flipped it and showed him her FBI badge and ID.

He looked at it.

The ID was behind a milky plastic cover. There was an FBI badge and an ID card. He read the Department of Justice, the big FBI letters, and saw her designation as a special agent, along with her Federal ID number and name.

She spoke as he read the name.

"My name is Alaska Rower. I'm an Investigator with the FBI."

Widow smiled and reached out his hand, offered it to her to shake.

He said, "Jack Widow. No fancy title other than that."

She stopped, froze, and stared at his hand.

*Trust*, she thought. *With an attempted murder suspect?*

She said, "I can't shake your hand."

"I know. I just wanted to see if you would."

He pulled it back.

She put the badge, ID, and wallet back into her jacket.

"You understand why you're here?"

"I do. But I shouldn't be in here."

"Why's that?"

"I did nothing wrong. 'Sides breaking down a door. I suppose."

"Why don't you tell me the story?"

"I already told Shostrom. I'm sure he told you."

"He did. But why don't you tell me?"

Widow repeated the story. The gas station, being abandoned, deciding to take the road less traveled, seeing the lights, finding the dog, the girl, and the rug. He told her about carrying her and finding his way to Overly's biker bar.

She listened. She didn't take notes.

She said, "That's it."

"That's it."

"And you're a drifter?"

"Yes."

"Why?"

"Why not?"

"You got money?"

"They took my bank card."

"They didn't show it to me."

"It's probably in a desk drawer along with my toothbrush."

"Toothbrush?"

"I carry one with me."

"Are you obsessed with your teeth?"

Widow said, "It's inconvenient to have to buy a new one all the time. So, I keep one on me as much as I can."

She stared at his face.

"They got your razor in that drawer?"

"I shave sometimes."

"You need to shave now."

"Think if I did, they'd let me out of here?"

Rower smiled, not a fake, flirty smile, like she might do to entice a male suspect to cooperate, a coercion tactic that she had used many times. It worked. Her mother used to say, "If it ain't busted, don't fix it."

"Tell me, Mr. Widow. What's with all the stamps on your passport? You a man of leisure?"

"I am, but the stamps are from when I was in the service."

"What service?"

"Shostrom didn't tell you?"

"No. Should he have?"

"Usually, it's mentioned."

"Usually?"

"I was in the Navy and the NCIS."

Rower cocked her head, shot him a questioning glance.

"You were in the NCIS?"

"Yes."

"Like the TV show?"

Widow shrugged and said, "Is your job chasing aliens?"

"Chasing aliens? Illegal aliens?"

"Aliens. You know? Little green men?"

"What on earth are you talking about?"

"That TV show. With Mulder and whatever."

Rower shook her head.

"Sculley. It's Mulder and Sculley. The show was The X-Files."

Widow stayed quiet.

Rower said, "No, I don't chase aliens."

"So, my job wasn't like the TV show either."

"Have you ever seen NCIS?"

He shook his head.

"Great show."

"Is it?"

"Number one on the planet."

"Really?"

"I think so."

Widow smiled and asked, "It got aliens?"

"No. No aliens."

Rower flipped open his passport, glanced through it again, and stopped on his photo ID.

"You were shaved here."

"In the Navy, they make you shave every day."

Rower leaned her face over the passport, out toward Widow, and took a couple of obvious sniffs of the air.

"They make you shower in the Navy too?"

"I shower."

"When was the last time?"

Widow craned his neck, leaned his head down the right side of his chest like a bird going to sleep in its feathers, and sniffed.

"I smell nothing."

"A shower wouldn't kill you."

Widow returned his head upright and smiled.

He said, "Alaska. Is that your real name?

"It is."

"Family name?"

"No. Just my name."

"It seems like I heard something about the name before."

"Yeah. Duh. It's a state."

"No. I mean something that has to do with a woman named Alaska."

They were both silent for a moment.

Widow asked, "You from Alaska?"

"Never been there."

"Damn. I can't remember where I heard the name before."

Rower shrugged.

"It'll come to you."

"So, what now?"

"You haven't asked me why the FBI is interested."

"Why is the FBI interested? It's not because of the interstates?"

"Could be."

"Nah. I found her on a country road, not the interstate. Shostrom's not gonna let you take his investigation from him."

"How do you know that?"

"I have some experience with sheriffs and jurisdiction."

"I bet you do."

Widow said, "I bet the reason you're here is because of her kidneys."

Rower's eyes opened wide, and her brow furrowed to one side, and her interest perked.

"Kidneys?"

"When I found the girl, she was wrapped up in a rug. Someone thought they'd killed her and they ditched the body. When I went to free her, I found she was all bandaged up, like she had major surgery. Right where one of her kidneys is."

"What do you make of it?"

"It's weird because someone tried to strangle her. Obviously. But someone else took her kidney and took great care of her afterward."

"Any thoughts?"

"My guess is that you can find out who by checking for the hospital where she had a kidney transplant done. She must've been taken from the hospital."

Widow shrugged and said, "I don't know why. It seems like it'd be risky to do something like that. Hospitals have staff, security, and lots of witnesses."

"If any of that is true, wouldn't my working theory be that a mental patient escaped, kidnapped her?"

"Am I the mental patient?"

Rower said nothing.

"That theory sounds stupid. A mental patient escaped and took a victim who just had major surgery? No-one stopped him? Why would I have been out in the middle of nowhere? In the middle of the night?"

"I don't know. You're the mental patient."

Widow stayed quiet.

Rower said, "No. I don't believe any of that. The reason you're here is how you busted into a biker bar with a half-dead girl. The reason I'm here is that this is an old case I had once."

Widow nodded. He recognized something familiar in her eyes, and he knew what it was immediately.

He said, "You've worked this case before."

She looked at him.

"What happened?"

Rower stared at him. She never broke contact, but she wasn't seeing him, not anymore. She wasn't at the moment. She saw something else, like a face from a distant memory.

She breathed for a long moment. Then she said, "A lot of cops work cases that haunt them. Cases that never get solved. Sometimes for months. Sometimes for years. The cases often hit brick walls and go cold. Most of them never get solved. They're cases that the investigators never shake."

"You ever work a case like that, NCIS?"

Widow nodded.

"I've got a few of those."

Rower turned away and stared down the hallway. Then she turned back to Widow.

She said, "I look you up, am I gonna find that who you claim to be, is real?"

"You already looked me up?"

"I didn't, actually. Shostrom just told me your name when I got here."

"They probably looked me up."

"No. They're not..."

She paused a beat and then said, "They're not the most thorough cops in the world."

"Better check me out then."

"I will. But first. Do you like coffee?"

Widow smiled.

## 16

Ty McCobb was named after the great baseball player—Ty Cobb, only with a Scottish twist on it. That's what he always told people anyway, even though it wasn't true.

The joke got a chuckle here and there. The truth was he hated baseball, but the bats came in handy for his job.

McCobb's job entailed recon and reaction based on results he found out. Sometimes this was passing on information. Sometimes it was giving out a warning. But sometimes, it was retaliation—his favorite.

Right now, he was being ordered by his boss, a guy named Holden from Rapid City. This was all Holden's region. Most of the Black Hills were.

McCobb was a kind of part-time problem solver and a part-time delivery boy.

He wasn't a drug dealer, per se, but he worked with and for a drug dealer.

McCobb's job was more on the execution side of things. He was charged with executing orders—problems too.

He walked into the hospital in Deadwood. It was a

redbrick, three-story building. It was no kind of major metropolitan hospital. But it was busy enough.

He left his car parked in the annex lot across the street. He wore a ball cap and sunglasses.

He entered through the emergency room entrance. He walked past security, which was an old guard behind a desk and a security camera that didn't move. It was planted up high on the inside wall and pointed right at the entrance and exit.

He was on camera. No getting around that.

McCobb had to leave the baseball bat behind in the trunk of his car. Couldn't bring it into the hospital—no way. They'd see something that big in a guy's hand.

But he could bring in a revolver.

Deadwood Hospital was no kind of top-security clearance place, like a bank or a prison or a military base. There were cameras, but there were no metal detectors. The hospital wouldn't fork over money for that. They had the elderly guard.

McCobb kept the revolver nestled in the single inner pocket of a denim jacket he wore. It was on the left side, which made for a right-handed draw. Not his idea of ideal since he was left-handed, but it was better than no gun.

On his way in, he nodded a polite hello to the elderly security guard and clocked the gun strapped to the guard's hip. It was in a holster in a belt with the safety button buckled. No way would the guard be able to draw on him before taking two to the chest.

McCobb passed the guard and walked past a full waiting room and past hospital staff and walked into a hallway until he found a large map of the hospital on a bulletin board.

He studied it and found where he was on the map. He found the right floor where they would keep someone like the person he was looking for.

McCobb walked down the hall to a pair of elevators. Only two. He hit the button for level two and rode up.

He got off on a floor that seemed busier than he had expected. There were staff doing things. He saw a patient engaging in physical therapy. She was walking along the wall with one hand planted against it, and the other draped over a therapist in scrubs.

He saw another woman in a wheelchair just rolling up and down the hall. There were nurses walking up and down the hall, some carrying trays, others pushing carts.

McCobb stopped at an open doorway and studied a sign on the wall that pointed the direction for recovery, which was more than half the floor.

He walked up and down the corridor, looking in every room that he could. He woke up one old man who was vocal about the disturbance.

The thought of shooting him crossed his mind for a moment.

McCobb couldn't find anyone who fit the description of the girl he was looking for.

After twenty minutes of searching, McCobb asked someone at the nurses' station. A risk, because then he would expose himself to a witness. But it seemed necessary.

So, he approached the station and asked about the donor. He gave her name and asked what room she was in.

One nurse, a black woman in purple scrubs, looked up at him from her chair. She pointed him to a white phone hung on the wall behind him.

She told him to use that for information.

McCobb thanked her and turned to the phone.

A sign above the phone read: *Pick up for information.*

He picked up and heard a voice instruct him to dial a

number that coordinated with the first letter of the last name of the patient he was looking for.

He dialed 6 for the letter O.

He waited, listening through a list of names. The list was pronounced slowly and dragged on in a monotone computer voice.

First, he had to wait through the Ms and then the Ns, until he got to the Os.

Finally, he got to the Os, and he listened. There was only one. Oxford.

That wasn't the right name.

He hung up the wall phone and pulled out his own phone. He texted Holden that she wasn't there.

He waited.

A good two minutes passed before Holden responded.

He responded with, "Check around again. Be sure."

McCobb texted back, "Okay."

He slipped the phone back into his pocket, and then he walked the floor one more time, checking the rooms for recovery patients and found nothing.

He decided that he'd better check the entire hospital, skipping places that wouldn't have an organ transplant patient recovering in, like the maternity ward.

McCobb went back to the elevator and started on the fourth floor and worked his way down.

The fourth floor was clear—no sign of anyone recovering from major surgery on that floor.

The third floor was the same.

On the third floor, he took the stairs down instead of the elevator.

He got out on the first floor, back where he'd started. He began searching the parts of the first floor that he could search. He had to skip the emergency room.

That didn't leave him much. Most of the first floor was the lab and technician and administrative areas.

Before he gave up, he saw something peculiar.

Through the windows on a pair of swinging doors to the ICU, he saw a uniformed deputy standing guard in an open room.

The deputy sat in a chair, reading a day-old USA Today. He had a pencil missing an eraser in his hand. He was doing the crossword—a man passing the time.

McCobb stepped to the side as a doctor and a nurse were pushing through.

As the door swung wide open, McCobb saw a young, twenty-something girl lying in bed in the room beyond the deputy. She was completely out and strung up to an IV drip and a heart monitor that blipped at a steady pace.

McCobb stepped back and pulled out his phone. He leaned against a wall and looked up and then down the hall for anyone who might get curious about him.

There was no one.

He texted back to Holden, told him he'd found her, told him she was under guard by the cops.

Holden was quiet for another long two minutes.

This time he came back with an order for McCobb to hold, to sit tight for now, while he got instructions on what to do next.

## 17

When Rower asked Widow if he "liked coffee," he smiled because he thought she was going to let him out so she could take him somewhere to get a cup of coffee, like a date. It was an impulsive thought, an instinctual miscalculation, he knew, but he wanted to think that she believed him.

He was partly right. She let him out, in front of the deputies, in front of the sheriff.

Rower turned to Shostrom, asked for the keys, which turned out to be keys and not an electronic lock system. The look on Shostrom's face was surprised, but that didn't compare to the looks on the faces of Rousey and Roberts.

The two deputies stood back and watched as if their boss wasn't opening a cell door for a man. They watched as if he was opening a cage, and they feared what was inside.

After Widow got out, he asked for his belongings, which they denied for the moment.

Agent Rower had possession of his passport and his bank card, and not his toothbrush. His coat was still in evidence.

Roberts cuffed him in the front, and they put him in an SUV and took him to get a coffee, as promised.

The coffee was hot, too.

Rower bought the coffee for him at the same gas station where he'd claimed to be the night before.

She convinced Shostrom to hand Widow over to the FBI.

Now, he was in her custody, technically, but the sheriff had assigned his two deputies to chaperone them while they stayed in his county, which Rower took as half extra protection for her from him, and half the sheriff keeping a watchful eye on Widow and herself.

She was in his domain, and he was going to make sure that she respected it, respected the unwritten rules.

Widow sat in the rear bench of a Lawrence County sheriff's SUV, a Ford Explorer painted with the sheriff's department colors, and a South Dakota state badge on each door. A big light bar was framed on the roof. There were lights embedded in the front grille as well. A black ram bar was mounted on the front of the vehicle.

The Explorer sat five people comfortably. This unit didn't have a third row of seats. Instead, it had a built-in cage, which Widow assumed was meant for a large cop dog.

Thankfully, there was no dog in it.

Widow liked dogs.

In the past in the Navy, he had worked with military dogs, mostly IED sniffing dog units, mostly Marines, and mostly huge German shepherds the size of small ponies, trained in police and military tactics like obeying commands, such as breaking the bones in a guy's arm in seconds.

He remembered the Marines treated the dogs like Marines. They gave them the designations of Colonel Rex and Commander Thor. He was pretty sure these were official names, but the dogs were considered the property of the USMC, just like the Marines, and they were given virtually the same treatment, minus the dog kennels.

Rousey drove with Rower in the passenger seat and Roberts next to Widow. They took the long way around to Old Highway Sixteen, a forty-minute drive. Widow didn't know why they didn't go the way he had come, back down the country road, where they could connect to the Sixteen a lot faster.

He figured Rower was waiting to search the country road last, like some big reveal. Or maybe she was just thorough. Maybe she liked to think linearly. First, this happened, and then that.

Maybe she was starting where he had started and following his story back to the part where he passed out from the exhaustion.

However, when they arrived at the Conoco, he suspected it might've been because no one believed him. They thought the country road was a waste of time because it had no landmarks—no signs. No structures to go by. How were they supposed to find the spot where Widow claimed to have found the girl?

He figured they knew they would spend the day combing through it all. And for what? His story wasn't true.

Maybe skipping it was more the work of the sheriff than Agent Rower. He wasn't sure.

Either way, she was going to indulge the sheriff over him. If the sheriff said they should go to the gas station first, that was what they would do.

When he realized they were going to the gas station, Widow asked about the security footage. Didn't Shostrom already order it to be messaged over? Or emailed? Or, however, they were going to do it?

Rower told him this was faster and left it at that.

They stopped at the station and parked near the rear in

front of a set of outside bathroom doors, white brick walls with graffiti in one corner, just past a dumpster.

Rousey and Rower got out of the front. Roberts stayed where he was, watching Widow like a hawk. He waited for Rousey to stand by his door before turning his back on Widow.

Out of curiosity, Widow tried the door handle on his side. It didn't open. They had the child lock engaged.

Rower opened Widow's door for him, but Rousey called to her to wait. She stopped and stood there, staring over at them.

The deputy popped the rear door and pulled out two Tactical Remington 870s. Big guns. All black finishes. Serious weapons.

Each deputy took one and loaded it and pumped the action. Rousey stared in at Widow, made sure he saw the shotgun, made sure he witnessed the pump.

Widow made no expression. He just waited.

Rousey told Rower to go ahead, and she opened the door, let Widow out.

Widow didn't want to get shot by whatever load the deputies were armed with, so he got it in his head to continue to play nice.

His suspicions nagged at him. Judging by the whole "Hannibal Lector" way that they were treating him. So far, the loads in the shotguns were probably Magnum slugs.

Why go all out with these weapons if you didn't have dangerous slugs loaded?

Rousey came around, stopped at the passenger side rear tire, and usurped Rower's control over Widow like he wanted to show her he was taking charge.

He barked at Widow to step forward.

Widow followed orders, no questions, and stepped

forward. He stayed cold: cold expression, cold gaze, and he was physically cold. He wondered if they would ever give him back his coat. He shivered in the borrowed thermal.

Rousey closed his door behind him.

Widow stared down at his handcuffs. For a moment, he expected Rousey to cover his hands with a jacket or something, but no one did.

"Let's go," Rousey ordered.

He waited for Widow to go first and stayed behind with the shotgun. It wasn't pointed at Widow, but it was there, pointed at the ground behind him, which made little difference in Widow's mind.

From Widow's experience, this looked more like a prisoner transfer than a simple witness pointing out where he had been the night before. But Widow didn't protest. Not once. Not so far.

Being a man with nowhere to go and all the time in the world to get there, he had a lot of patience. Why not? He considered himself lucky. Most people in this world dealt with tremendous nuisances every single day. Although being in handcuffs for doing the right thing was worse than mundane, daily nuisances, he still considered the whole thing an inconvenience.

He followed behind Rower. They walked into the gas station. Roberts held one of a set of double glass doors open.

Rower stepped in first and then Widow, followed by the deputies.

Behind the counter stood two employees of the gas station. One was an older woman with white hair. She was petite to the point of being a borderline little person. The second was the young guy from the night before.

Dark circles surrounded the under part of his eyes. He hadn't been to sleep yet.

Rower had Widow stand four feet from the counter and asked, "You recognize this guy?"

"Yeah. That's the dude that got left here last night. The same guy, I told Rousey about."

They knew each other. Widow figured most people from around twenty square miles probably knew who Rousey was, being that he was the full-time deputy stationed in this area.

Rower asked, "You guys got last night's surveillance footage?"

The lady with the white hair answered.

"I already sent it to the sheriff."

"You got a copy here too?"

"Of course."

"Let me see it."

"Who are you?" the lady with the white hair asked.

"Pardon me; I'm with the FBI."

Rower took out the same badge Widow had already seen and showed it to the woman and then the young, tired clerk. After they were satisfied, she flipped it closed and stuck it back into her jacket.

"Come on then. It's back in the office."

Rower followed the lady back behind a door marked "Private," but the lady stopped and looked back.

The deputies were pushing Widow forward like they were all going back.

The white-haired lady said, "We can't all fit back there."

Rower turned to the deputies and said, "I'll take him."

Rousey said, "What?'

Rower stepped up to Widow and grabbed one hand under his bicep. She tugged on him, pulled him away from the deputies.

"I'll take him. Don't worry."

Rousey looked over at Roberts, who stayed quiet.

"You boys stay here. Stand guard."

The deputies were ordered to follow Rower's instructions. Nothing they could do. No grounds to argue. She had given them a clear order.

They both nodded and stayed back.

The white-haired lady's reaction was different. She wasn't under orders by the sheriff. She had no obligation to follow any orders at all from the FBI.

She said, "I don't want him to go back there."

"He's gotta go back. I want to see him and the guy in your footage together."

The white-haired lady frowned in protest. She said nothing, but the resistance was obvious.

Rower said, "It'll be fine. Don't worry."

And she pulled open her jacket, showed the white-haired lady her Glock 22.

Widow smiled, because he knew that wouldn't reassure the woman. He knew she had two guns herself, at least. One was under the counter. It was probably packed beneath the cash register. And the other was in the office. Probably duct-taped to the bottom of a desk.

He figured neither of them was a Glock. They were both probably closer to the rocket launcher family than the nine-millimeter family.

He smiled.

The white-haired lady nodded and led them both back.

The office was more cramped than Widow thought. He barely fit in behind Rower.

She stayed close to the white-haired lady, who sat in a rolling chair at a desktop attached to the wall.

She clicked on a laptop computer and pulled up the file for the cameras with the right times. She had already set it up, all ready to go.

She clicked play, and they watched on the screen in four split screens as Widow's story unfolded, just as he had described it.

He arrived in a car with two other passengers. He climbed out and headed inside the station, as he had said. A minute later, the two in the car could be seen arguing, not heavily, but disagreeing about something. Next, they slowly backed out of the space and drove off.

On the other screen, they watched Widow staring out the window near the register. His expression stayed stagnant, unemotional, not angered, not bent out of shape. He just looked opinion less, like it didn't matter to him.

They watched as Widow did as he said. He bought a coffee and drank it, right there in front of the gas station, out near an icebox. Finally, they watched him throw away the empty cup and saunter off out of the close camera's view. Next, he appeared on the most external camera, pointed at the interstate.

They watched as he looked at the interstate and then back towards a long set of unmarked country roads, like it was a tempting choice.

In the end, he chose the country road, and just like he had claimed, he vanished down one, trekking over the light snow.

Rower said, "So, you were telling the truth?"

"Did you doubt it?"

"I'm an FBI agent. I always doubt everything."

"Can I get out of these cuffs now?"

"Not so fast."

Widow's face was the same as on the screen—emotionless and unaffected.

Rower said, "But, I owe you a coffee like I promised."

She thanked the manager and followed Widow back out

into the store. Roberts and Rousey stood near the entrance, shotguns ready.

Widow walked toward them, presuming that was Rower's next order.

"Hold on," she called out from behind him.

Widow stopped, turned, and faced her.

"Wait for us outside."

"What?" Rousey asked.

"Give us some space."

Rousey looked at Roberts. Both men paused a long beat.

Rower said, "It's not a democracy, guys. This is my case. My prisoner. Wait outside."

Roberts said nothing. He turned and left the gas station. Rousey followed, but paused first and stared at Widow again.

"That guy's got a stick up his butt."

Rower said, "They've got tough jobs. They all have sticks up their butts."

Rower signaled for Widow to follow her, and she walked to the register. The manager moved behind them and skirted her way behind a complex of display cases and impulse buys until she was standing behind the guy behind the register.

The manager moved in front and waited as if she was needed to wait on the FBI over an hourly employee.

"What else can I do for you?" she asked.

"Where's the coffee?"

"Back counter."

Rower nodded a thank you and led Widow down a junk food aisle until they were at the coffee station, which was as he remembered it from the night before.

"Can you pour your own cup in those?"

"I can. But..."

"What?"

"I don't have any money."

"I told you. I'm buying."

Widow nodded and smiled. He stepped up, took a medium cup, and set it down. He picked up a half-full pot and poured it carefully into the cup. Then he returned the pot.

"You didn't spill any."

Widow smiled and said, "Not my first time."

"Cream and sugar?"

"No. Coffee is perfect already. You don't add to something that's perfect already."

Rower nodded, stepped up, and grabbed a lid for the cup.

"Better put that on. Those deputies won't be happy that you have an open container of hot coffee. It could be seen as a weapon."

"It is a weapon. Hot coffee is like a grenade only instead of shrapnel; it sprays hot liquid."

"Are you trying to make me regret buying it?"

"No. Thank you."

Rower signaled for Widow to step ahead of her, back to the front.

"You're not going to get some for yourself?" he asked.

"I don't drink coffee."

Widow froze. His face finally turned to an expression that she had expected on the man in the surveillance video when his ride abandoned him. It was an automatic reaction of disappointment. It was almost one of being insulted.

"You don't like coffee?"

"It's not good for you."

"Pretty good for me."

"It's bad for the heart."

"If you say so."

"Come on."

They returned to the front. Rower moved in front of Widow to the cashier and the manager.

"That's all. How much?"

The manager said, "Nothing. Don't worry about it. It's on the house."

"Are you sure?"

"Yes. Anything for law enforcement."

"That's kind of you."

"Of course. We're just glad you get guys like this off the street."

Widow's face returned to emotionless. He was often misunderstood and feared for no reason. Not the first time, wouldn't be the last time. There was no reason to make a big deal out of the erroneous opinions of complete strangers.

Rower felt differently.

She said, "He's not a criminal."

"Why he in handcuffs then?"

Rower shrugged and said, "That's merely a formality. For your local boys, out there."

The manager said nothing to that, which was probably because she didn't know what to say. But her face said a lot, more than Widow's had been saying, that was for sure.

She looked like she just realized that Rower was an outsider, and she wasn't that fond of outsiders. An ironic disposition for someone running a service station on an interstate where practically every patron who stopped for gas was an outsider.

Widow made no comment about it.

Rower did not wait for a reply. She signaled for Widow to follow her, and they walked back out to the lot.

"Wait for us," she ordered the deputies.

They made no protest, but they walked over to the Explorer.

Rower put up a hand.

"Not here. Wait over there somewhere."

She continued back to the Explorer.

Widow followed and stopped.

Rower leaned against the rear tire of the vehicle and waited for Widow.

He stopped five feet away, stayed out in the lot, and pulled the coffee up to his lips, took a pull. It was hot, as advertised.

"So, you're telling the truth? So far."

"I got no reason to lie."

"We'll go check out the road in a few minutes."

"What is this? Bad cop, good FBI agent?"

Rower paused a short beat.

"I believe you're telling the truth."

"So why the song and dance?"

"Your story is insane; that's why. You just wandered down a dirt road in the middle of the night, middle of nowhere, and stumbled upon a dumped woman that someone tried to kill?"

"That's what happened."

"It's unbelievable. You gotta admit."

Widow stepped slowly, kicked up some dirt with his boot. He stayed back a few more feet from Rower, still thinking in the back of his head that he might get shot by one of the deputies.

He asked, "What's her name?"

"Her name is Laine Olsen."

"She gonna be okay?"

Rower looked off at the forest, her eyes laid out over the snow-covered treetops, and back at Widow.

"I think so. Are you telling us the truth?"

"I am telling the truth."

Widow took a long, double pull from his coffee, realizing

that she might wait for him to finish it before getting into the vehicle with him.

"I am telling the truth."

She was quiet for a moment and then she said, "I believe you. You saved that girl's life."

Widow stayed quiet.

"Come on. Finish up. Let's get this over with."

Widow took another drink.

"Why is the FBI here?"

"This case falls under our jurisdiction."

"No, it doesn't."

"It does."

"Why?"

"For a couple of reasons."

"Like?"

"Where you found the body, might be federal land."

"Federal land?"

"Yeah. Ever heard of the Black Hills?"

"That's the mountain range over that way," he said and pointed two-handed with the coffee cup.

"It's more than that. It's a national forest."

"Why?"

She looked at him like a schoolteacher looking at a student, asking a dumb question on purpose.

"What?" he asked.

"Think about it. What's famous around here?"

"Rushmore."

"Rushmore," she nodded.

"Shit. I didn't even think about it."

She nodded and said, "That's why it falls under FBI jurisdiction."

"You could pass it off."

"I could."

"Why don't you? What else is going on?"

"Did you notice bandages on Laine Olsen's body when you found her?"

"I did."

"Not only did someone try to kill her; they took her kidney."

Widow froze and stared at Rower.

## 18

Rower stared off into the Black Hills, over the forests and the mountains.

Widow asked, "What else are you not saying? What is it you didn't want the deputies to hear?"

"What makes you think that?"

"You don't know me from Adam. These local boys don't want to believe me, but you just said you did."

"The security footage corroborates your story so far. Why wouldn't I believe you?"

"You didn't tell them to wait back there for me. You told them so you could tell me about the kidney. What's going on?"

She turned and said, "Jack Widow. Former Navy SEAL."

"I already told them that."

"But you didn't mention that you were really an undercover NCIS investigator."

"I didn't think it was needed."

"They'd let you out faster. Probably."

"They'll let me out, anyway. I didn't take that girl's kidney."

"I know. I believe you. But we gotta go look at the road where you found her, anyway."

"You didn't answer my question. What else is going on?"

"The FBI has an ongoing case."

"About what?"

"Organ trafficking."

Widow paused a beat, and then he asked, "That's a real thing?"

"Of course, it's real. Haven't you heard of it?"

"Like that story where a man wakes up in a bathtub full of ice?"

"No. Not like that. Here, the man in the bathtub doesn't wake up. Usually, he's murdered for his kidneys. You get two for one that way."

"Someone stole this woman's kidney and dumped her in a ditch?"

Rower shrugged.

"Come on. Let's go."

Widow drank the rest of the coffee, walked back to the station, and tossed the paper cup into a trashcan.

The deputies watched him the whole time. They followed him back to the Explorer.

Everyone loaded up, and they headed to the country road.

19

McCobb waited for further instructions while sitting in the hospital cafeteria, which was a room small enough to fit inside the cafeteria back in the hospital in Rapid City. He knew that because he'd been sent there before, too.

On a TV mounted on the wall, he watched a program about the making of nuts and bolts in a factory, a sleepy affair. The TV was muted, but the whole thing was so boring that it almost put him to sleep twice.

The machines banged and pummeled metal into nuts and bolts. It was like closing his eyes and imagining the inside workings of an old clock.

Suddenly, his phone rang in his pocket.

He answered it and didn't bother leaving the room.

"Yeah."

"It's me," Holden said.

"Did you call them?"

"Yeah. Just got off the phone."

"What they say?"

"They said to leave her there. I gotta meet them at the airport tonight."

"They're coming back?"

"Yep. Apparently, they want to handle this themselves, like a preemptive thing. Before it gets out of control."

"They think the cops will be onto them that fast?"

"They do. I'm sure they think the FBI will be onto them."

"The Feds?"

"Yeah."

"Why?"

Holden paused a beat because he realized McCobb didn't know what exactly it was the boys in Chicago did, what they took from the girl.

He said, "Don't worry about the details. Just know that the FBI is bad for them, bad for us. We're the low men on the totem pole here, you and I."

Which McCobb took to mean that he was the low man on the totem pole.

If the boys in Chicago get caught, arrested, and prosecuted by the FBI, they'll get plea deals, surely, then Holden will get arrested, and he'll probably rat out all his boys just to save his own ass. Typical.

"What do we do?"

Holden was quiet for a minute, then he said, "We tread lightly, but we need to know what they need to know."

"Which is?"

"Who knows what? And what's happening?"

"What do I do?"

"We do what they told us."

"Which is?" McCobb asked.

"They want me to check around with the local cops personally. Like I got some kind of connections with them."

"They don't want us to do nothing about the girl?"

"Like what? She's being babysat by a cop, right?"

"Yeah. A local deputy."

"Then leave her—for now."

"Want me to check around with the local cops instead?"

"They said to keep my distance from them. They said to use back channels."

"Back channels?"

"Yeah, stupid Chicago pricks think that I'm like a connected man. Like I got those kinds of resources. Like Al Capone or something."

"So? What you want me to do?" McCobb asked again, realizing that Holden was spacing out, not living up to his side of their criminal dynamic.

Holden said, "Go down to Reznor. See what's going on."

"Want me to talk to the cops?" he repeated.

"Not unless you know someone there."

"I do. We got a client."

"We do?"

"Yeah."

"He trustworthy?"

"Maybe. I sell him meth, sometimes."

"Okay. Poke around. But don't push him. No specifics, either. Just cause a bored cop does meth from us doesn't mean he's gonna give up secrets of an investigation."

"Okay. What're the Chicago boys gonna do?"

"Told you. I gotta pick them up from the airport tonight."

"What are they gonna do when they get here?"

"I imagine they're gonna kill some folks."

"We could do that ourselves. Make it easier for them. Easier for us."

"I'm not saying to do that. But I'm not telling you not to either."

"Affirmative," McCobb said, and they got off the phone.

McCobb smiled at a woman who was staring at him like she had heard both sides of the conversation.

He got up and left the waiting room, passed by the ICU once more, and peeked in. He saw the same deputy sitting there in front of the girl's door.

He smiled at him too, but the cop didn't see it.

McCobb left the hospital back through the emergency room entrance and walked back to the annexed parking lot and to his car. He took the revolver out of his coat and stuffed it between the seat and the console.

He started the car up and drove west to Reznor.

## 20

The former SAS man was called Paul Gade. He decided not to tell his boss about their developing problem in South Dakota, not yet.

Instead, he sent his two guys back, but by plane, not the long drive back. And because witnesses were a huge threat to their organization, he decided it would be best if he went along.

Normally, he wouldn't go along for cleanup, but being that time was a factor—because the first twenty-four hours were the only twenty-four hours in these matters—and being that they didn't know what was going on, he had to go along; no reason to be a huge step behind the cops, if there were cops involved.

He couldn't send his men back to check it out and then wait for them to report back and then wait for them to take care of the situation. They had incidents in the past, incidents that almost led to investigations, which would lead to the Feds snooping around.

He didn't want that again. Better if he went along.

Gade's boss, the owner of the company, wasn't the forgiving type. In all the years that he had worked for the man and his family, he had never known them to be merciful, not one of them, and not once. It wasn't in their DNA. After all, they were from the side of the world that still beheads their enemies, including men who fail them, and beheading wasn't something that Gade wanted to be a part of.

On the plane, he slipped off his coat and laid it neatly over a high-backed leather chair next to him. He sat near the window, away from the other two.

It was late afternoon for him. They would arrive in Rapid City in two-and-a-half hours. If they arrived in the town of Deadwood shortly after that, they could find out what was going on, eliminate the problem, and be back on the plane by midnight. He could be back in his own bed in the morning by the time his boss woke up.

Being that he was taking steps to eliminate the problem before it spiraled into the hands of the FBI didn't mean that he kept secrets from his boss, which was good because right then, he got a text message from him.

The name on the screen of his phone read "The Prince," which was a nickname but was almost true as well.

The text read: *Where are you?*
Gade replied: *Plane. Taking off.*
The Prince replied: *Problem?*
*Taking care of it.*

Gade waited for a long second for a reply. Even though he knew the Prince trusted him completely, and he knew he was the highest man in the organization next to the Prince, he still felt fear of what might happen to him if he didn't resolve the problem.

The Prince texted back: *Good.*

And nothing more.

Gade sat back and stared out the window as the plane took off.

## 21

Widow stood exactly where he remembered he had found Olsen rolled up and naked in a rug.

Roberts and Rousey stayed back by the Explorer on the orders of Rower, who stood next to Widow.

The snow had stopped falling, but on their short drive down the lonely road, it started up again, light and inviting.

Widow looked over the leafless trees and the terrain.

He pointed down with two hands at tracks in the snow. They were deep, but half covered from a slow snowfall and the hours that had passed.

"There. That's probably our tracks."

"They survived the night?"

"Sure. It snowed, but not bad."

"Still, how do you know those are your tracks?"

He pointed next to the deep tracks at tiny ones that were almost gone.

"See those?"

"Yeah."

"They're her dog's. He followed us all the way to the bar."

"Then he ran off?"

"After we got to the bar."

"Show me the ditch."

Widow stepped, heavy in the snow, next to the tracks he'd left to show her the depth of his boot print, which she noticed because she nodded and saw the same size track in the snow.

Roberts followed behind, while Rousey leaned against the Explorer slowly. He fidgeted with his phone, which must've been vibrating in his pocket.

Widow looked back and saw Rousey texting on it, intensely.

He turned and continued on down a ways, trying to recall the path he had taken the night before in the darkness. He stopped once, looked left, looked right.

Up ahead, he saw a tree he thought he recognized but wasn't sure.

He took a right and continued trying to picture where he had walked to.

Finally, he stopped at a ditch and stepped in. His boot sank into the snow like it had the night before.

They walked a few minutes until he stopped and stared, dumbfounded.

"Something wrong?"

Widow was stone-cold quiet.

"Widow?"

He stared down at white, wet snow, brushed from side to side, sloppily, but still fleecy and brushed.

It was gone. The rug, the duct tape, the shape that should've been left behind. It was all gone.

The only thing left was the trail of paw prints and the trail of boot prints he'd left behind.

## 22

McCobb remembered what Holden had inferred. It was in everyone's best interest to clean this up. They were at risk right along with the Chicago boys.

He had worked as a freelancer for Holden for years. He knew the man's tells. Holden left it ambiguous for him not to take any action, but it wasn't ambiguous, not to McCobb. To him, it was big and bold and obvious. He was supposed to take action if he was given the opportunity.

And the opportunity was presenting itself.

After he got to his car in the hospital annex parking lot and stowed his revolver, he made a phone call, which led him to a voicemail. He hung up and texted instead.

He stood and waited for a response.

He got none, so he drove twenty miles up the road toward Reznor.

He still waited for a response, and he should've gotten it. It might've saved someone's life, but he didn't get it, which made her life forfeit because unless Holden gave him a direct order not to kill her, then he was condoning for McCobb to use his best judgment. That was how it had always gone.

Deep in Reznor's rural areas, McCobb turned the wheel and drove over muddy snow. He slowed and turned down a dirt road that led to another dirt road.

He passed one cluttered, unkempt lot with an old, white trailer on it. It was a doublewide. The yard had a chain-link fence boxed all around it.

Two large pit bulls barked at him from the yard as he passed.

He drove up another hundred yards, past another trailer and lot on the other side of the road. It was completely different in that it had a cleaner yard and different upkeep, but it was the same in terms that he could not care less about either.

McCobb reached over and jerked his revolver out from between the seat and the console and set it on his lap.

She would know he was coming because she had seen his car before. Most of the neighborhood had. Every week, twice a week, he drove through, selling meth and collecting payments. But this was an unscheduled stop. She wouldn't be expecting him.

She would probably wonder why he was stopping at her place.

McCobb drove another hundred yards and pulled up to a fenceless yard with a doublewide trailer parked up on cinderblocks, hidden behind a shoddy lattice of thin wood.

The trailer was green and hadn't been painted in a decade or more. It was Lainey and Kylie's family trailer.

Two sisters. Their parents were dead—no other family. This was where they were born, and this was where they'd lived all their lives, and this was where they would die.

He was sure about one of them.

McCobb pulled up onto a snowy drive and parked the car. He left the engine running. No need to kill it.

He got out, tucked the revolver into the waistband of his jeans.

He pulled a beanie off his head and tossed it back into the car.

Wisps of breath fogged out in front of his face. He looked around, scanned the yard. He knew they had a dog, not a big thing, but a little one.

He didn't see it. It might've been indoors.

He expected her to come out, but she didn't, which was unusual because normally she was always the first to greet him. Usually, she came barreling out before the damn dog did, her and her boyfriend. They would come out, smiling, foaming at the mouth like kids waiting around all day for the ice cream man.

She didn't come out. Neither of them did.

McCobb checked his phone again. No messages. He was getting angry. Cop or not, the guy should text him back.

McCobb bent down and grabbed a lever by the floorboard and pulled it. The trunk lid popped, making an audible noise.

He paused, looked at the front door, at the porch, and at the windows, thinking he'd see her face appear. But it didn't.

McCobb left the driver's door wide open and walked back to the trunk. He pulled out a Louisville Slugger. It was made of thick brown wood. This one was old. He had used it before.

He also left the trunk open.

He snapped a peek down and saw a box of latex gloves and rolls of plastic garbage bags. He didn't need the gloves because he was already wearing winter gloves, but the garbage bags might come in handy.

He looked over his shoulder at the road for cars or pedestrians. There was neither.

He walked past his car and over to the side of the trailer.

On the side, he found her car, which was really the boyfriend's car; both of their vehicles belonged to him.

The car was parked on the side, as it usually was when he dropped by. The trunk was open, not wide, but left ajar, like it wouldn't shut all the way.

He folded his fingers into the lip and pulled it open. It squeaked, loud and brash.

He looked around. No one came out of the trailer.

He saw why it was ajar. It wouldn't close because it was packed with an old rug. There was dirt and muddy snow all over it.

The rug was ruined.

He wondered what it was for.

He looked at it once more, looked over the car once more, and left them there. He walked around to the backyard.

He saw some grass and some snow and trees and not much else.

There was a backdoor on top of a short set of concrete steps. The steps weren't properly lined up with the trailer. There was no railing.

Suddenly, he knew the dog was there, but not because it was barking, like he had expected, like anyone would've expected. He knew it was there because it was whining near the back door.

It was faint, not because it was muffled by the door, but because the dog sounded weak.

He knew the cries of sick, weak dogs. His kid sister had fostered them. She lived in Utah. She would take in all kinds of dogs from the shelter. She made him volunteer whenever he went to visit her. He hated dogs.

McCobb didn't knock on the back door. First, he pulled open a screen door. It creaked open.

He tried the knob on the back door. It was locked, but the

knob shook. It had a weak lock. Why wouldn't it? Who was going to rob them?

He took another look back over the backyard and the trees surrounding the property. There were no neighbors to the back, and basically no neighbors within earshot. The ones she had were close enough to hear a gunshot, but not a bat.

McCobb stepped up and propped open the screen door with his body. He reared the Louisville Slugger back and slammed it into a window on the center of the backdoor.

Glass shattered and cracked and sent shards into the trailer.

The dog whimpered a little louder, like it wanted to bark but just didn't have the strength.

In an explosion, McCobb reached in, fast, and unlocked the door and jerked it open. He stepped inside and let the screen door slam behind him.

He lowered the bat with his left hand, and drew his revolver with the right, pointed it straight out. No one came out. No one came at him with a shotgun or any gun.

He called out the girl's name.

He knew the boyfriend wasn't home because his Explorer was gone. He would be busy anyway. His job had a lot on their plate today.

The dog was in the kitchen, whining.

He had expected to see it unfed and scrawny, as they had neglected it. He had seen that before, but with children. Sometimes, meth-head women get too high and forget about their kids. Once, he found a dead woman in her own house and a baby on the verge of death.

He had gone to collect payment that she had been late on, only to find her dead.

McCobb liked to do bad things. That was why he loved

this job, but he wasn't a savage. He called the police when he found the baby, anonymously, of course.

The dog wasn't neglected or sick, as far as he could tell. It looked sad.

The kitchen bled into the dining room. There were small appliances, and a table filled with clutter.

He moved on, swept the rooms, one by one, with the revolver out in his right hand and the bat in his left. It was leaned over his left shoulder, casually.

In the next room, he found more clutter, an ugly green carpet that needed to be steam cleaned if he was honest with himself.

There was old, secondhand furniture everywhere, a sofa, a couch, a coffee table, and a TV stand with an old box TV on it. A pair of rabbit antennas were sticking out the top, one bent and one broken off at the end.

The TV was on, set to a channel with static and the grainy sound that came with it.

The couch looked like it was made up as a temporary bed for a third guest who was not here.

*Lainey slept there*, he thought.

He ignored it and moved down a short hall, but he stopped near the front door. There was dirt and snow and mud all over the tile.

The floor looked stomped down on like someone came in from dancing around in the snowy woods, somewhere, and just stomped the mud off the boots. Which he confirmed a second later when he looked at a boot rack behind a lounge chair. There was a pair of boots in it, covered in mud.

They were women's snow boots.

He found a bedroom, piled with thrift-store clothes and laundry baskets and old watercolor paintings of no value but sentimental.

The next room was a tiny bathroom. The door was wide open, and the room was empty.

He moved on to the last room with another wide-open door. It was the master bedroom. He saw more secondhand furniture, all a bedroom set. There were photographs everywhere.

There were clothes everywhere; dirty laundry spilled out of a hamper.

So far, he saw no sign of anyone home.

He moved on to the master bath, where he found women's clothing on the floor.

The light was on from under the door.

He tiptoed over a pair of muddy jeans, worn socks, and panties and a bra and pushed the door open with the muzzle end of the revolver.

He shoved, and the door creaked open, slow.

The bathroom had a white-tiled floor, which was also dirty in places, not as bad as the entrance, but noteworthy.

Inside the bathroom, he saw two other things that were quite shocking, but only one was shocking to him.

First, he found Kylie Olsen. She was dead.

Her naked body was laid out in a bathtub full of murky water right up to the faucet.

The water was red and brackish. It was colored with her blood.

Her wrists floated in the water.

She had long, deep slashes down them, vertical, not horizontal like in the movies.

Suicide.

There was no note.

She had done it the right way, in McCobb's opinion.

Her eyes were open and lifeless. They stared at him.

"Why?" he asked out loud.

He tucked the revolver into the waistband of his jeans.

He found a pipe and other drug paraphernalia on top of the toilet seat. He recognized all of them. Looked like she had done more than one thing. There were even two empty bottles of pills.

He looked at her eyes. The pupils were huge, like two lifeless black holes.

Whatever was her reason to take her own life, it consumed her, unlike anything he had ever seen before. She had no intention of being resuscitated, not by anyone.

The only thing that can make a person commit suicide like that was guilt, but McCobb wouldn't understand that. He felt no guilt. He had no room for guilt when money was better.

And that was the second thing he found, and it did shock him.

On the floor, in the center of the bathroom, laid out on horrid white tile, was a turned-over duffle bag and a heaping stack of cash poured out of it.

## 23

Rower put her hand on her Glock. Out of training, out of habit.

She stood behind Widow, who wasn't answering her and was taking a long time.

"What's the problem?" she asked.

"It's gone."

"What is?"

"The rug."

"What happened to it?"

Widow turned and looked at her.

"They came back for it. Had to have."

Rower stepped left and looked at where he had been staring.

"I believe you."

He looked at her, but said nothing.

"I do," she said, "I'm not stupid. I can see that someone tried to wipe away the tracks. Did someone come back to clean up?"

"That's what it looks like."

"And it wasn't you?"

"How could it be me? You guys have had me behind bars for sixteen hours."

Rower nodded.

"I believe you."

"That's good to know. But what now?"

"Now, we talk about who could've known that Lainey was found. Because my take is someone knows that you found her and rescued her and they came back to clean up."

"It's a little bizarre though."

"How do you figure?"

"Because whoever dumped her last night was complete amateurs. They killed no one in their lives. We know that because they didn't kill her at all."

"Unless their plan was to leave her to die."

"I doubt it. Why bother strangling her at all?"

"So what do you think? I know you were NCIS. You must think something?"

"I think what you think."

"What's that?"

"I think between the bar filled with witnesses, the sheriff's department, and Deadwood Hospital, there's a leak."

"Or an inside man?"

"Maybe."

"Let's look at the road again."

"What for? Now, you want to follow my tracks all the way to that bar? If they're still there."

"Tire tracks," she said.

They turned and walked back up the trail, through the snow, to the road.

Roberts and Rousey were standing by the Explorer.

Roberts was standing at attention, shotgun down in a safe position, but Rousey was weird. He seemed weird to Widow.

He was messing with his coat sleeve like he had been with

his shirtsleeve the night before. The bags under his eyes were worse, darker, like the last time he slept was more than twenty-four hours ago.

Not once, but three times. Widow had taken part in a SEAL Special Op, where one of his guys had been injured. He and the other guys had got them back to safety under hostile fire, and back to base, and all three times they had been medevacked back to Germany, the US Air Force Base, for surgery.

But the first time that had happened to him, he demanded to go along. Normally, this would've been denied, but he had pulled rank, pulled strings with his secret NCIS Unit Ten CO, Rachel Cameron, and she had made it happen.

He remembered being in the waiting room for thirteen hours, waiting for the guy to pull through. He had the guy's wife on and off Skype all night.

The guy died in surgery, but Widow remembered the wife's face when he met her at the funeral, two days later. She had those same huge bags under her eyes. It was two nights of insomnia.

That's what Rousey looked like.

His shotgun was laid out across the hood of the Explorer, and he was too busy to notice that Rower and Widow were walking back.

Widow's cuffs seemed to tighten around his wrists like the cold was expanding the metal. He felt them.

He kept his eyes on Rousey.

Rousey had his face down, texting on his phone.

## 24

Gade didn't speak to his men the whole time he was on the jet. He just stared out the window, occasionally twisting in his seat, or looking at a five-thousand-dollar Rolex on his wrist.

One hour down. One hour to go.

He hoped that whatever was happening with the girl in South Dakota, that they could find out, solve the problem, and be back in the air.

He hated working at night like this because his boss required him to be up and at 'em every morning. He didn't get days off unless his boss took them.

He glanced over at the other two guys. One was asleep, head folded against the window. And the other was reading a magazine.

He stared back out the window.

Thinking about being inconvenienced was making him angry. He wasn't sure what the issue was on the ground, but he was pretty sure that the best option was going to be just to kill all the parties involved and be done with it.

When you got fleas in your house, you don't shampoo the carpets; you bomb the whole house.

25

Widow sat on the left rear side, his head out the window, and Rower was to his right. She had moved closer to him, leaned up and over his shoulder so that she could see out past him.

Rousey drove the Explorer slowly.

Widow and Rower were watching the ground, tracing what was visibly left of his boot prints from the night before and the tire tracks that Widow claimed were from the night before and a new set.

They figured the new set was from whoever had come and tried to clean up, only they left the tire tracks behind.

*Amateur*, Widow thought, again.

Rousey was driving straight and normal, so Widow disregarded his obvious sleeplessness.

Roberts was talking to Rousey in the front. They went on about baseball and football, and then they repeated the conversation.

Rower half-whispered to Widow.

"So, you left the Navy and the NCIS, and now you're just a vagabond?"

"I prefer violent nomad, but sure."

"Why 'violent'?"

"It's a SEAL thing. We're all violent nomads. It's like a group nickname like you're a Fed."

"Oh. Okay. Weird."

"Not really. We're supposed to be terrifying. It's like the whole deal. A nomad is a wanderer, someone without a home, and therefore has nothing to lose. And violent because...well, you get that part."

"Do you have nothing to lose?"

He felt her Glock under her coat push against his bicep, under his borrowed thermal. It caught his attention and imagination, as a beautiful woman in uniform who carries a firearm often does. Even though her uniform was a suit, it counted.

"That's right."

"So then you have nothing to live for, right? I mean by that logic?"

Widow looked over his shoulder at her. Her face was close—close enough to kiss. But he didn't.

"Not so."

"Why's that?"

"I have the most important thing to live for."

"Which is?"

"Freedom."

"I have freedom."

"Do you?"

She stayed quiet.

Widow said, "I don't have bills to pay, debt, I answer to no one. I go where I want when I want."

"You're untraceable?"

"Yeah. But I'm not talking about that. I'm talking about choice. I have pure, free choice."

"I have a choice."

"True, but not like I do. You answer to a SAC."

She thought of Bukowski for a quick second.

"Yes. So what? Are you like a cowboy? A loner?"

"Pretty much."

She smirked and looked at the snow outside.

"How much longer?" Roberts asked.

"Till what?"

"How much longer you want us to drive along like this?"

"Till I tell you different."

Roberts looked forward and said nothing.

Widow said, "Can I ask you a question?"

"Sure."

"Why Alaska?"

"What about it?"

"Why did your parents name you after a state?"

"They didn't name me after a state. They named me after a person."

"Who?"

"My dad was a Fed. His dad was a beat cop, and his uncle was a Fed. He wanted me to be a Fed."

"Okay."

"So he named me after Alaska Packard Davidson."

"Who is?"

"The first female FBI agent."

Widow looked back at her. Not realizing she had leaned closer, his face almost touched hers. His lips almost touched hers.

He paused a beat and asked, "That true?"

"Yeah. That's true."

"Alaska?"

"That's true."

Widow turned back to watching the thin tire tracks, and the thinner tire tracks flash slowly along the ground.

## 26

McCobb debated whether he should call Holden and tell him about the money that he'd found. He debated it hard.

What made it even harder for him to make the phone call was the fact that he had counted it twice. There were a hundred and fifty thousand dollars here. It was hundreds and fifties. It was real, and it was unmarked, and it could all be his.

While contemplating this decision, he did text the boyfriend again after he received a text. They had a heated exchange.

He told him he was onto him, and the boyfriend had denied everything.

McCobb wasn't a rocket scientist, but he knew a scam when he saw one. Even though the boyfriend was a local sheriff's deputy, he was no mastermind criminal.

It didn't take McCobb two seconds to figure out that Kylie and her boyfriend, Deputy Rousey, were in on this together. Lainey was Kylie's sister, and they had stolen her sister's money, which they must've known came from dangerous people.

McCobb was pretty sure that Shostrom didn't know that

Rousey was dating a junkie, which wasn't because Rousey was smart enough to hide it. It was because Shostrom was an old man, and he had a lot of territory to cover. He didn't pay attention to who his deputy was dating and living with.

McCobb smiled, thinking about how oblivious to things his county sheriff was. Rousey and Kylie had plotted right under his nose. Then again, they were doing meth under his nose too. Plus, Holden sold a lot of product out there, the benefits of living on the rural side of Lawrence County.

McCobb started piecing it together. He figured the two lovebirds must've been present when the transaction took place. He had not met the two representatives of the buyer personally, but he had known Holden for years. Anyone he feared was worth being terrified of. No getting around that.

However, McCobb wasn't the same as Holden. The guys from Chicago might never even find him. He could just toss the money back into the bag, zip it up, and run off with it.

He could just stash it somewhere. Keep it for himself, and when the Chicago boys came calling, he could deny ever seeing it.

How would they even know?

In the end, McCobb came to the only sensible conclusion. He couldn't take it. He couldn't deny it.

He had heard that the Chicago boys were a part of a huge bio conglomerate, and they made their money on organ trading.

The kinds of guys who deal in that trade weren't to be crossed.

He might get away with the money, but they would certainly kill his kid sister trying to find him. And Holden would give her up, too.

Better to turn the money over and let them give him a reward.

Maybe he could cut Holden out of that deal somehow.

For now, he zipped it up and kept it to himself. He told Holden about the dead sister.

Holden told him to track down Rousey and take him alive for the Chicago boys. That way, all they had to do was step off the plane, see that Holden had taken care of it, and be back on the plane with no fuss.

McCobb texted one last time to Rousey: *Where are you?*

A moment later, Rousey texted back the location from a screenshot of Google Maps off his phone.

"What a stupid, stupid cop, you are," McCobb said to himself.

## 27

The Explorer drove slowly, with all four people inside. It seemed to slow down, even slower than Rower had asked Rousey to drive.

Widow asked, "Think you can take these cuffs off now?"

"I will soon."

"When?"

"Make you a deal."

"What's that?"

"Come with me to meet Lainey, and I'll take them off when we stop."

"Why do you want me to meet with her? You want her to identify me as the guy who tried to strangle her?"

"I told you I believed you."

"What about Shostrom?"

"It's not his call."

"Sure, I'll go with you. What choice I got?"

"You could say no. You're the one with choices, remember? You could just say no."

"And what? Stay locked up?"

"We'd let you out, eventually. I'm a good agent. I'm not gonna put an innocent man away. Trust me."

Roberts looked over his shoulder. Just a quick glance. There was judgment in his eyes.

Rower saw it too, but said nothing about it. She moved back away from Widow.

She said, "Rousey, speed it up. Just follow the tracks."

Rousey looked at her in the rearview.

He sped the SUV up to around twenty miles an hour.

"You can go faster than that."

What they couldn't see was that Rousey's phone had multiple messages on it, asking where he was, who was with him. He'd replied that the FBI was there with a witness.

He was told to stall and wait on the road for McCobb to show up.

## 28

McCobb drove on the Interstate Ninety, which allowed him to step on the gas. He had his phone in a cup holder. A voice gave him instructions and updates on where to go.

Traffic was normal, not empty, not crowded.

He looked at his watch. The sun was starting its climb downward over the mountains to the west. It shone in his face here and there, but the cloud cover helped to block it out for most of the trip.

Doing fifteen miles over the limit, he calculated he would meet with Rousey and his passengers head-on.

In his messages, Rousey sounded tweaked out and very much on edge.

McCobb had no reason to tell him about his dead girlfriend. No point. He didn't tell him he had seen the money, or that he had taken the money. It was stuffed back into the duffle bag and packed into his trunk under the Louisville Slugger.

He wasn't nervous, but he was excited and anxious. He'd never killed an FBI agent before.

Rousey had told him they had a witness and that he and

Kylie had planned to pin the whole thing on the guy. All he'd said was that he was a drifter and nothing else.

McCobb came up with a similar plan. A plan that he messaged Holden about and got Holden's approval.

All they both knew was that the Chicago boys were coming, and they wanted Rousey alive. They didn't need anyone else alive.

McCobb would be a hero as soon as he handed over the man who plotted to ruin their business. Plus, he would show them he, single-handedly, solved the whole problem, on top of handing over their money. That last part, he wasn't sure yet. He hadn't decided.

He looked at his watch again.

Fifteen minutes.

29

Fifteen minutes later, Rousey slowed the Explorer nervously. The shotguns were in the back, and he was in close quarters that were too close for shotguns, and he was right-handed. His .38 Special was in his holster on his right hip. No way could he grab it and shoot Roberts and Rower before one of them got him first.

All he knew was that McCobb was onto him and was coming to help him with the FBI agent and the witness, and, unfortunately, Roberts, whom he had known for a long time.

He would venture to call them friends, even, but he didn't need friends. He needed the money, so he could buy drugs and get the hell out of Reznor and Lawrence County.

If McCobb wanted to help him, fine. Why did McCobb want to help him? He wasn't sure. Somehow, his drug dealer had found out about what they were up to. That made little sense to him because they had been so careful.

He felt the need coming on. He had been staving it off all day with pills. No one had noticed. He had been careful when popping them.

He hadn't heard from Kylie all day. He wondered if he should be worried about that.

He just realized what if she ran off with the money?

She hadn't been answering his calls or texts.

No way would she betray him. She was solid. He knew it.

She went back to the dumpsite and clean up, after all. She had told him she took care of it. She told him not to worry.

His mind, and he thought about the money. He had big plans for that money.

He'd probably have to kill Kylie, but later. Right now, two heads were better than one.

"What the hell is happening?" Rower called from the back.

He had to focus on getting rid of this problem first. Then they would have to get rid of her sister too if she pulled through. That would be harder, but it could be done. He could pick up that shift tomorrow after he dealt with this problem.

He planned to kill all three and blame this Widow guy. He'd shoot Widow first. The guy was handcuffed. What was he going to do?

So, he executed what he thought was a brilliant plan. He faked the steering wheel, pulling and jerking. He started pulling the SUV over to the right.

"The steering wheel is shuddering."

Roberts said, "What's wrong with it?"

"Must be wheel alignment."

"Could be a tire?" Rower said from the back.

"Let's stop here and check it out," Roberts said.

Rousey slowed and pressed the brakes.

The sun was still up, but already in its sunset flight path. The light was low around them. The trees and the clouds grayed out the sky and dulled what was left of sunlight.

Widow stared straight ahead.

Rousey brought the Explorer to a dead stop and put the gear in park, killed the engine, took the keys out, and got out.

"Need help?" Roberts asked.

"Yeah. Probably."

"Okay," Roberts said, and he opened his door and hopped out too, leaving the door open.

Rower opened the door on her side, but it was childproofed.

"Hey. Guys, let me out."

Rousey put his head back in the driver's side door.

"You stay inside."

"I want to look."

"No need. It's cold out here. You stay there. Stay warm."

Rousey bent down and pulled a lever and popped the hood. Then he stepped out and shut his door.

Roberts lifted the hood and set it up.

Rousey and Roberts both disappeared behind it.

"I told him to let me out," Rower said to Widow.

Widow stayed quiet. He closed his fists and opened them again, cracking his knuckles.

Widow twisted in his seat, slowly reached down, and undid his seatbelt.

"You should keep that on."

"We're not moving. And you're not wearing yours."

Rower looked at him.

He asked, "What?"

"You're a prisoner still."

"So?"

"So, I don't feel afraid of you."

"You were before?"

"I mean, I trust you more than I should."

They were quiet for a beat.

Rower said, "I trust you more than these clowns, anyway."

"I'm not so sure that's a compliment."

"Why not?"

"Because I don't trust them either. Something's not right."

"How's that?"

"Last night, Rousey was on duty with me all night."

"That's his job."

"He brought in Olsen's sister, Kylie."

"Kylie?"

"Yeah. Don't you know about her?"

"No one told me. Why did he bring her in?"

"So she could identify me as this mysterious guy that her sister had been dating."

Rower looked at him, confusion on her face.

"Shostrom didn't tell me. She IDed you?"

"Sort of."

"What do you mean?"

They heard voices up in front of the SUV.

Roberts appeared and said nothing but walked around the vehicle, stopping at each tire well, looking down, bending down, inspecting each tire.

Rousey followed behind him. He smiled at Rower, a big, hearty smile. He lifted his thumb.

"We'll figure this out."

Widow looked at him, then looked back over his shoulder at the cargo. He could see the shotguns, both loaded. They were out of reach for him. The dog cage embedded in the back was a close-patterned wire mesh. He could barely reach his fingers through it, much less his arms long enough to reach one of them.

Rower had a Glock. He knew that.

"Kylie was there with Rousey. She hid behind him like she was afraid of me."

"That makes sense if she thinks you tried to kill her sister."

"There was something strange about it."

Widow thought back.

He said, "She shivered, and she's definitely a meth-head."

"How do you know that?"

"Come on! You know how I know. You could see it."

"So she does drugs. That's probably why Shostrom didn't tell me. She sounds unreliable. Besides, I'm sure she's wrong. I told you I believed you."

"There's something else."

Widow leaned forward and looked over the driver's seat. Roberts and Rousey moved to the other rear tire behind him.

Rousey stood back and looked past Roberts. He put his hand on his .38 Special. He could shoot Roberts now, but then he stopped. It would look bad if Roberts was shot in the back of the head by his gun. He was driving. How would Widow grab his gun?

He holstered it.

"These tires and tire wells look fine. You sure it's pulling?" Roberts asked.

"It was pulling. You saw it."

"Let's check under the hood again."

The two deputies walked back to the front of the Explorer and out of sight.

Widow made eye contact with Rousey, who seemed to grin at him.

"Something's not right," Widow repeated.

"What?"

Widow looked down at the front seat again. He looked at the ignition.

"Why did he take the keys out?"

"I don't know. I'm not a mechanic."

Widow looked down at the console, at the cupholder. He saw a pill bottle. He jerked forward, fast, and grabbed it, and pulled it back.

"What are you doing?"

He spun the pill bottle and looked at the label.

The label read: *OxyContin*.

"Look at this."

Rower grabbed the bottle and read the label.

"That's not right."

"Rousey has been taking this. He's been tweaking ever since I met him yesterday."

"It's not right, but this is a prescription bottle."

"Read the label."

"I did. It says OxyContin."

"Read the name."

Rower looked at it and read the name out loud in a slow, lingering voice, like it was hitting her all at once.

She said, "Lainey Olsen."

## 30

Fast-two gunshots rang out from the front of the Explorer.

The hood, the engine block, it all shook as loud metallic gunshots slammed into the hood. The windshield cracked from the impact of bullets.

Widow grabbed Rower by the head and shoved her down and hard behind the front seats. He twisted violently on his back and turned and slammed his boots through the window as fast and as hard as he could.

He knew it was possible that the police package on a Ford Explorer might have double pane glass or some kind of upgraded glass for the windows, but judging because Rousey had been issued a weapon that he had last heard of being used in the nineties he felt okay with taking the chance that he was stronger than the glass in this older model.

His boots shattered through the glass.

Rousey shot Roberts out in front of the SUV.

Once! Twice! In the chest.

Roberts gripped his chest as he fell back against the front grille. Rousey shot him a third time right there.

Roberts was dead.

Rousey should've kept moving, but he froze for a moment, like the realization of what he had done was just dawning on him.

Quickly, he came around the passenger side of the vehicle and fired into the windshield. He fired through the window into the Explorer and into the rear.

The .38 Special is a deadly accurate weapon, but slow compared to a semi-automatic handgun like a Glock 22, like the one that Rower had.

The front windshield was severely cracked from the bullets wildly passing through it.

Widow squeezed himself down and waited.

Rousey had fired three rounds into Roberts and three into the Explorer. He was out of ammunition.

Widow reached up with his cuffed hands and grabbed the grip on the roof, and hauled himself up and slid out of the broken window about as fast as a baseball player sliding to home plate.

On the other side of the door, he toppled forward onto the snow and paused for a fraction of a second and rolled under the Explorer.

He knew that Rower would have her Glock out by now. He hoped she hadn't been shot.

Widow stayed prone and Army-crawled under the SUV, past the front tire. He paused and saw six .38 cartridges drop to the ground and land in the snow.

He saw Rousey's feet.

"Come on out, FBI?" Rousey said.

Widow could hear the delusion in his voice as if revealing himself to them as an enemy had set his high free.

Rousey even chuckled.

Widow heard new bullets go into the revolver, and the cylinder slam shut.

Just then, Rower was in that action, a little slower than he had expected.

He heard return fire from her Glock 22.

She fired two rounds in his direction, but Rousey was behind the hood. She missed.

Rousey ducked down, his knees exposed to Widow.

Widow looked at Roberts' body. He had planned to go for Roberts' gun, but Rousey was too close.

He twisted and Army-crawled backward, keeping his eyes on Rousey's feet.

"Widow? You okay?" Rower called out from inside the cabin.

Widow didn't answer.

As high as Rousey was, he wasn't stupid. She'd just told him that Widow was out of the vehicle.

Widow picked up the pace.

Rousey got down on one knee and looked under the SUV and saw Widow.

"There you are!"

Widow crawled to the back and shoved himself out, and moved his feet behind the rear tire just in time to miss a bullet.

Rousey fired once under the Explorer.

The bullet slammed into the rear driver's side tire. It exploded with Widow right next to it.

The sound of the tire was louder than the gunshot.

Widow stayed where he was. He looked around the road. There were rocks and tree roots and branches everywhere, but one rock, in particular, caught his eye.

Sticking up out of the snow was a baseball-sized stone. He

leaped out and grabbed it and jumped back behind the tire, which was now just a rim and some rubber.

He called out.

"Rower!"

"Yeah!" she called back.

"Cover fire!"

She didn't hesitate. She fired in Rousey's direction in a fast triple-round burst.

Rousey cried out and ducked down close to the tire again.

Widow jackknifed to his feet and reared his hands up over his head and slammed the rock down on the back windshield, shattering it.

Glass sprayed over his arms and face.

He dropped the rock and reached in and jerked out one of the Tactical Remington 870s. He hoped it was the same one that Rousey had pumped in front of him earlier. He hoped that because Widow had a thing for poetic justice, in any form.

Rousey fired back into the vehicle at Rower—once, twice!

Widow pumped the gun with one hand, and his other was off the trigger housing because of the handcuffs. A slug flew out. He ignored it because he didn't need it.

He returned his hand down the gun, back to the trigger housing, ready to fire it.

He stepped around the opposite side of the Explorer, the side that Rousey was closest to, and stopped.

Feet planted, he stood straight up and called out.

"Rousey!"

"Yeah!"

"I'm going to kill you with your own gun!"

"How you figure? I'm still holding it!"

Widow pounded on the back side panel of the Explorer

with the nose of the Remington, loud enough to get Rousey's attention.

Rousey heard it and stepped up and out. Either he was the dumbest criminal ever, or he was stoned out of his mind.

Widow suspected he was both.

Rousey stepped out and came face-to-face with the barrel of his own Tactical Remington 870.

Widow could've said something clever or ironic, but that wasn't real life. In real life, he preferred to let the shotgun do the talking.

He squeezed the trigger and watched most of the top left side of Rousey's torso and shoulder and heart blow out the back of him.

Rousey flew back off his feet so fast it left his revolver right where he had been standing.

The gun clanged and bounced down somewhere into the engine block.

Widow called out.

"It's okay! You can come out! He's down!"

Rower popped her head up and stared at Widow.

"He's dead," Widow said.

"Open the door."

Widow lowered the shotgun and opened her door.

Rower stepped out; glass was in her hair and in her coat.

Widow had just noticed that the front windshield wasn't just cracked; it was gone. Thousands of shards and pebbles of broken glass littered the front and back seats.

"You okay?" he asked her.

"Other than having a cop shoot at me, yeah. I'm fine."

Rower brushed herself off and pointed the Glock at Rousey's corpse. She approached him.

"That's not necessary. He's dead."

"You sure?"

She kept walking anyway and saw for herself.

She lurched back and looked at Widow.

"That's horrible."

Widow shrugged.

"It's a Magnum slug. The guns were loaded out with them."

"That's not normal."

"It's not illegal. Or against police policy."

"I don't think so."

"Forty cents a slug," Widow said.

"That cheap?"

"Sure. Or more. Depends."

Rower holstered her weapon and went over to Roberts.

Widow joined her.

They looked at him—no reason to take his pulse. He was dead, too. His eyes were wide open and completely lifeless. Blood pooled everywhere, all over three holes in his chest, under him. Even the surrounding snow was dyed red for a few feet out in all directions.

Rower said, "Now what?"

"This means that Kylie Olsen is probably guilty."

"You think?"

"My guess is her sister got hooked up with some organ traders. They offered her substantial money for her kidney. A young woman like her could probably get twenty grand."

"Try a hundred and fifty."

"A hundred and fifty?"

"Sure, or more, if the buyers are some major players. They'd pay well. It's better to make the donor happy to keep them quiet."

"Cheaper to kill them and take it. You get two kidneys."

"Better to not kill them. Murder racks up faster than

buying and trading kidneys. People take notice of a bunch of dead bodies missing kidneys."

"Wasn't that actually happening in Chicago or somewhere?"

"It did. In Chicago. Last year. But we busted the operation."

Widow nodded.

Rower said, "This isn't that. We've suspected major players with an organization like a corporation."

"Looks disorganized to me."

"He's not a part of whoever the buyers are."

Widow shrugged.

Rower pulled out her phone.

"Who you calling?"

"The sheriff. We need a ride, and his men are dead."

"Think you can uncuff me now?"

Widow smiled and held his hands up.

31

Rower and Widow stood in the snow and the dirt out in front of the Explorer. The two dead bodies of the Reznor side of the Lawrence County sheriff's office were laid out ten feet behind them.

Widow held onto the shotgun in the trail carry position with one hand south of the trigger housing and the muzzle pointed down.

He stood three feet from Rower, but he didn't have to. He wanted to.

Compared to her five feet four inches, Widow stood a whole foot taller. She looked up at him a little more than she did most men. He could tell because she seemed to strain a bit. The polite thing to do would've been to back up a foot or two, but he didn't. He liked being close to her.

Rower holstered her Glock after double- and triple-checking that Rousey was dead. She never checked his pulse or breathing or listened for a heartbeat. She just looked at his missing northeast torso. Widow didn't know why she had to look three times, but she did.

After she holstered her Glock, she took her phone out

of her jacket pocket and called Sheriff Shostrom first. She told him what had happened. He was in complete disbelief, which was understandable. In less than five minutes, his entire department in Reznor had been decimated.

He said he was on his way and commanded them to preserve the integrity of the crime scene, which rubbed Rower the wrong way. But she said nothing about it.

She called her SAC next and explained to him what had happened. He suggested she keep Widow close, and they should search for the sister. Maybe she could explain and confirm Widow's theory.

Bukowski said he would send two more agents if she needed it, but she declined.

"I'll be fine on my own for now."

"You sure?" Bukowski asked.

"I've got Widow."

He was quiet for a moment. He had already looked Widow up and found out all he could, which was that there were redacted files, courtesy of the United States Navy, and the DOD.

He found Widow had served in the SEALs and was officially an NCIS agent, but with a sixteen-year career, the man only had six years accessible, and even those had redacted sections.

"Be careful."

"I will. I'll call you later."

They both clicked off their lines.

Bukowski made one more phone call and ordered two agents to be on standby. They were posted in different locations. The closest one was in Sioux Falls.

Bukowski ordered the man to head to their satellite office in Rapid City, just in case.

Rower slipped her phone back into her jacket pocket and turned to Widow.

"Guess we're waiting for Shostrom."

"Do we have to wait? Shouldn't we get over to the sister's house?"

"We can't leave dead bodies out here unguarded."

"Why not? They're not going anywhere."

"We have to stay. At least until Shostrom gets here."

"That's not how we do it."

"How who would do it?"

"The Navy. We'd leave them when there're still bad guys out there."

"Didn't you say Kylie was scrawny?"

"Ninety pounds, if that."

"You worried about a ninety-pound junkie?"

"I'm not worried about her, but whoever else is involved. If Rousey was her boyfriend or whatever, there could be others. I only thought I saw two people in that car last night. There could've been three or four."

"We can't leave, anyway. He shot the tire out."

Widow shrugged and said, "We can walk. I did it."

"How long did it take you?"

"Little over an hour, but I was carrying a woman who was out cold. She was dead weight. And it was colder than it is now. If we wait much longer, it's going to get worse. The sun is going down."

He pointed to the sky. Not because she needed to know where the sun was, but because he wanted to use his arms and his hands. He was no longer wearing handcuffs, and it felt good.

"You're right."

"You're the agent in charge here. You make the call."

"Technically, I'm in charge of me. You're free."

"Free to go?"

"You can go. I need you to stay in town, though."

"I'm not leaving you. Think you know that."

"I do. But I had to say it, anyway. That's the law. Can't detain you for no reason."

Widow looked at the sun peeking through the trees.

He said, "Sun goes down early here."

"It's winter. It started vanishing around four-thirty."

Widow nodded.

"I'm going to check the truck for a flashlight."

Rower said, "Good idea. Check for flares."

She took out her phone and called Sheriff Shostrom again. She wanted to get an ETA.

Widow walked back to the rear, back to the cargo bay of the truck, and checked around. He found road flares under the floorboard, as well as a spare tire, but he ignored it. She would make him do all the changing of the tire and still insist that they wait. Plus, there was steam hissing out of the engine. He was pretty sure the Explorer wasn't going anywhere anyway, not on its own.

He didn't find a flashlight, only an empty case where it looked like one was supposed to be stored. He found backup batteries for a flashlight, but no flashlight.

He grabbed five flares and went around the Explorer, cracking them and dropping them around the truck. When he reached the nose, he held onto the last one, in case he needed it.

He met with Rower. She hung up the phone.

"He's on his way."

"We waiting?"

"Of course."

"Okay."

"You worked the Chicago thing? Earlier, you made it sound personal."

"It is. It happened in Chicago. It was headed by a different office, but we had a task force that spread out across state lines. They asked me to join. I flew to Chicago."

"What happened?"

"Bodies turned up all over Chicago. Missing organs. Mostly poor people. Mostly black. Mostly men."

"Sounds like a serial killer."

"That's what we thought, but why the missing organs?"

"Hannibal Lector took his victims' organs. He cooked them."

"I know. I saw that movie."

"The book is more graphic."

Rower said, "This went on for nearly a year."

"What happened?"

"We caught the guy."

"And?"

"Dr. John Jay Holcomb. A retired Marine surgeon, actually."

"Really?"

"Yeah. But that was ten years earlier. Then, I think he was selling stereo equipment at a Best Buy."

"He should've gone into the Navy."

"Would that have made a difference?"

"Maybe. Or the Air Force. Lots of tech skills learned. That's popular nowadays, right? He would've been the manager of the Best Buy instead."

"It's not funny."

Widow asked, "Why the dramatic decline in jobs?"

"His medical license was disavowed, and the Marine Corps dishonorably discharged him. He was doing unsavory things. Nothing like later on, but bad shit."

"Then he sold stereos?"

Rower said, "He quit that job, anyway. When we caught him, he was living in a houseboat on Lake Michigan."

"How did he afford that? Must've been a piece of shit."

"Then it was a million-dollar piece of shit."

"How?"

"That's how we noticed him. Someone called in a tip and told us he was spending large amounts of money, more than he had. He quit his job. And started living it up on the boat. He bought it with cash."

"How?" Widow asked again.

"He was killing poor black men, harvesting their kidneys, sometimes their hearts, and he sold them."

"On the black market?"

"No. He sold them to one buyer. They turned around and sold them for more money."

"Who was it?"

"That's the thing. We never found out."

"Did you offer him a plea deal?"

"The DA refused to. His name was in the paper, on TV. People were terrified of him for a year. The mayor wanted him hung out to dry. No immunity. No deal. Not even a lenient sentence. Just the death penalty."

"Illinois doesn't have the death penalty."

"No, but that's what everyone wanted. He got life."

"Did he ever say who he sold the organs to?"

"He died. Three black inmates from a local gang beat him to death. Retribution, they claimed."

Widow nodded.

"John was sick in the head, but I always felt that we were arm's length away from someone worse. Whoever bought the organs was organized, like a corporation."

"How do you know?"

"Because we didn't even get a whiff of them. He murdered ten people. That's probably twenty kidneys if they were all healthy. Plus, he took two hearts."

"If there's a corporation that deals in organ theft..."

"Black Market Organ Trade," she corrected him.

"Right. If there's a company that deals in that, then there must be a lot of money in it, but aren't organs fairly cheap on the black market? I read something about this once in Time magazine. I thought it was cheap to fly to the Middle East and get kidneys."

"In Iran, you can buy a kidney for five thousand bucks. American."

"See, cheaper to just fly to Egypt and then buy a ticket to Iran."

"True, but that's the prices for people in Iran. You can't fly to Tehran with an American passport."

"You can. I've done it."

"Not from America, you can't. Besides, you don't know what you're gonna get if you go through all that trouble. And a five-thousand-dollar black market kidney in Iran is just as likely to be useless as replacing your kidney with a tennis ball. Often, American businessmen with the right connections have gone through all that trouble and ended up dead. I heard of one who got a goat's kidney."

Widow made a face like he was grossed out.

"Goat?"

Rower shrugged and then looked down the road for Shostrom. Nothing was coming.

She said, "That's what I heard."

"So how much to get a black market kidney in America?"

"Depends. They range from fifty thousand to a half million."

"Half million?"

"That's for top quality. They match them, do the procedure with top medical staff, and there's actual customer service provided."

"If you don't know who the company is, how do you know all this?"

"We've seized websites, and there's some witness testimony out there. Plus, Interpol has busted warehousing of organs. So, have we, but not like they have. They found a huge facility in Spain last year."

"Who owns it?"

"It's a dummy corporation. All the trails anyone has ever followed have led nowhere."

"Could be different corporations out there."

"There are, but someone is the head of the snake."

"How come no one's talking about this?"

"It's complicated and complex. It's like the sex trafficking trade or the drug trade. It's huge and touches all corners of the earth. There are a lot of greased hands, and it's old too. The media has a short attention span. They want instant news stories. The organ trade has been around since the invention of the scalpel.

"Hell, since the invention of ice."

Widow nodded.

They both looked up to see the sun take one last shine over South Dakota, over the Black Hills, and then it set in the west.

After sundown, they saw a pair of headlights beaming and bouncing on the road ahead.

32

Rower stepped forward and stared at the oncoming lights. Widow stayed back a little because of his cautious nature, and a little because of experience, and a lot of the primal brain that his genealogy never evolved away from.

He said, "Careful."

Rower stayed quiet, but he saw her reach up under her jacket and unsnap the safety catch on her gun holster, all from standing behind her. He knew the movements she made, and he heard the faint whisper of a click from the button.

She stepped up and reached out her left hand up over her face to dim the lights.

When the car was in sight, she began flagging it down.

Widow pumped the shotgun, ejecting the casing for the slug that had blown a major chunk of flesh and tissues off Rousey and replacing it with a live Magnum slug.

The car that pulled up was an old Buick. Widow didn't know the model, not by sight, but an old Buick was an old Buick, reliable, big, clunky.

The car rode fine over the snow and dirt. The driver's face

was not visible because of the headlight beams shining at them.

As the car came closer, Rower reached into her jacket and pulled out her FBI wallet and badge, flipped it to show the badge.

The Buick driver saw her and slowed the car.

He rolled a window down and stuck an elbow out, rested it on the sill. He leaned out a little and came to a stop.

"What's going on here?"

Rower walked up to the window, but not too close.

She said, "We've had an incident."

"Like an accident?"

The driver leaned out a little farther and looked.

"Oh, my! Are they dead?"

"I'm afraid so."

"You FBI?" The driver looked at her badge.

"That's right."

"Is that James Rousey?"

Rower closed the badge and put it back in her pocket. The driver stared at her Glock as her jacket whipped open.

Widow noticed.

The Buick's bumper was a good twelve yards from Widow.

"I'm afraid it is. Did you know him?"

"We all know him."

"You got a license, sir?"

"Oh. Of course."

The driver turned and reached for his wallet. Widow watched.

The driver wiped a brown leather wallet open, like Rower had done, and jerked out a driver's license, handed it to her.

Widow heard a noise just to his right. It was a buzzing sound, like a pager.

He looked down and saw Rousey's phone was half hanging out of his coat pocket. The screen was cracked. It faced upward to Widow.

He stepped over one big step and bent down. He scooped it up.

There was a late text message alerted across it.

It was from some guy named McCobb.

Just then, he could hear up ahead of him Rower read the driver's license.

"Ty McCobb."

"That's me, ma'am. Sorry, I mean, Agent."

Widow read the rest of the message.

It read: *Almost there. They dead?*

Widow looked up and saw McCobb holding a Ruger GP11 with a short three-inch barrel. It was a palm-sized weapon that packed a powerful punch with .357 Magnum bullets.

McCobb pulled the hammer back with his thumb and aimed it right at Rower's head and pulled the trigger.

The muzzle flashed a bright fireball, and a bullet rocketed out of the barrel.

The gunshot *boomed* in the snowy silence.

## 33

Widow raised the Remington shotgun fast and pointed it at the driver through the windshield.

He yelled at the top of his lungs. That old cop training came back, and the bass down deep in his chest took over.

"TOSS THE GUN! TOSS IT!"

Rower toppled over, clutching her ears. Her left eardrum had burst open in a painful explosion, as if it had been prodded with a stiletto. Blood seeped out between her fingers.

She racked her jaw up and down, out of reaction. Her Glock lay on the ground. She had tried to draw on him when she saw the barrel of the Ruger, but he ambushed her.

The Glock was in her reach, but her ears throbbed and her head pounded. She couldn't stop thinking about the pain.

McCobb had fired a warning shot right past her head, a shot across the bow. He ducked down fast, and the driver's door swung open. He hopped out, stayed tight behind it, and pointed his Ruger over the sill, down at Rower.

"Hold it! I'll kill her!"

"THROW THE GUN!"

McCobb pulled the hammer back again.

"Three seconds!" he shouted.

Widow froze. He knew he could hit McCobb from this distance, but he could also hit the Buick and miss completely.

McCobb had a shorter distance, a clear line of sight, and an incapacitated target.

"Two!" McCobb yelled.

Widow looked at Rower. She rolled back and forth, slowly over the snow. She couldn't hear the countdown.

"Drop your gun! Last chance!"

Widow shouted, "All right! All right!"

He let up his aim and showed the Remington to McCobb. He took his right hand off the gun, away from the trigger housing.

He tossed the shotgun up and ahead of him about ten feet, which he made look like it was accidental.

McCobb wasn't stupid, however, because he called out further instructions.

"Step forward past the gun!"

Widow stepped forward, past the shotgun.

"Keep coming!"

Widow kept walking.

"Come on!" McCobb said.

Widow continued.

"Come up to the hood of the car!"

Widow walked slowly to the hood of McCobb's Buick.

"Put your hands on the hood!"

Widow bent forward and put his hands on the hood.

"Keep them there!"

Widow stayed quiet.

"Move them, and I shoot your girlfriend! Got it?"

Widow nodded.

McCobb stepped out from behind the door and walked

over to Rower. She saw him coming and rolled on her back and grabbed her Glock. Blood pooled in her ear canal.

"No! No! Sweetie!" McCobb said, and he stepped on her Glock, pinning it to the ground.

"Roll back over!" he said, and he nudged her with his boot.

She rolled over onto her stomach.

He knelt and put a knee in her butt. With one hand, he frisked her.

"You got any other weapons, honey?"

She couldn't hear him. One ear was busted, and the other rang—hard.

He found her phone and pulled it out and tossed it into the woods.

He found her handcuffs, and then he found the ones she had taken off Widow.

He stood up and backed away from her and tossed a pair of cuffs to Widow.

They landed behind Widow's boot.

"Pick those up!"

Widow backed off the hood, slowly, and turned slowly, and bent down, picked up the cuffs.

"Cuff her!"

Widow walked over slowly to Rower.

She said, "You're going to prison for this! It's a life sentence for assault on a federal agent! Automatic!"

Her voice was loud because she couldn't hear herself.

"Cuff her!"

Widow bent down behind her and turned her over onto her back.

"From behind!"

Widow stopped and took her hands one at a time and cuffed her.

"Tight!"

He tightened the cuffs to their maximum.

McCobb stepped closer and looked down, double-checking Widow's effort.

"Okay. Good. Now back up!"

Widow stood back.

McCobb tossed Widow the second set of cuffs, the same ones he had already worn.

"Put those on."

Widow put his hands behind him.

"No. You can do yourself in the front. So, I can see them and not just hear the clicks."

Widow did as he was instructed. He didn't wait for the command to tighten them. He tightened them all the way.

"Now what?" he asked.

"Stay back," McCobb said. He aimed the Ruger at Widow and stepped forward, stopped at Rower, and reached down. He grabbed her cuffs and hauled her up.

He pulled her close to him and stayed behind her like she was a human shield, like she would shield him from Widow, who was unarmed.

McCobb was close to her, very close, close enough to whisper a secret into her ear.

He looked at her ear from over her right shoulder and said, "Whoa! That looks bad!"

He let out a hearty chuckle like a cartoon villain.

Widow stayed quiet.

"Okay. Now, you two killed Rousey?"

"I killed him," Widow said.

"And who are you?"

McCobb aimed the gun from around Rower's arm at Widow.

"Me? I'm nobody."

"Well, Mr. Nobody. Know who I am?"

"McCobb. Rousey's drug dealer."

McCobb stared at him in disbelief.

"Now, how do you know that? You hear my name from all the way over there when she said it?"

"Rousey programmed you in his phone as McCobb. Drug Dealer."

"Ah. You saw his phone?"

Widow nodded.

"Where is it?" McCobb asked.

"On his dead body."

"Better get that. Don't want to leave Shostrom any evidence."

McCobb hauled Rower by the cuffs and towed her backward with him as he waddled over to Rousey's corpse. He kept the revolver aimed at Widow.

McCobb stopped over Rousey and turned and looked down at the mess that used to be a living, breathing deputy.

"Damn! You killed him well!"

Widow said nothing.

McCobb let go of Rower and bent down to pick up the phone. He grabbed it and came back up on his feet. He stuffed it into his pocket and shoved Rower forward.

"You two are coming with me."

Rower stumbled forward.

She came up on her feet and shot Widow the look that he was waiting for.

She turned and stared at McCobb.

Her voice loud, she shouted at him.

"You think you're some big bad man?"

McCobb watched her, amused.

Rower puckered her lips and said, "You're a backwoods hillbilly!"

He gave no reaction.

"You're nothing!"

No reaction.

He just watched her, still amused, but a little confused.

Widow inched back and to the left until he stood over her Glock.

"You some kind of big drug dealer out here? Selling to hillbillies?" Rower taunted. It was all pretentious, and a little fake, but it distracted him.

He said, "FBI, you get brain damage from that warning shot?"

She walked closer to him and pointed down at his groin with her chin. She wasn't sure if he was getting it.

So, she said, "Bet it's tiny?"

His amusement turned to frustration.

"You trying to intimidate me?"

"I'm sure you're always intimidated, like a mouse."

McCobb said nothing.

"Is that it? You got a mouse down there?"

She stared at his groin.

"Bet it's teeny-tiny."

McCobb punched her across the face with the Ruger in hand.

"I'll kill ya! You think you're funny?"

Rower went flying off her feet like it was on purpose, and she fell back on top of her hands in the snow. She stared at McCobb and smiled.

"What?"

"McCOBB!" Widow called out.

McCobb looked back at him.

Widow stood in the firing position, the Glock in his hands aimed at McCobb. The handcuffs dangled from one of his wrists.

McCobb's eyes widened.

"How?" he asked, but it was too late.

Widow squeezed the trigger, firing two rounds.

McCobb's chest blew open from the front. Blood sprayed out into a red mist like his exhale had turned red.

He fell back, dropped the Ruger. His hands clutched at his wounds, desperately.

He said, "How?"

Moments earlier, when Rower was on the ground getting handcuffed, she wasn't fighting back. She wasn't trying to stop Widow from cuffing her. She rolled around on the ground to hide the fact that she had reached into her pocket and pulled out the handcuff key. She slipped it into Widow's palm.

McCobb finally figured it out when Widow walked over to him and stood over him as he bled to death because he saw the key locked into the dangling handcuff.

Rower hopped to her feet and walked over. She was supposed to save his life, but she didn't.

She asked, "Who's your boss?"

"Help?" he begged.

"Who?" she said.

He gasped once and said nothing, and then he was dead.

## 34

"I shouldn't have done that," Rower said. She stood over the body of McCobb.

Rower had short brown hair, lower than her ears, but higher than her shoulders. It rustled in the wind, and Widow watched.

He walked behind her and stopped.

"Done what?"

"Killed him. It's murder. Technically."

"Not for you."

"I let you do it."

"He was going to kill us."

"You don't know that for sure. He might've led us to his boss. Or whoever is higher up the food chain. I doubt his boss was the man I'm after."

"Turn around."

She turned around, stared up at him.

"Let me take those off you," he said. He reached out and gently grabbed her by the forearm, spun her around like a dance move, and used the handcuff key to unlock her.

After the clicks, she turned back around.

"Funny," she said.

She took back the cuffs and the keys and returned them to her jacket pockets. Next, Rower held her hand out and took back the Glock, holstered it.

"There's nothing for you to feel bad about. The guy was going to murder us. It was him or us. Simple."

"You don't know that. Besides, I should've helped him."

"How?"

"There's a medical kit in the back of the truck. Has to be. Mandatory."

Widow looked down at two gaping holes in McCobb's chest; then he looked up at the lifeless look in his eyes.

"You can still try."

"He's dead now."

"He would've been dead before, too. Nothing in the back of the truck or in a medical kit was gonna save him. Not unless there's a time machine in there that can take us back to before he fired that Ruger next to your head."

Instinctively, Rower reached her hand up, touched her bloody ear.

Widow asked, "How is that ear?"

"Feels like hell, but I'll live. My eardrum's busted. Definitely."

"You can hear me, though."

"My left ear had a ringing in it. That's all. It works."

"That's what we should get the medical kit for. We can gauze that ear."

Rower nodded and said, "We should call Shostrom, tell him."

"We should call nine-one-one for you. Get a paramedic out here. Could mean the difference between you hearing again or not."

"It's a busted eardrum."

"You don't know what it is."

She said nothing to that.

Widow said, "He was going to murder us, Alaska."

She stared at him.

He said, "Look. Come here."

She walked over to him. He turned and led her back over to Rousey's body, and he bent down and scooped up the dead man's phone.

He clicked the lock screen. The last text message notification came up.

*Almost there. They dead?*

He showed it to her.

"That's from him," she said and pointed at the dead guy, and then she read the name *McCobb. Drug Dealer*.

"He was coming to kill us if we weren't already dead. See, nothing for you to get bent out of shape about."

"I'll have to lie on my report."

"Why?"

"I lured him in. I baited him. You shot him because of what I did."

Widow lowered the phone.

"Get over it," he said and shrugged.

"You ever lie on a report?"

"It's not lying. Just tell the truth. You don't have to give every detail."

"Lying by omission."

"McCobb might be wearing underwear with hearts on them. You're not gonna put that in the report, are you?"

She cracked a smile. It was fast and short, but Widow saw it.

"No," she said.

"So? Is that lying by omission?"

She didn't respond to that. Instead, she shrugged and asked, "You sure you were in the NCIS and not DAG?"

"It's JAG, not DAG."

"That the one with the lawyers?"

"That's the one with the lawyers."

Rower reached out her hand.

"Give me the phone. It's evidence."

Widow handed it to her.

He said, "You gonna bag it?"

"No. I'm gonna use it. Unless you can find my phone," she said and turned and pointed into the brush.

Widow nodded.

McCobb had tossed her phone in that direction.

"You know Shostrom's number by heart?"

"No," she said and stopped as she tried to go through Rousey's phone, but didn't know the passcode.

She said, "I'm sure it's in here, but I can't unlock it."

"That thing got fingerprint access? We can use his finger to unlock it."

"I don't think so. This model is old."

"We can ask him for the passcode," Widow said.

"Not funny."

Widow shrugged.

"I can still dial nine-one-one, though. Don't need a code for that. It's a standard feature," she said because she wasn't sure if Widow knew.

"Okay. You call them. I'll get the medical kit. Shostrom might show up before them, anyway. I think we'd better find Kylie."

"And check with Lainey to see if she's okay or awake yet."

Widow left her standing over Rousey's dead body, and he went to search the back of the Explorer for a medical kit and gauze to bandage her head.

## 35

THE PRIVATE JET Gade was flying in wasn't owned by BioWaste, the company he worked for. Instead, it was owned by the Saudi royal family, technically by his boss's father.

Gade looked at his phone out of habit, but there was no signal at forty-one thousand feet, not for him.

He pocketed the phone and stood up and walked to the cockpit.

His boss employed a steward for the plane, but not for Gade and his men. There was no steward on this flight, just Gade, the two Smiths, and the pilots.

Gade stopped in front of the door to the cockpit and pulled it open.

He stepped in and stopped in the doorway.

He looked at the pilots. One of them turned back to him.

"Can I do something for you?" he asked.

Both pilots were terrified of the owner of the company, like most of the men who worked for BioWaste. They were equally afraid of Gade. The owner might be the one to order rendition and torture and death to anyone who betrayed him, but Gade was the one who did the torturing and killing part.

"How much longer?" Gade asked.

The pilot turned and looked at the other one, who answered.

"We'll be down on the ground in forty-five minutes."

Which was not accurate, but close enough.

Gade nodded and turned around and left. He shut the door behind him.

He walked back to the Smiths and sat across the row from them. They both sat up and turned to face him.

He said, "I wanna be back tonight. No horsing around. We get to the ground, load up, and kill everyone."

One of the Smiths said, "I thought that was Plan B?"

"It is, but it's a close Plan B. First, we rendezvous with our guy and then find out what's happening."

"Are we going to make bribes?"

"No. We already paid the girl. She breached her agreement with us the moment this all got out of hand."

The other Smith said, "I'm sure it's her two friends."

"Friends?"

"Yeah, I been thinking about it. She brought two chaperones with her. They seemed sketchy."

Gade said, "Why did you go through with it? Didn't you vet them?"

The second one said, "We did."

The first one said, "One was her sister. The other was the sister's boyfriend. It was all legit."

"He's a cop," said the second one.

"A cop?"

The first one said, "A local guy. Holden confirmed it by phone. He vouched for the guy. They buy drugs from Holden. They weren't sketchy, just a little nervous."

The second one nodded along and said, "Nervous, is more accurate. Borderline sketchy."

Gade said, "Holden doesn't sell them drugs."

"He says he does."

"Not him. One of his guys sells them drugs. Holden's a two-bit drug dealer, but he's got a large territory. He's not going to sell drugs to some broke cop in the boonies."

The Smiths said nothing to that.

Gade said, "So, now we got a third party involved or technically a fifth party."

The Smiths didn't argue with that.

Gade said, "I think it's best to cut our losses."

"Want us to kill Holden too?"

"Let's wait 'til he leads us to the rest."

They both nodded.

Gade returned to his seat, looked at his watch, and calculated that with drive time and all, he could be headed home by midnight.

## 36

It was full dark by the time Shostrom showed up; the paramedics got there first.

The headlight beams from a Deadwood city ambulance lit up the path in front of it, revealing the two dead deputies, the dead drug dealer, the Lawrence County sheriff's Ford Explorer, and the blown tire.

The ambulance driver left the sirens off, but the light bar on the roof rotated blue and red flashing lights. They danced across the trees and the snow and into the sky.

The sheriff showed up with his sirens and lights flashing to match.

When he arrived, the paramedics were already looking into Rower's right ear and re-bandaging her from the first attempt Widow had made.

Shostrom was upset and visibly livid. He wanted to recuff Widow, but Rower argued against it. The whole thing made Widow feel like an object and not a person, but he had dealt with plenty of small-town sheriffs before. He knew to keep his mouth shut since Rower was on his side, and Shostrom was not.

The whole time they were arguing, Rower sat on the back floor of an ambulance with the rear doors open. The paramedic was packing and gauzing one ear, while Shostrom was arguing with her in the other.

Widow had wandered to McCobb's Buick.

The keys were still in it. He could slip in and drive away before they noticed. He thought about it. The opportunity was tempting.

He would have to put it in reverse, keep the lights off, and swing around, drive past the sheriff's car, and then hit the gas when he cleared the cluster of vehicles.

He could be on the I-90 before they knew it, but he wouldn't get away. The sheriff could radio in backup, set up roadblocks in both directions. Eventually, they'd stop him unless he took to the back roads.

Not worth the risk.

Widow stepped up to the driver's door of the Buick and reached in and popped the trunk.

He walked around and pulled it open and stared at a zipped-up duffle bag and a Louisville Slugger with some marks on it, like it had been used a lot. Knowing McCobb's profession, Widow doubted he hit homers with the bat.

He reached into the trunk and unzipped the duffle bag.

He stared at the contents and backed away.

"Alaska!" he called out.

She didn't respond. He heard her and Shostrom arguing still.

"Alaska!" he shouted.

No response.

"ALASKA!"

The two of them stopped arguing.

"Get over here!" Widow said.

Rower moved the paramedic away and walked to the Buick, past Shostrom's car. The sheriff followed.

They all stopped and stared at the duffle bag full of cash. There was blood on it.

"How much is that?" Rower asked.

"A couple hundred grand, I guess," Widow said.

Shostrom said, "Drug money. How can it be so much?"

"It's not drug money," Widow said.

"What's it for?"

"A kidney."

"What?"

Rower said, "It's for Lainey Olsen's kidney. This guy must've stolen it."

"From who?"

Widow said, "Must have taken it from Kylie Olsen. Who took it from her sister after she and Rousey tried to kill her."

"Rousey?" Shostrom said.

"They're dating," Rower said.

"Probably were dating," Widow said, "They were probably living together."

He turned to Shostrom and said, "You'd better get someone over to their place."

Shostrom nodded and walked over to his car. He opened the door and dumped himself down in the seat, left one leg out, and the door wide open. He got on the radio and made the call.

He got one of his deputies who was posted in Deadwood and ordered him to stop at Rousey's. He told him to get in no matter what and to be on the lookout for a female.

Widow turned to Rower and said, "We should get to the hospital. Check on Lainey."

"What about Kylie?"

"She's dead."

"How can you be sure?"

"McCobb's got the money. He was going to kill us. I'm sure he paid her a visit already. He was probably going to hand Rousey over to his boss."

"Who is his boss?"

Widow looked over at Shostrom, who wasn't paying attention. He pulled a different phone out of his pocket. It was old and gray and worn down. It was a burner phone.

"Whose is that?"

"McCobb's."

"And?"

"There's no passcode on it."

"Did you look at it?"

"Of course."

"And?"

"These guys were pretty stupid. I'm surprised they operated at all."

"Why?"

"He's got phone calls and messages from his boss, a guy named Holden."

"He named him?"

"Yep."

"Could be a fake name."

"Maybe. But he put Holden' The Boss'."

Rower rolled her eyes.

Widow handed her the phone, and she went through it. It didn't take long before she had a link on the top of the food chain.

"Check this out. There are references to the 'Chicago boys,'" she said and read to herself.

After a minute, she said, "They seem afraid of these 'Chicago boys.' They must be the buyers. Probably using Holden for transportation and clean up."

Widow nodded.

"So, we find Holden, and we take him in. I can squeeze him for a name higher up."

Widow said, "Congratulations. Seems like you'll get your guy."

"Yeah. But first, you're right. Let's get to Lainey. They might send more guys to stomp her out."

"We need a car."

Rower said, "We can ride with the paramedics. They're pushing me to go to the hospital, anyway. I might as well kill two birds and all."

"What about me?"

"Aren't you coming?"

"Shostrom seems pissed."

"He is. Two of his men are dead, and one of them did it."

"He going to arrest me again?"

"Don't worry. I got you."

Widow smiled.

She said, "You will have to stick around, though. We'll need a statement. Don't worry, though. I'll back up your story. As long as you keep being useful."

He nodded along.

"Okay. Come on," she said, and she led him back to Shostrom and the ambulance.

She stopped and said, "We're headed to the hospital in Deadwood. Bag and tag what you can."

Shostrom was out of his car and staring at her.

"What? You can't leave! He can't leave!"

Rower said, "Sheriff, I'm the FBI. I tell you what you can't do. This is my case. You got a problem with it, call the Bureau."

Shostrom stared. His face registered something between frustration and anger and helplessness.

Rower said, "Oh, call my phone."

Shostrom looked at her a second more, and then he pulled his cell out of a coat pocket. He hit redial and called her.

Widow already knew what she was doing, and he walked to the area where McCobb had tossed her phone and waited for it to ring.

It did. He stomped through the snow and dead, fallen branches and twigs, and found it in the dirt.

He picked it up and clicked the button to end the ringing.

"Got it," he called out.

He joined Rower at the ambulance.

"Take us to the hospital," she told the paramedic, who nodded. She, Widow, and the two paramedics climbed back into the ambulance.

The driver K-turned and slowly drove around the dead bodies and the parked vehicles and took them back to I-Ninety and to Deadwood.

## 37

On the ground, Holden stood to wait in front of a Lexus LS 500, which was the most expensive vehicle that he had in his fleet of stolen vehicles.

It was black and freshly washed at a local automatic car wash he drove through after filling the tank.

He waited on the tarmac to the airport in Rapid City. He was on a private runway that wasn't used to getting visitors. It was all technically a part of the airport, but was a mile away. There was a single large airport hangar behind him. It was empty.

The runway was asphalt, but the drive to the hangar was dirt, which pissed him off since dirt and muddy snow had kicked up onto the tires and in the undercarriage.

It made him wonder why he'd bothered getting the thing washed at all.

He was worrying too because McCobb hadn't called him in a while, but that wasn't anything to be bent out of shape about. Lots of the rural parts of the Black Hills had spotty reception.

Holden waited and watched the plane come in and land. Three men climbed out, down a door that doubled as steps.

There was one white man he didn't recognize and the two buyers that he had already seen the day before.

He waited for them to get halfway to him, and then he walked ahead and joined them.

Holden wore his best clothes, which were jeans, boots, and a button-down shirt. No tie. He wore a simple winter coat and gloves.

The three men were in suits, tailored, fancy suits.

They met him in the middle, and all three shook hands and introduced themselves.

The Smiths gave the same stupid aliases, but the white man said his name was Gade. He was the leader, obviously.

Holden pointed to the car, but Gade interrupted him.

"Wait. John?" he said.

One of the Smiths nodded and returned to the plane. He waited near the wing for two pilots to come out with two twin duffle bags, both black. Both looked heavy.

Holden wondered if it was more cash.

Smith took one bag, slung it over his shoulder and around his back. He lifted the other and carried it the rest of the way until he got to the other Smith, who took it.

They joined Gade and Holden at the Lexus.

"Pop the trunk," Gade said.

"Sure."

Holden popped it with a button on the key.

The Smiths loaded the bags into the trunk and shut it.

"Okay. Let's go," Gade said.

Holden walked to the driver's door and opened it.

"No," Gade said.

Holden stopped.

"No, what?"

"Not you."

One of the Smiths walked around and snatched the key from Holden.

"Hey?"

"Shut up," Gade said.

Holden protested, but the Smith, with the key, punched him in the back of the head.

Holden toppled forward and slammed his face onto the roof of the car.

"What the hell!" he shouted.

"Shut up," Gade repeated.

Smith grabbed Holden by the arm and frisked him. It was a quick, one-handed frisk. He found a nine-millimeter handgun stuffed in his inside coat pocket. He took it out and tossed it to Gade.

Next, he found a phone and took it out, held onto it.

Gade ejected the magazine from the gun, racked the slide, and ejected a chambered round. Then he threw the gun off into the distance.

"Hey! That's my gun!"

"No shit?" Gade said.

One Smith opened the rear door, and the other shoved Holden down into the car.

Gade climbed in on the other side and sat next to Holden. Both Smiths were in the front.

The Smith driving asked, "Where to first?"

Gade asked, "Where are they?"

Holden said, "My guy's taking care of the witness now."

Gade paused and frowned and reared his hand and elbow back and punched Holden in the chest with a right jab. It was hard and violent, but not life-threatening.

Holden coughed and spattered and tried to catch his breath.

Gade said, "Okay. Okay. You're okay. Now, we told you we'd handle it. Isn't that what you told him?"

Gade looked at the Smith in the driver's seat.

Smith said, "That's what I told him."

Holden said, "I...I...Sorry. Things happened."

"I don't care about what happened. Now, we gotta clean all this up. Where is your guy?"

"He's not answering his phone."

Gade's face turned more frustrated.

"He's not?"

"No."

"Do you know what that probably means?"

Holden said nothing.

"It means that he's probably been arrested by the cops."

"He said there was an FBI agent."

Gade looked up at the Smiths, and then he said, "Where is he?"

"He's passed a town called Reznor. He's out taking care of the witness and the Fed."

"What happened?"

Holden sat back in the seat. Black leather creaked behind him. His face was bloody from hitting the roof of the car. His gums and teeth were red.

He said, "It looks like the girl's sister and her cop boyfriend tried to steal the money. The payment. After your guys left her."

"Go on."

"My guy said that the cop told him they strangled her and dumped the body out in the middle of nowhere."

"Where?"

"Just some road. I don't know. It's dead out there. There's lots of no-name roads that lead nowhere."

"What happened?"

"The morons didn't kill her. They're a pair of tweakers."

"A tweaker cop?"

"Yeah. This is South Dakota. And they're out in the country. It's what happens when you grow up out there."

Gade said, "Where's the girl now?"

"Hospital in Deadwood."

"How did she get there?"

"Some nobody found her."

"So, this tweaker cop and his tweaker girlfriend didn't kill her properly, and they didn't dump her properly?"

"I guess not," Holden said.

"Tell me what your man was supposed to do to take care of it."

"The cop took the Fed and the witness who found her out to that same road. He was going to shoot them both and then meet with my guy who will bring him to us."

"And you haven't heard from your guy?"

"I told you. Reception is spotty out there."

"When's the last time you spoke to him?"

The Smith in the driver's seat took out the phone and thumbed through it.

He said, "Looks like two hours now."

"What's this guy's name?"

"McCobb," Holden said.

"Call him."

The Smith in the driver's seat hit redial and handed the phone to Holden.

Holden took it and held it to his ear. It rang and rang and went to voicemail.

"It's voicemail."

Gade snatched it from him and clicked off the call. He returned the phone to the Smith in the driver's seat.

"Since we don't know where they are, what about the sister? Where's she?"

"She's dead," Holden said.

"How? Your guy do that?"

"She killed herself."

Gade nodded.

"Guilty conscious then?"

Holden answered, "Guess so."

"Where's the money?"

"What?"

Gade jabbed him again, in the same spot on his chest, and got the same gagging and coughing reaction.

"Stop! Stop! Please! I'm on your side."

"Where's the money?"

"I don't know."

The Smith in the passenger seat said, "McCobb must be trying to steal it."

Gade nodded and said, "Probably. We'll deal with him."

He looked up at the Smith in the driver's seat.

"Take us to the hospital in Deadwood.

## 38

Rower sat on a hospital bed in a small room that reminded Widow of a bunk on a submarine, tight quarters, and no privacy.

The room wasn't really a room so much as a cubby in a larger room. They had a curtain to close them off from everyone else.

Widow stood with the curtain to his back.

Rower was on the bed, sitting up and cupping the huge bandage wrapped around her head.

"I feel like I'm wearing a helmet," she said.

"It looks like a helmet," Widow said.

Her jacket was draped over the back of a steel chair. When she took it off and set it there, she suddenly was reminded of her briefcase, which was still on the back seat of the Ford Taurus, parked at the Reznor sheriff's station, which no longer had any employees.

Suddenly, she got a little paranoid thinking that someone might steal it, and she knew where the paranoia came from. The doctors had given her some painkillers to help with the throbbing eardrum. The effects were kicking in.

Before the nurse wrapped her head in a helmet made of bandages, the ER doctor had looked into her ear and told her that her eardrum had been ruptured. He said it probably would heal on its own, or they'd need to do surgery on it, but he couldn't be sure until her swelling went down. But the good news was that, in time, it would work again.

She felt lucky.

Widow said, "I'll go check on Lainey."

"No. No way. You're not leaving me here. We'll both go."

"Can you?"

"I'm not gunshot. I can walk."

"Okay." Rower stood up and stumbled a little. Widow grabbed her by the arm.

She shook him off and said, "I got it."

"Your ear controls your balance."

"I know that."

"Okay. No reason to shout at me."

She lowered her voice.

"Sorry. I didn't mean to."

Widow smiled.

She asked, "What?"

"You're not shouting. I'm messing with you."

She punched him in the arm and got up with his help, and walked to the chair.

She pulled her Glock out of its holster and tucked it into the waistband of her pants. She untucked her shirt and draped it over the gun to conceal it. She didn't want to scare the patients.

They walked out into the ER. There were nurses in scrubs and doctors in scrubs and orderlies in scrubs. Everyone seemed busy, casual, but busy.

She said, "I wonder which way she is?"

"Let's find out," Widow said. He pulled aside someone in

scrubs. It was a man, but that meant nothing. It didn't identify his position, just that he worked in the hospital.

"Where's Lainey Olsen?"

"I don't know who that is," the guy said.

"Woman with missing kidney."

Rower stepped forward and said, "She's under guard. There's a cop in front of her door."

"Who are you?"

"FBI." She went for her wallet and badge and realized they were still in her jacket.

The guy didn't wait to see them. He said, "Oh, okay. She was moved to the fourth floor."

"Why?"

"She woke up."

They stepped away, and the guy in scrubs went back to doing whatever he was doing.

Rower said, "Get my badge, please. It's in my jacket."

Widow nodded and left her standing there. He went back and got the badge and returned to her. He handed it to her. She slipped it into her back pocket and thanked him.

They left the ER, and walked to the elevator, took it up to the fourth floor.

## 39

Snow fell in Deadwood—small, light flakes of snow. It was light and calming. Up above, the dark clouds loomed over and blocked out the stars above.

The Lexus drove through the annex lot that McCobb had parked in earlier that day. It drove in and through and then out. It entered the main lot and pulled around to the back of the building, where they found no one, no security guards posted. Back there was a loading bay with a metal sliding door that was wide open. There were pallets of boxes on top. It looked like the loading crew had left it open to go grab dinner, maybe.

Gade told the Smith who was driving to park there.

They parked, and they all climbed out.

One of the Smiths hauled Holden out. They all met at the trunk, and the other Smith opened it. He pulled out the duffle bags and set them on the ground.

Gade unzipped one and pulled out a wad of zip ties and a roll of duct tape.

He looked at Holden.

"Guess what, Mr. Holden."

"What?"

"You get to live."

Holden said nothing because he didn't feel relieved by the declaration.

Gade zip-tied his hands and duct-taped his mouth. They shoved him into the trunk and slammed it shut.

They could hear him kicking and pounding on the inside.

Gade looked around. There was still no one. But there was a single security camera. It was facing the approach. The car would be identified, but not their faces.

He said, "Load up here."

They unzipped both bags and pulled out three black ski masks, put them on.

The three men took off their coats and set them on the rear bench of the car.

They took out three sets of Kevlar and put them on. The straps were Velcroed, and they each pounded on their vests like a signal that each was on tight.

Next, they checked their handguns, which were in hip holsters. All loaded and ready to go.

Last, they reached into the other bag and pulled out three Heckler and Koch MP5SDs submachine guns, the Special Forces kind.

The MP5SD is built with a suppressor into the gun. The barrel is ported internally for extra soundproofing.

Bullets ignite from a gun and burst into loud sounds, because they travel faster than the speed of sound. Thus, making a sonic *crack*. The only way to avoid this side effect is with subsonic ammunition, but not with the MP5SD. The weapon was built to turn the cheapest nine-millimeter rounds into subsonic rounds.

They were using nine-millimeter parabellums.

Each man checked the rounds, checked the magazines, and loaded them.

They each had a single backup magazine with thirty rounds each, totaling sixty a man, for a grand total of one hundred eighty bullets.

"Parameters, boss?" one of the Smiths asked.

"Find Olsen. Kill her. Kill any cops."

"Everyone else?"

"Shoot anyone who gets in the way," Gade said.

He set the MP5SD to single round burst for precision and led the way through the cargo loading bay to a back elevator.

## 40

On the way to Lainey's room, Widow saw an offer he couldn't refuse.

At the nurse's station, down a different corridor, and after the elevators there was a countertop with a coffee thermos, with the top screwed down tight to keep it hot.

There was a sign that read: *Hot Coffee* and *Free For All*.

He said, "I'll join you in a minute."

Before Rower could object, Widow was headed down the other hallway.

"Okay," she called after him.

She headed on.

Lainey Olsen's room was obvious because the uniformed deputy was sitting out in front, in a folding chair. He had a USA Today with him and a pencil. The paper was folded up under his chair, and the pencil was on top.

Rower stopped close to him. He looked up and then stood up.

She reached for her badge, but the deputy spoke first.

"You Rower?"

"Yeah."

"The sheriff called. He said you'd be coming by."

"Did he tell you to give me shit?"

"No. He said to assist in any way that I can."

"Good," she said, surprised because she hadn't expected that.

She asked. "What's your name?"

"Wallace."

"Okay, Wallace. My associate went around the corner for coffee. He's a big dude. Kind of looks like a combination of the worst mugshots you ever saw and a pretty boy. Or a guy who used to be pretty like when he was a baby."

She felt the painkillers adding a little extra commentary that she didn't mean to say.

"I saw him," Wallace said.

"Good. He's with me. So, don't give him any shit either."

"Okay."

"You're doing a good job," she added.

"Okay. Thank you."

She nodded at him, and she stepped past him, pushed open a big, heavy door, and entered the hospital room.

The door closed behind her, slowly.

Lainey Olsen was seated upright. Her head was bandaged from a head wound.

She wore a hospital gown. There was an ID bracelet on her wrist.

She said, "Who are you?"

"I'm FBI. Rower is my name."

"Oh," she said and looked down at the humps in a blanket that covered her. It was her knees. She pulled them up slowly.

"Careful," Rower said.

"I'm okay."

"You had a kidney removed. Doesn't it hurt?"

She nodded.

"They gave me pills."

"I see," Rower said. "I know the feeling."

"What happened to you?"

"Long story. A buddy of yours tried to kill me."

"What? Who?"

"A lowlife named McCobb."

"Oh."

"You know him then?"

"He's a drug dealer. My sister got mixed up with him."

"Yeah."

"Where is she?"

"I don't know. We're looking for her now."

Lainey stared down at her blanket and knees again.

She looped two hands up and around them.

"Not sure you should sit like that," Rower said.

Olsen stayed quiet.

Rower said, "Because of the kidney."

Silence.

Rower stepped forward and pulled up a stool meant for the doctor, she supposed. It rolled along the tiled floor on wheels.

She sat on it.

"Listen, Rousey is dead."

"Oh," Olsen said again.

"How?"

"Well, he tried to kill me. He killed his partner. I saw it all happen."

Suddenly, Rower wasn't sure she should relay the information. Her head felt okay. It must've been the painkillers.

She said, "Tell me what happened."

"Don't I need a lawyer? I mean, don't I get a lawyer?"

"You're not being charged with a crime. What do you need a lawyer for?"

"Oh."

"No. No crime. But we need to know the truth."

Olsen stared off around the room.

She said, "You promise? I'm not in trouble?"

"Not yet. Unless you don't cooperate."

Which wasn't quite true, but she said it anyway.

"I sold my kidney."

"How? Give me some details."

"I hate it here. I want to go. I figured the best way to make a lot of money was to do something drastic."

"How did you link up with someone who'd pay for it?"

"The dark web."

"The dark web?"

"Yeah, you can find anything online. I posted an ad on a website. Took me months to find someone telling the truth. A ton of people emailed me. Then they found me. I looked them up, spoke to them, and met with them. They seemed real."

"Just a website?"

"Yeah."

Rower shrugged and said, "Guess that's the only way to connect for something like this. You remember the site?"

Olsen told her the link.

Rower nodded. She knew it. The FBI already monitored it, but it kept going down and popping up with variations of the same name.

She couldn't do anything about the site. It was owned and operated in the Middle East.

"What else? Who are they?"

"It's a company."

"What's the name?"

"BioWaste was the only name I got."

"Okay."

Olsen said, "I don't know much else."

"How much money did they give you?"

"It was supposed to be $250,000. But I never got it. My sister was supposed to accept it."

Rower didn't tell her about the money in the duffle bag inside the dead drug dealer's trunk.

Olsen asked, "What happened to me?"

"Is that all you remember?"

"I remember going to the warehouse."

"Warehouse?"

"No," she paused, and then she said, "I mean garage. It was a big garage."

"What kind? Like for a house?"

"No. A tire garage. Used to be."

"Where is it?"

"West. Before Reznor."

"Okay. What else?"

Just then, the lights in the hospital went out.

41

Downstairs in the hospital in Deadwood, Gade stood behind one of the Smiths as he cut all the cables and wires that he could find in an electrical room.

The aim was to cut the phone lines and the internet network because hospitals have backup lights and generators.

The generator was on the roof and not in the ground-floor electrical room.

Gade clicked on a flashlight from out of his pocket and shone the light on the Smiths.

"Let's go," he said.

They walked out past the lock they had shot and continued out to the bottom floor hallway.

"Great," one of the Smiths said.

"What?"

"We can't take the elevator."

Gade said, "Doesn't matter. We need to go floor by floor till we find someone who knows where she is."

Just then, a set of double doors up ahead opened. A maintenance worker walked through the doors.

"What the hell now?" he said out loud to himself.

Gade pointed his MP5SD in the guy's face along with the flashlight beam.

"What floor is Lainey Olsen?"

"Wait. Wait."

The worker put his hands up in the air. An unlit cigarette fell out of his mouth as he had just been savoring the idea of smoking it, even though he couldn't smoke it anywhere in the hospital.

It bounced on the tile below his feet.

"Floor?"

"I don't know who that is."

"How can we find out where she is?"

"The directory. But it's going to be off."

"How else?"

"I don't know. Ask a nurse."

Gade shot him twice in the chest, center mass. Blood sprayed in a red puff of smoke.

The guy fell back, dead.

"You boys split up. You take the first floor," he said to one. "You the second. Work your way up. I'll start at four and work my way down. Call me when you find her."

They nodded, and all headed for the stairs to take their assigned floors.

## 42

Widow tried to pour a hot cup of coffee out of a coffee thermos. That's all he wanted. He had a long day. Was that too much to ask?

Widow stood at the counter. Two nurses worked behind it. One was on the computer. The other was reviewing a chart or notes or something. He didn't know. All he knew was that it was paperwork, paper-clipped together.

He stopped at the counter and read the sign three times to himself and asked, "This coffee is for everyone?"

The nurse at the computer looked up and over a pair of reading glasses.

"That's what it says."

"I know, but for anyone?"

She smiled at him.

"Sir, that's what the sign says."

"I read it, but you know that old saying when something's too good to be true?"

"It's true," she said, and she went back to her computer.

Widow pulled a Styrofoam cup off a stack and readied his other hand like that scene in Indiana Jones where he swaps the bag of dust for the gold statue. He did it, and he thought of the reference at the same time like he was goofing around.

He picked up the thermos, unscrewed the lid with a flick of his thumb, and started pouring the coffee into the cup.

Steam came out, and he got hit in the face with an alluring aroma, which to him was like a siren's seductive call.

After he filled his cup, he replaced the thermos and tightened the lid and drank.

Suddenly, the power went out, and he was surrounded in darkness.

"Hell!" one of the nurses said.

"What now?" the other said.

Widow stood frozen. He had the cup, but couldn't see to put it to his lips.

He waited like it was a power outage, but after a minute longer of waiting, a pair of backup lights on the top corners of the halls flicked on.

"The emergency lights?" a nurse asked.

"Guess the power's out for good."

"Damn!" the other said.

Widow did not drink the coffee. He turned and looked back down the hall. He walked to the end with the coffee brimming and spilling out over the top lip.

He stopped at the end of the hall and turned and looked at the deputy who was posted out front of Olsen's room.

He joined the guy and checked out his nameplate.

"Wallace. I'm with Agent Rower."

"I know. She described you."

"What's happening?"

"Could just be a power outage."

Widow looked past him, out the window. He walked to it and looked down at the street.

"Then why is that gas station across the street lit up?"

Wallace said, "You think it's something else?"

"Better safe than sorry."

Rower came out of the room and stopped between them.

"What's going on? Power out?"

"Don't think so. The lights are on across the street," Widow said.

Rower said, "Is it him? Holden?"

"No. I doubt it."

Wallace asked, "Who?"

"Drug dealer," Rower answered.

"Could be them," Widow said.

"Them?"

Rower answered, "Bad guys."

"Very bad," Widow said.

"We better check it out," Rower said.

"We'll do it. You stay with Lainey."

"I'm the FBI."

"That's why it's better you stay and protect her."

"You benching me?"

Widow said, "Really. Alaska, you should stay and protect her. She's no good to your case if she's dead."

"What about you?"

"We'll check it out," Widow said and looked at Wallace.

Wallace shrugged.

"Here. Take my gun."

She drew her Glock and reversed and tried to hand it to him.

"Keep it. You need it."

"What the hell are you going to do if there are bad guys?"

He showed her the coffee and said, "Coffee grenade. Remember?"

She smiled and re-holstered her Glock.

"Be safe."

Widow nodded and led Wallace down the hall.

Rower went back inside the room.

"What's happening?" Olsen asked.

"Don't worry. I'm taking care of it."

She turned to the door and looked for an inside lock. There wasn't one. She searched the room for the heaviest thing that wasn't bolted down. There was nothing. All she could find was another chair and a roundtable. She moved both in front of the door like a makeshift barricade.

"What's happening?" Olsen said. She looked nervous.

"Someone might be coming. We're just taking precautions."

## 43

Widow stayed behind Wallace because he had the only gun between them, which was another revolver, a six-shot.

"We should check the stairs. That's going to be the only way for anyone to move around," Wallace said.

Widow stopped him at the intersection and pulled him back down the hallway with the nurse's station and the free coffee.

He stopped at the station.

"Where are the stairs?"

One of the nurses said, "There's a set on each end of the floor."

She pointed in opposite directions.

"Guess we should split up," Wallace said.

"Yeah."

"I'll take the south."

Widow left him, and they went in opposite directions.

Wallace went north. Shadows covered a lot of the floor between him and the stairwell door.

He stopped at the door and drew his gun. He opened the door and powered through.

The stairwell was wide and dark except for emergency lights that only lit up cones of space.

He walked down a flight, his weapon in hand, pointed at the ground. He didn't want to shoot anyone if he didn't have to.

At the next landing, just above the third-floor stairs, he heard footsteps. They were light, but fast.

"Someone there?" he called out.

The sound stopped.

"It's the police."

He walked down the next set of stairs until he was in front of the door for the third floor.

"Show yourself," he called out.

A voice from the shadows said, "You're police?"

"Yeah. Come out."

"What's happening?"

"Step out."

Wallace raised the weapon to point at knee-level.

The voice said, "Is it a power outage?"

Wallace said, "Come on. No reason to be afraid."

The voice said, "Are you here to protect Lainey Olsen?"

Wallace raised the gun all the way.

"How did you know that?"

Wallace never heard gunshots, but he heard three slow purrs like whispers in the dark.

Three bullets erupted through his stomach and chest, fast, before the pain could even register in his brain. He dropped the revolver and slumped down to his knees, stared up to the shadow.

A man stepped out. He wore a Kevlar vest and expensive slacks and shoes. His watch looked like a Rolex.

Gade pointed the MP5SD at Wallace and stepped closer to him.

He said, "Sorry, amigo."

Wallace slumped forward and was dead.

Gade left him there and walked up to the fourth floor.

## 44

Widow descended the stairwell slowly. He had been serious about the coffee grenade, because that was all he had.

The coffee slurped and brimmed with every step down.

He stopped at each landing and each door. He saw a few staff members sashaying, but no one who fell into the category of a bad guy.

On the ground floor, he stepped out of the stairwell and looked around to see if he could locate the electrical room.

There was a dead guy sprawled out on the floor, and the lock was shot out.

He checked the dead guy. It was a maintenance worker—no phone on him.

Widow turned and went back to the stairs. He had to get back to Rower.

He entered and heard shouting and screaming above him. People came down the stairwell. He stepped aside and saw people in scrubs and a few patients.

Widow pushed past them and climbed.

He went past the first floor to the second-floor landing. It was quieter.

Suddenly, the door burst open, and a hospital security guard, an old guy, tumbled backward. He had two bullet holes in his chest. Widow hopped back and hugged the wall on the opposite side of the door.

The door swung open, and he saw a gun barrel suppressor dart out, followed by a MP5SD.

The guy holding it wore a ski mask. He wore expensive clothes under a Kevlar vest.

Smoke pooled at the end of the MP5SD's muzzle.

Widow waited till the guy was in the doorway and slammed the hot coffee into the guy's face.

The liquid scalded and burned him.

Widow didn't stop there.

He grabbed the muzzle with his left hand and jerked the guy forward and kicked him hard in the groin.

The guy screamed. His eyes shut, and his face burned, even through the mask.

Widow ripped the MP5SD out of his hand, reversed it. He pointed it up behind the guy, in case there was another.

He saw no one else, just shadows and two more dead hospital staff on the floor.

Widow jerked forward and jerked the guy's mask off his face. He was Middle Eastern.

The Middle Eastern guy clutched his groin with one hand and his face with the other.

Widow kicked him again in the solar plexus hard because he wanted him to feel it through the vest, which he did.

The guy fell back and rolled around on the tile, squealing in agony.

Widow stepped into the hall and sidestepped. So his back had a wall behind it. He didn't want any surprises.

He lifted his boot high and slammed it down into the guy's groin again.

The guy's eyes shot open like someone had slammed an adrenaline shot into his heart.

Widow shoved the barrel of the MP5SD into his face.

"How many?"

"What?"

Widow moved the gun and fired one round into the guy's kneecap.

He squealed again, loud and painful.

"How many are with you?"

"Two others."

Widow looked up again, checked the hall, and saw no one.

"Where?"

"One below us and one above."

"What floors?"

"First and four."

Widow looked back into the stairwell. It was automatic.

The guy shouted at the top of his lungs.

"JARRAH!"

Widow turned back and shot the guy twice more—both in the face.

The guy's head slammed back down on the tile. He was dead.

Widow backed up into the corner. He heard footsteps running up the stairs.

A voice called out, "Idris?"

A second later, another masked man stepped onto the landing and saw his friend on the floor—dead.

Widow switched the MP5SD's fire selector to full auto. He stepped out with it from behind the doorway and shoved the muzzle of the weapon into the guy's vest.

"You must be Jarrah?" he said and squeezed the trigger.

The MP5SD fired faster than he could count, and Jarrah went flying back into the stairwell.

His MP5SD dropped to the ground.

Widow stopped firing and checked Jarrah. The guy lay on the stairs, sieving around like a turtle on its back.

Widow bent down and picked up the other weapon, ejected the magazine from it with one hand, and dropped the gun. He kept the MP5SD trained on Jarrah and knelt down, scooped up the extra magazine, pocketed it.

He stepped into the stairwell.

Jarrah was pulling a Glock out of a hip holster.

Widow squeezed the trigger, and three more rounds blasted out into Jarrah's vest.

He dropped the Glock.

The guy was coughing blood. It seeped out from the mouth hole in his mask. And more blood pooled around him onto the concrete.

Widow said, "How many?"

"Go to hell."

"You're Jarrah. That's Idris. Who's the other dude?"

Jarrah stayed quiet.

"There are three of you, right?" Widow asked.

Jarrah looked at him, fast, like a reflex.

"Good enough," Widow said.

He took it for an answer, and he pointed the MP5SD at the guy and squeezed the trigger.

The gun purred and fired bullets until it purred nothing.

All the shots went into Jarrah's Kevlar vest.

Widow stared at him. More blood pooled everywhere, and he coughed and gasped until he stopped gasping and coughing and breathing.

Jarrah was dead.

Widow ejected the magazine, fed in the new one, and loaded the chamber.

He switched the fire selector to his favorite, which was a three-round burst.

He knelt down and scooped up the Glock, too. He stuffed it in his pocket.

That's when he noticed that the borrowed thermal shirt he wore was not white anymore. It was red. Blood had splattered on it and virtually dyed it.

Widow turned back to the one called Idris and saw the mask on the floor. He bent over, scooped it up. Then he looked at Idris's Kevlar vest. He went for it and unstrapped it and pulled it on. The vest was snug on him, but they come in one size fits all. He buckled it and slipped the mask on over his head, kept it pulled up in case he ran into Wallace.

He ran through the open doorway to the stairwell and headed back up the stairs, taking big, giant steps.

## 45

Rower stood in the center of the room, Glock pointed at the door. She waited.

She heard screams from down the hall.

"What's happening?" Olsen asked.

"Quiet!"

Suddenly, someone knocked on the door from the other side.

"FBI, are you in there?" a voice asked.

Rower said, "Don't come in! I'll shoot you."

Silence. Then Rower and Olsen heard multiple soft purrs and wood cracking sounds.

The door rattled and shook. Parts of it pelted out like someone was stabbing it from the other side.

"What was that?" Olsen asked.

"Quiet!"

Rower knew what it was. It was bullets from a silenced submachine gun. Had to be. They were dead quiet and too fast to be fired by trigger pull from most people, anyway.

"I'm armed!" she shouted.

"That's okay. So are we."

"I've called for backup!" she lied. And suddenly she thought, *why not call for backup?*

She reached for her phone until she realized it was in her jacket pocket, downstairs.

"Shit," she muttered.

"Liar," the voice said. "Come on. Nobody's coming for you."

"The FBI is! They'll be here soon!"

"Now, I know you're lying. I'm counting to ten. Then I'm coming in. If I have to come in, I'll kill you both."

Gade didn't count like he said. Instead, he kicked the door open and unloaded the MP5SD's magazine. Full auto, like a madman.

He fired until the purrs dulled down to empty bullets.

Smoke filled the air.

## 46

Gade ejected the spent magazine from his MP5SD and let it fall to the floor. Quickly, he pulled the backup out and slipped it home and chambered a round.

He called into the room, through the smoke.

"You still alive in there?"

He sidestepped to the right, in case Ms. FBI fired at him and aimed down the sights of the gun. He swept left to right, but couldn't see completely through the smoke.

From behind him, he heard a sound at the other end of the hallway.

He stepped back and looked. It was the other stairwell door, slamming open.

He saw one of his guys' barrels through it and stop and bend over. The guy put his hands on his knees like he was out of breath.

"You okay?" he called out to him.

The guy stood up tall, taller than he recognized. The guy put up a hand and waved at him with one finger like he was trying to tell Gade to hold on.

"You look like you're out of breath."

His masked guy stayed quiet.

"Jarrah, what's up?"

The masked guy kept walking to him, passing through shadows, staying out of the cones of light from the backup bulbs.

"Jarrah? Why'd you run?"

The masked man kept pounding on his chest and having a hard time getting the words out, but he kept walking.

As he got thirty yards away, Gade squinted his eyes and stared at the guy. He seemed really tall.

Gade saw blood all over the guy's mask and Kevlar vest.

"Damn! You been enjoying yourself down there?"

The masked man kept waving his left hand, his right hand on his MP5SD.

Gade saw the guy's trigger finger go into the housing like he was waiting to fire it.

Gade stepped closer, stepping into the doorway.

Suddenly, the masked man raised the MP5SD like he was going to shoot it.

Gade jerked his up and fired, but several gunshots rang out from inside the hospital room.

Rower fired until her Glock ran empty.

Widow fired two sets of three-round bursts.

Gade fired zero shots.

Instead, his Kevlar vest took several shots from the front and the side. His legs and neck took the rest.

Widow pulled his mask up, left it on like a beanie.

Gade dropped his MP5SD and clutched at his throat, which was spraying blood and running out like a geyser run dry.

He dropped to his knees.

Widow stopped dead over him and stared down.

Gade released his neck and clutched at Widow's legs and jeans.

He tried to speak, but no words came out.

Widow looked into his eyes as he died.

## 47

Widow tossed the MP5SD and pulled up the Kevlar and dropped it to the ground.

He walked into Olsen's room, through a dying halo of gun smoke.

He saw Rower lying up against the bed. She was clutching her stomach and chest.

She was hit.

He ran to her.

"No. Alaska!"

He grabbed at her, using his hands to cover the bloody holes. There were too many for him to plug, and he couldn't determine them all. So, he pressed down on the stomach one and the chest one. They were the two that seemed the worst.

"Alaska! Stay with me!"

She grabbed at him. She pulled on his shirt and squirmed and gasped.

Blood came up out of her mouth.

"Alaska!"

She stared into his eyes.

He heard Olsen moving around. She had hidden behind the bed.

"Is she dying?" she asked.

"GET A DOCTOR! NOW!"

Olsen jumped out of the bed. Her bare feet hit the tile. She pulled off the medical patches that were hooked up to measure her heart rate and ran back into the hall, past Gade's dead body. She vanished from sight.

Widow held onto Rower.

She looked up into his eyes.

She tried to speak.

"Don't speak. Save your strength," he begged her.

She said, "I got him."

He smiled down at her.

"Yes. He's dead. You got him."

She smiled a big smile, all teeth, and all blood.

He smiled back at her.

A second later, she stopped smiling. She stopped moving. She stopped clutching. And she stopped fighting.

Her arms fell limp.

Her head fell back.

The life in her eyes was gone like that. One second she was there, and the next she was gone.

## 48

Olsen returned one minute later that seemed like ten. She brought with her doctors and nurses and people in scrubs that Widow couldn't identify.

They took Rower from Widow, but it wasn't easy. He held her for a long, long time. He wouldn't let go.

He finally did, and he backed away.

Blood covered him from head to toe.

The doctors and nurses and other scrub people took Rower away on a gurney on wheels.

Widow stayed in the room for a long moment more. Olsen stayed with him.

She felt responsible, but she said nothing.

Widow stared at his hands.

Finally, he spoke.

"Who did this?"

Olsen said nothing.

"WHO?"

"I don't know. That guy."

She pointed at Gade's dead body.

Widow looked at her.

"Who's at the top?"

"I don't know. But the company is called BioWaste like I told Agent Rower."

Widow nodded and stepped away, out of the room.

He knelt down and bunched Gade's vest in his hand and jerked the body up in the air.

He searched the pockets.

He found a set of Lexus car keys and a wallet. He took them both.

He walked back down the hall, stuffed the keys and the wallet into his pockets.

He slammed into the stairwell and jogged down to the first floor, and entered the hallway. He went to the emergency room where they had gone to patch up Rower's eardrum.

People in scrubs passed him and didn't bat an eye. They were all panicking from rumors of gunfire. Most were trying to work on patients who were shot, but alive—patients who were also hospital workers.

Widow walked to the cubby and found Rower's jacket. He sifted through it until he found her phone. He looked at the screen. He couldn't unlock it. It was passcode protected.

There were two missed calls from a guy named Agent Bukowski.

Widow figured he'd call back. So, he pocketed her phone, and then he sifted through the last pocket and found his passport and his bank card. He pocketed them in his back pocket.

Widow left the emergency room, back down the stairs, and back to the ground floor. He walked past the same dead maintenance worker and kept going.

He figured that had been the dead guy's first stop, which meant they were parked out back, behind the hospital.

Widow found a black Lexus LS 500 parked at the loading bay.

Widow took out the wallet and stared at it. A license inside said the dead guy who killed Rower was called Gade. He was a resident of Illinois.

There was an address, but Widow doubted it meant anything.

He shuffled through credit cards until he found something of interest. It was an ID card with a chip in it, like a security card to open doors at the Pentagon.

He took the license and security card and two credit cards that looked like they had huge limits and tossed the wallet.

The security badge read: *William Gade. Security. BioWaste.*

Widow pocketed the cards and IDs.

He took the keys out and clicked the button to confirm that the car was the dead guy's.

The Lexus LS 500's lights flickered and beeped. It was right.

Just then, he heard something shuffling in the trunk.

Widow walked around and clicked the trunk button on the key. The lid opened. He pulled it open.

Inside was a guy all tied up.

Widow reached down and ripped the duct tape off the guy's mouth.

"Who are you?" he asked.

He must've looked like a nightmare, because terror filled the guy's eyes. He turned white.

"Who are you?" he asked again.

"Get me out of here, man. These crazy guys kidnapped me."

"Who are you?"

"Name's Holden."

Widow stared down and smiled.

"What, man? What?"

"Holden Drug Dealer?"

"Yeah. I know you."

Widow looked around the lot. He saw no one.

He pulled the Glock out of his pocket and pointed it at Holden.

"What, man? What?"

"Who's the head of the snake?"

"What?"

"BioWaste. Who?"

Holden looked at Widow and knew he wasn't joking around. So, he answered the question.

Afterward, Widow dropped him off in front of Deadwood's sheriff station, unconscious from a head wound the size of Widow's fist.

He left him on their doorstep, still zip-tied.

Shostrom would find him, eventually.

Widow got into the Lexus. He had a long night ahead, with a long drive.

## 49

In the morning, nine hundred forty-nine miles from where Widow had started, plus one time zone ahead of where he'd started was Chicago. One of the several Saudi princes in the world was named Mohammed Al Serafi, and he lived in Chicago.

Serafi stared out over Lake Michigan. He watched the morning schooners set out on the water. He watched the late-night yachts sway back and forth over the waves, their owners and passengers still asleep from the night before. He watched the fishermen line the shore and the piers below.

Serafi smoked a cigar and leaned against the glass railing. He tapped the ashes over the side and exhaled the smoke up into the air toward the clear skies overhead.

Life was good for the former prince who kept the title in name only, and only from his staff and employees, whom he saw as his subjects. Therefore, he demanded that they call him Prince Serafi every time they addressed him. The only exception to this rule was his top lieutenant, a man called William Gade, and no one else.

The only reason Gade was given such privileges was that

the man had saved his life once. And now, his savior was given special considerations over everyone else.

Serafi enjoyed a morning cigar, as he did every morning. This one was Cuban and possibly illegal in the US, possibly not.

Did the US still have an embargo on Cuba? Or did it not?

He didn't know because he couldn't keep up with trivial things like that. He had no intention of keeping up with trivial things like that.

Life was short, as he well knew.

Serafi enjoyed cigars, and he enjoyed morning views, like this one.

From his penthouse apartment in the Fordham Building, Serafi could see all of Chicago from a three-hundred-sixty-degree view. Every room in his two-floor apartment had a clear view of one compass direction or another.

He had purchased the apartment from some dead movie star's estate, on the cheap, too. He paid five million, US, for an apartment that was worth double that in today's market. And he'd only purchased it ten years ago, right after the American economy had its biggest stock crash since the Great Depression.

One of the good things about being a Saudi prince was that he didn't care about the American stock market. His father had. He remembered that.

His father cared a great deal because he had a lot of money invested in stocks. But their family had plenty of wealth. So why care about one bad year of stocks?

From a passerby, Serafi did not look the part of a Saudi royal prince, which technically made sense because he no longer was in the line of succession. That's what happens when you're banished from the kingdom.

Serafi took another puff of his cigar, held it, and exhaled

one more time before one of his servant girls, nineteen and getting old for his taste, stepped out onto the balcony. She carried a serving tray with a freshly brewed pot of Turkish coffee and one empty, pristinely clean mug—white, as he demanded.

The serving girl was platinum blonde, dyed that color every week because that was the look that Serafi preferred in his girls. She had blue eyes, also fake. They were colored contacts, nonprescription because she had 20/20 vision, naturally.

Most of that stuff she didn't mind. Not that hard.

Her lips were puffed out and big. The word that Serafi used to describe them was voluptuous.

They were fake too. She had them injected with collagen every month to make them appear the way he preferred.

She hated doing it, but it could've been worse. He required one of the other girls to get breast implants. So far, she had not been required to do that, maybe because she was naturally endowed in that way.

The serving girl wasn't American, but she was white and spoke fluent English. She was Ukrainian born, like the other two girls who worked in Chicago with her. They all had the same basic life stories.

Their country faced hard economic times. Her family was poor. Her father was poor. They were indebted to the prince for choosing their daughter.

Her father put her in contract with Serafi. She was to be his servant, and in exchange, her family got a monthly stipend.

At first, it was scary for her. At sixteen, when she first joined Serafi's entourage, it was a living nightmare. But after a time, it wasn't so bad. It wasn't like she was abused violently. Serafi had never hit her or any of his servant girls.

She was designated to his Chicago residence. He had other homes in other locations, none of which were in Saudi Arabia. All of which were Western countries and Western cities: Chicago, New York, Miami, Toronto, London, Paris, and Rome. Those were just the ones that she knew of specifically. She knew he had properties that were more secluded, in the mountains, or on lakes. She also knew there were boats. She didn't know how many, and she had never been invited to work on one.

Serafi didn't take any of his girls with him when he went out of town. She knew he was never anywhere without one. The way she figured it, Serafi had dozens of servant girls under his employ.

In Chicago, he had three—her and two others, both younger than her. She was the oldest.

She tried not to figure out how many he had. She guessed it was more than twenty, maybe even as high as fifty.

Being nineteen, her biggest fear was what would happen when she got too old for him. He already no longer showed her much attention, not like he had three years ago.

Serafi stayed in Chicago a lot. He spent a lot of time there. It seemed he spent well more than half of the year there.

She didn't understand why.

It wasn't because of his business, which she pretended to not hear about. That was one of the first lessons taught to her by the girl who trained her in New York, three years ago.

Don't ask questions.

The less you know, the better.

Don't make waves.

Eventually, she dismissed his business as being the reason that Serafi spent his winters in Chicago.

She hated the cold weather. It reminded her of home. The

snow was overbearing. The wind was severely chilling. And the lake froze over every year.

But this was her life now.

She was his servant. In exchange, she had room, board, a salary, and her family was taken care of. Her father was honored. She never thought about escaping. But lately, it was hard not to think about the future because she knew she was getting too old for him. She didn't know what he did with girls when they got too old.

The serving girl set the tray down on a stone patio table behind Serafi and began pouring his morning coffee.

Serafi turned around and glanced at her. She was dressed in American clothes that he preferred: a tight-fitting, sleeveless white top and a tight pair of shorts that left little to the imagination.

The serving girl wore sneakers, also white.

He said, "Why those shoes?"

The girl stood up straight, placed the coffeepot down on the tray before addressing him.

She kept her head down, didn't look him in the eyes.

She said, "Pardon me, Prince?"

"I asked, why do you wear those sneakers?"

He stared down at her.

The girl's height stopped at his chest, but not because Serafi was a foot taller than her, which would've made him six-foot-two-inches tall.

Serafi wasn't that tall. He wasn't over six feet tall. He wasn't over five-foot-ten-inches tall. And he wasn't over five-foot-nine-inches tall.

He appeared tall because he wore special Italian-made shoes with special Italian-made lifts in them.

The serving girl kept her eyes down, staring at the ground.

The wind blew hard across the deck of the balcony. The gust caused her to shiver.

Serafi stood straight, walked over, and stopped right in front of her. She felt his morning breath hot and smelling of cigars on her face.

He wore white silk pajama pants and a white pullover fleece top.

"I asked you a question?"

"The shoes are for comfort, Sir."

Serafi did not reply, but she sensed a frown coming over his face.

For a moment, she thought he might strike her. But he didn't.

Serafi stared past her at the coffee and the tray.

Pinched down, snug between the coffee mug and the steaming coffeepot, was the day's copy of the New York Times.

"I see you remembered today's paper."

"Yes, Prince. Of course."

He nodded at her. Then he reached out and touched her chin. He gripped it like it was a lever on a machine and pulled it up, forcing her to look up into his eyes.

Serafi's face was hard to see underneath the bristly, thick, black beard he wore. At that range, she saw enough of it.

Even though Serafi was Arabic, his skin was pale white, as if he had never seen the sun. She saw he wore makeup over his skin—a pale foundation. He colored himself pale on purpose. He avoided the sun on purpose. Anything that reminded him of Saudi people, he avoided like the plague.

Serafi stared into her eyes for a long, frightening second.

He said, "You're growing up."

A shiver surged down her spine, which she disguised as just the cold weather around her, but it was fear.

He said, "I don't like the sneakers. It makes me think you are preparing to run from me. Is that what you're doing? You're planning to run away?"

"No, Prince. Never."

He remained quiet, just nodded, and studied her eyes.

"You know I can tell when someone is lying to me?"

"I know that, Prince."

"Are you lying now?"

"No, Prince. Of course not."

"Are you sure?"

She nodded, trying to keep the shivers of fear at bay.

"Do you love me?" he asked.

"Yes."

He paused a beat and then let go of her chin, of the lever, and stepped back, and puffed once again on the cigar. He exhaled the smoke up and away out of her face.

"Finish pouring my coffee."

The servant girl nodded and smiled a fake smile at him. He couldn't tell because of her lips.

She poured the remainder of the coffee and stepped aside.

Serafi sat down on a heavy stone chair and stuck the cigar into a thick glass ashtray. He opened the paper, sipped the coffee, and read about the day's news.

The servant girl walked away.

Serafi called out to her. She stopped and turned.

"Get Gade up here. And bring him some breakfast too."

The servant girl didn't call back. She knew better. She walked back and spoke.

"Mr. Gade is gone."

"What do you mean? Did you check his quarters?"

Gade lived in quarters under the penthouse. Serafi wanted him close.

She said, "He never came home."

Serafi said, "Leave."

She turned and left.

He took his phone out. It was gold plated—the cover, the shell, all of it except for the gorilla glass.

He pulled up Gade's phone number and called it, waited.

Nine hundred forty-nine miles away, Gade's cell phone rang in an evidence bag, on an evidence table, in Sheriff Shostrom's head office, in Deadwood.

Serafi got Gade's voicemail.

He said, "You'd better have a good reason for your absence. For not answering. If any other man ignored my call, I'd kill him."

Serafi clicked off the phone.

In the kitchen, a private service elevator door opened, and Jack Widow stepped out onto the tile. He had his Glock out, and a round chambered.

He walked into the most luxurious and gaudy apartment that he had ever seen.

Everything was gold—the countertops, the floor, the walls, the fixtures—everything. Even the knobs on the two huge stovetops were gold.

"What the hell?" he said to himself.

He walked into the kitchen and swept all directions with the Glock. He kept the security badge in his front pocket. It had let him into the private parking garage entrance down in the alley, and it had started the private service elevator he found down there. So far, no guards. But the expensive, high-tech badge made it impossible for anyone but the possessor to get into the apartment, to begin with.

Widow looked left and looked right.

He searched the apartment, room by room, until he came face-to-face with a young girl, carrying a tray and wearing some kind of outfit that looked like she was playing a part in a rap music video.

She froze, stared at him, wide-eyed. She dropped the tray.

It fell to the floor and bounced on the tile, making a loud metal sound that echoed through the apartment.

Widow pointed the gun in her face.

She stayed quiet.

He was going to ask for Serafi, ask where he was in the apartment, but he didn't have to because Serafi spoke.

"Did you break something? That's gonna cost you, my dear!"

Widow put his hands up to his lips and told her to shush.

She nodded.

Widow stepped close so she could hear him and no one else.

He asked, "He on the balcony?"

"Yes."

"He alone?"

"Yes."

"You want to live?"

"Yes."

She spoke with a Ukrainian accent.

"You Russian?"

"Ukraine."

He looked her up and down, the fake eyes, fake hair, fake lips. He asked, "You a slave?"

"Yes."

"Traded to him?"

She nodded.

"How young?"

"Teenager."

He lowered the Glock.

"Go to your room. Get dressed. You got money?"

"No."

"He got cash around?"

She shrugged.

Widow reached into his pocket and pulled out the credit cards from Gade. He handed them to her.

"Take these. I'm sure you can find a way to get cash out."

She nodded and stared at him.

"Whatever you hear, don't come out on the balcony. Just go to your room, change, and get the hell out of here and never look back."

She nodded and smiled and took the cards, and ran down the hall out of sight.

Serafi called out from down a different hall that led out to the balcony.

"Are you listening to me?"

Widow walked down the hall, out to the balcony. He stepped out and found a short, thin Middle Eastern man smoking a cigar and reading a paper.

"Who the hell are you? How did you get in here?" Serafi said.

Widow smiled at him and took Gade's badge and license out of his pocket, tossed them on Serafi's lap.

"How did you get these?"

"I'm friends with Alaska Rower."

"Who is that? I don't understand?"

Widow pointed the Glock at him.

"Stand up."

Serafi's eyes went wide. He started looking around, desperately, as if someone was coming to save him.

No one came.

Serafi didn't stand up, so Widow grabbed him by the robe and hauled him to his feet.

He took him to the ledge to the railing and stared out over Lake Michigan.

Widow said, "Great view."

"I have money, girls, whatever you want."

Widow leaned forward with Serafi and looked down over the railing.

"How far down would you say that is?"

"What do you want? I have gold."

"Looks far."

Widow turned Serafi around and stared into his eyes.

"I want my friend back."

"Who? I can help."

"Alaska Rower was her name."

"Was?"

"You killed her."

Serafi's eye opened wider than Widow thought possible.

Widow threw him off over the railing, off the ledge, one-handed. Then he leaned forward and watched as the robed Saudi prince who'd killed his friend went falling to his death on a street in Chicago.

## 50

Widow hung around the fancy penthouse apartment long enough to shower and find clothes in Gade's closet that fit.

He knew it was Gade's because it was the only room that wasn't gold.

The clothes he chose were snug, but fit well enough. He found a pair of socks and an expensive pair of jeans and an expensive button-down shirt and a very expensive leather jacket. He also took a pair of shades off the dresser and one Rolex watch. He couldn't help himself on that one.

He had to settle with the same boots because Gade's feet were a size twelve, too small for Widow.

After he was finished grabbing some new duds for himself, he checked the rest of the apartment and found no one else. He heard the girl leaving. She wasn't alone. He heard two other female voices; both sounded like they had been asleep.

He figured it was the rest of Serafi's girls who lived in the apartment.

After Widow was sure that no one was left, he walked

through and wiped down everything that he remembered touching and took the service elevator down.

He kept the ski mask and wore it over his face on the way down and out of the building, the same as he had on the way in. That was for the cameras.

He fired up the Lexus and pulled out of the garage into the alley.

There, he heard a phone ring. It was Rower's. He had left it in the cupholder.

He answered it.

"Hello?"

A voice asked, "Is this Widow?"

"Depends. Who's this?"

"I'm Bukowski, Special Agent at the Minneapolis FBI Field Office."

"Yes?"

"I know about Rower."

Silence.

"I heard you were helping her. That you were there when she died."

"She was brave."

"She was a damn good agent."

"Yeah. I'm sorry."

Widow heard a *crack* in the guy's voice, the kind he had heard a million times in the Navy.

"Losing an agent is hard."

"It is."

Widow stayed quiet.

Bukowski said, "It never gets easy."

"No, it doesn't."

"Okay. So, what's next for you?"

"You're not gonna ask me to come back. Give a statement?"

"Would you come back?"

"I never go back."

Bukowski paused a beat and repeated his question.

"What will you do?"

"I don't know. Guess I'll see where the road takes me."

"Well, then. Good luck to you. I'd better go. We got a lot of cleaning up to do. A lot of paperwork. More investigations."

"Call up the Chicago office. Tell them to look for a guy named Serafi."

"Who's that?"

"Tell them to look through his life. And make sure they know that Alaska Rower found him. Make sure she gets the credit. Got it?"

"How will they find him?"

Widow heard sirens in the distance.

"Tell them. Okay. They'll find him."

He clicked off the phone—no goodbye.

Widow tossed the phone out the window and drove to the end of the alley. He stopped at a street that went in two directions. He looked left and looked right. He thought about which way to go.

THE STANDOFF: A PREVIEW

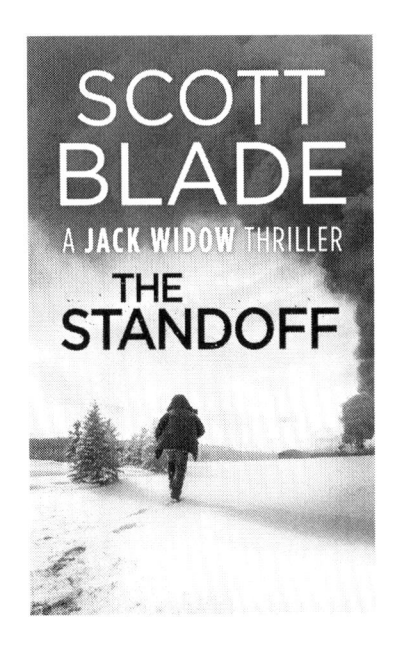

Out Now!

# THE STANDOFF: A BLURB

**A police raid gone horribly wrong.**
**A band of deadly cult-terrorists on the run.**
**A family held hostage.**
**One man no one counted on to be there—Jack Widow.**

When an ATF raid on a cult compound goes horribly wrong, the cult leader and his band of deadly terrorists escape.

On the run and desperate, they need a place to hide. A remote family farm makes for the perfect place. But there's one big problem. The family that lives there has a guest—a drifter they picked up by the name of Jack Widow.

*Widow, the ultimate loner, comes to a Standoff with pure evil in the million-selling action-thriller series.*

*Readers are saying...*

★★★★★ Dare I say it? Yes! Better than Jack Reacher!
★★★★★ Fantastic read....fast-paced!

# CHAPTER 1

Joseph Abel palmed a heavy, jagged rock in one hand and followed behind the guy he intended to bludgeon over the head with it, staying five feet back, giving the guy enough space to tempt him to make a run for it, but staying close enough to taunt him.

The guy wasn't young, wasn't old, but was right at the cusp of forty, which he considered to be the peak of his athletic lifespan. He played baseball in high school, which got him into college on a scholarship. But it didn't get him into the major leagues. It didn't get him into any leagues. He didn't play anymore. He made a different occupational choice.

His hair was fair, cut short. It was up off his ears, but coiffed and swirled like nature had decided that he would never need any hairbrush other than his own fingers to style it.

In regular life, he was a good-looking man, almost to a fault. His peers often referred to him as "Pretty Boy."

However, he wasn't that pretty anymore, not now. There was dried blood in his hair mixed in with the swirls. His nose wasn't broken, but it was swollen. He was certain that they could've broken it easily enough. But they didn't. Not so far. That could change.

Abel said things to tease the guy.

"Think if you run, you can make it to the trees?"

The guy stayed quiet.

"I dare you. Go for it."

The guy did nothing. Abel continued taunting him.

"You sure? Just take off. Go for it. Who knows? Maybe you'll get lucky."

Silence.

"We could give you a head start?"

Nothing.

"Would you like that? I can have my guys close their eyes and count to ten, like hide-and-seek. Think that's enough time for you to make it to the trees?"

The guy did nothing.

What Abel said or did to the guy depended on what the guy said or did.

So far, the guy said nothing and did what Abel told him to do. No protest. No conspiring to run. No plotting to fight back.

The guy knew that it didn't really matter what he did. Abel was never going to really give him a head start. If he took off running, he'd get a bullet in the back.

Either way, Abel was going to smash that rock over his head. There was no stopping it. *An unstoppable force meets an immovable object.* The rock was the unstoppable force, but his head was no immovable object. It was just an object, like pottery—very easy to smash with a big rock.

The guy was Abel's prisoner. He had been for eighteen long hours, ever since they set a trap for him, a trap he walked right into like a rookie cop like it had been his first time.

The trap involved a two-way radio that the guy thought

was well hidden in one of several abandoned structures that stood on the compound grounds. The structures were all there when they moved in. They came with the property, sort of an as-is kind of deal, like buying a house and having to take an old car that came with it.

The prisoner chose an old shed to hide the radio in. He had chosen it before he had ever even been there. He had seen it from aerial photographs, taken by drone. It was part of his preparation before coming to the compound.

The radio was a thin thing, black rubber with a hard plastic case.

The same remote-controlled law enforcement drone that took the recon photographs flew over the compound overnight and dropped the radio from less than a hundred feet in the air. It flew in quietly, emitting no more sound than a hum. It flew just over the tree line in order to avoid being seen.

Pretty Boy snuck out on his second night, while everyone else was asleep, and waited for it to show up overhead at a preset of approximate coordinates he had memorized before going undercover.

The drone flew overhead right on time and dropped the radio. It landed in the snow, between trees. Not exactly where Pretty Boy had rehearsed where it would land with his handler and agent in charge, but these things never went exactly according to plan, almost never. In fact, whenever something did go as planned, he usually questioned it as too good to be true. In undercover situations, when something's too good to be true, it doesn't just mean that it probably isn't true. It also means that it is probably a trap. Things didn't go off exactly how he planned, but it was close enough.

He stumbled right into the radio on his way to the shed. He should've taken it as an omen.

He should've known better.

Everything seemed fine for a while until one of the children caught him sneaking out on another night. He had been heading out to make one of his nightly radio checks. He couldn't make the radio check from inside the compound. At night, he slept in a huge room on a cot with twenty other cult initiates, all on cots like military boot camp.

At first, he thought his cover was intact because the children weren't supposed to be out after curfew, either. He and the children had converged accidentally, a stroke of bad luck. They met on the same exit point in the main building.

They all stopped dead in their tracks, the children too. They thought their parents had sent him out to find them, like a search party. And he thought he was dead in the water, busted right there. They were all concerned with covering their own butts.

Like a good undercover cop, he struck a deal with them. He made them promise not to say anything, and he would say nothing, silence for silence. It was a good trade. They had feared punishment from their parents if he turned them in. And he feared death. So, they agreed. He thought it was a solid agreement—a verbal contract, but children were the worst assets to have in an undercover situation because they're unpredictable and unreliable. Plus, kids don't keep secrets very well. He should've known, but he thought he was in the clear. He thought that if he could trust anyone, it would be the children. They wouldn't turn him in. He thought they would keep their end of the bargain. And they did...for almost one whole twenty-four-hour period—almost.

He was busted the next night.

The compound crowned the top of a thick forest in the middle of nowhere in northern South Carolina, twenty miles south of the border with North Carolina. It was nestled between a town called Carbine and a small county with miles and miles of half-abandoned farmland, dirt roads, and long stretches of unprotected forestland called Spartan County.

Spartan County met all of Abel's needs when he was picking out locations for his militant cult, which originally didn't start with the purpose of raising an army, but it evolved that way. Abel didn't start out with an ironclad purpose. He just started the cult and people came—unexplainably, the way cults often go. Families came. The lost came and joined—willingly, happily.

Over the years, he grew more and more ambitious. Leading a cult was supposed to be part of his retirement, a new chapter of life, but the longer time passed since his days in the Army, the more militant he grew.

Pretty Boy knew this. He had read the files over and over. He had memorized them. The good thing about the Army for law enforcement was that they kept impeccable records. They had files on Abel the size of the Oxford Dictionary. This included comprehensive psychological records and tests. Apparently, the Army had thought it prudent to force him to meet with a psychologist for a period of months, during his tenure in the military. Perhaps, it was because his unit had had the highest body count in Baghdad during Operation Iraqi Freedom perhaps because they had the highest number of allegations of cruel misconduct of any other security team during the long transition from the old Iraq to the new democratic version, post-Saddam Hussein.

No one knows the whole story, the whole picture, of why they had had enough of him. It was a where-there's-smoke-there's-fire kind of situation. Something about him rattled the brass because they did assign him and his team members to psychological observations.

Either way, none of it mattered now. None of the records

he read, none of the preparation he did, made any difference. He was caught now. He was Abel's prisoner.

Both Pretty Boy's hands were zip-tied tight behind his back. He knew the attack was coming. He knew that Abel wasn't marching him battered and broken just to set him free.

He was a condemned man.

To have hope at this point would almost be a blatant betrayal to himself, but he couldn't help it. Hope clawed at him. A human brain is a problem-solving machine, and self-preservation is the brain's number one priority. As he marched to his death, his brain continued to work out ways to survive. It calculated and assessed every option to get away that came along.

Hope is a tricky thing. It's hardwired deep in the brain like roots. It can't be shaken loose. It's too deep, too hardwired. Even though he knew that hoping was futile, his brain latched onto that hope like a bad drug that can't be beaten—once hooked, always hooked.

Pretty Boy couldn't make a run for it. But that was what he kept thinking about over and over.

*Go! Run!* His brain shouted to him. It taunted him as much as Abel had done as if they were working together, partners in torturing him. But he kept thinking it all out, calculating the odds.

If he ran flat-out as fast as he could, could he make the tree line? Could he make it to safety?

His instincts kept telling him to go for it—pushing him, but it would be pointless, and he knew it.

He would never make it—not in the snow, not in the cold temperatures, not in his weakened state, and not with his shattered morale. That was the biggest gut-punch. They had broken him the night before. Abel and his guys had stomped out most of the hope he had of being rescued. They literally stomped on him until he had nothing left.

Making a run for it wasn't going to work.

They would shoot him in the back.

No way could he outrun a bullet, and Abel and the six guys who followed behind him had plenty of bullets.

Pretty Boy didn't count all the bullets present, but he did count four fully automatic weapons and two shotguns, and that didn't cover all the guns on them.

He knew that Abel had a holstered Glock, which told him that the six guards also had sidearms. Altogether there must've been thirteen firearms among them. That meant possibly hundreds of loaded rounds with four of the weapons firing full auto—if they so wanted.

Not to mention the shotguns, which he figured were loaded with buckshot, most likely.

Buckshot is deadly at close range and often still deadly at mid-range and can even be deadly at the mid-to-long range. The guys with the shotguns behind him were close enough in range to cut him down before he ran to mid-range.

They would shoot him dead without having to reload.

There was no running away, not this time. His only hope was his backup swooping in at the last minute, like the cavalry does to save the day in a movie.

But real-life never works out like the movies.

He had no chance to run and no chance of fighting back.

Pretty Boy wore the same thick garb as the rest of the cult's newcomers: brown tunic-like clothes, somewhere between robes and medieval peasant gear. From the looks of it, the clothes they all wore was picked straight out of a cult catalog.

The cult's winter fashion line, he remembered joking

with Adonis when he first saw the clothes that he would be wearing.

The cult's garbs came in tiers, like military uniforms, each specifying one's status in the chain of command.

He was dressed in the lowest level of clothing offered to the cult's newest members, which meant that his outfit screamed to everyone that he was a newbie.

Even with the right garbs, Pretty Boy stuck out like a sore thumb to Abel.

Abel was suspicious of him almost straight away, which was sad for Pretty Boy because he had been an undercover agent for five years.

Ten days ago, he showed up at the gate with a group of outsiders, all wanting to get in, all wanting to join the cult.

In general, newbies showed up several times a month in small groups wanting to join. Many of them were militia rejects, the kind of people too extreme for typical militia groups.

Most militia groups tended to walk a fine line between extremism and simply having a fear of government. Most were in the business of knowing weapons, learning survival skills, and engaging in an overall sense of family. They tried to avoid extremists because they weren't in the business of terrorism. They only wanted to live their lives in the tradition of the American revolutionaries. Despite their political slants, they tended to live and let live. They kicked out extremists.

Therefore, extremists tended to be the people who showed up at Abel's gates. They were lost souls looking to belong, but lost souls with extreme views.

Abel didn't take on everyone who showed up. Unlike most militia groups, he sought out the extreme-minded as well as those who would die for their beliefs. Nothing's more dangerous than crazed martyr-like followers seeking someone to follow.

Many of those who sought out Abel was turned down. They didn't believe enough or didn't pass the smell test.

Pretty Boy wasn't the first undercover cop to try to infiltrate Abel's group, but he was the first to succeed.

When newbies showed up, the cult performed tests on them to make sure they were who they claimed to be. They wanted to make sure that newbies were earnest about their intent. They wanted to make sure there were no narcs.

The cult accompanied the tests with an unofficial background check. Pretty Boy was the first undercover agent to pass. He passed the background check and all their smell tests. No problem. He was in.

One of the tests was a series of questions. And one of the questions was how he had found out about the cult in the first place. The second was how he had gained entry to the testing phase.

Pretty Boy had learned the answers back during the briefing phase, preparing to go undercover.

Newbies heard of Abel and his followers in all kinds of different ways: the internet, the dark web, social media groups, and good, old-fashioned word of mouth.

Word of mouth generally came from outside militia groups who were like-minded. Often people who joined militia groups were kicked out because they were too extreme or unhinged, or they were searching for a religious element.

That was when someone in the group would take them aside and tell them about this place in South Carolina.

Someone would ask, "Have you heard of Joseph Abel?"

It was the story of Abel that interested people, but it was his unexplainable, undeniable charismatic persona that captured them.

Abel was a myth among the militant, among the conspiracy theorists, among the backwoods survivalists.

New recruits came from all over. Most of them were lost souls with nowhere to go. Some of them felt misunderstood in their own lives. Some of them knew of the anti-government positions of Abel, and they wanted to join for those reasons. They shared the same sentiments.

Whatever the reasons for joining up, everyone who came turned into a true believer before long—all but one. And now he was caught, beaten, zip-tied, and marching to his own death.

The undercover agent had ridden in with a small group from fifty miles north of Atlanta at a designated recruitment center, which was an old, run-down church with a pastor who favors the extremist side of religion.

A building attached to the back of the church existed as a halfway house, used by the state for battered and abused women, as well as former junkies, and other lost souls.

As soon as Pretty Boy got there, they tested him.

It all went down like the whirling water in a draining bathtub. Before he knew it, he was sucked down the drain with the rest of them.

First, he passed their tests. Next, they took all his earthly possessions.

"Shake loose your mortal ways," Abel preached the newbies, "This is a fine day for you. You're no longer lost. We're your family now."

Once Pretty Boy was sucked down the drain, they tore off his clothes and shoved him into brown garbs, like a new inmate joining the general population of a maximum-security prison for the first time.

He believed they made all their own clothes. Later, he

confirmed this when he saw the women cutting and sewing and cleaning fabrics.

The fabric and many other goods were picked up by two of Abel's guys who went to Carbine, he guessed. They must've had several large P.O. boxes restricted for deliveries and shipments of materials they needed.

The guys who went never came back empty-handed. There were always shipments of something—grains, ingredients, supplies, and fabrics.

After they clothed him, Abel's men asked him to do two things.

First, they gave him back his old clothes and his wallet and his cheap burner phone; he had bought it at a gas station. It was packed with fake contacts, and phone calls made to numbers that correlated with his fake undercover identity—in case they went far enough to check all that out, which they didn't.

Over a roaring backyard fire, they made him toss his old things into the fire, including the burner phone, which the agency he worked for had anticipated—naturally. That's why they gave him general coordinates of where he could expect the tiny radio he got to be airdropped in during the night.

The radio was all he thought about as he watched his fake stuff burn.

The second thing they made him do—over the fire and over his burning possessions—was pledge his undying allegiance to Joseph Abel and to the Athenian cause. All of that done in some weird half-religious, half-militant ceremony.

He wished he could go back and turn down this assignment. But hindsight was always twenty-twenty.

Wasn't it?

Pretty Boy started at the lowest level and, therefore, wore brown, representing the muck and the dirt.

The Athenians considered all newcomers to come from the muck. All those from off the street, all those who were newly pledged, were the uninitiated, the unenlightened, commoners, the filth.

Joseph Abel, however, wore all-pristine, all-white garbs—white pullover under a white winter coat and white pants with newly washed white underwear underneath. He wore all white all the way down to the laces on his boots and the threads in the socks over his feet.

His uniform signified that he was the highest-ranking member of his cult, higher than a bishop in a church. He was the pope. Therefore, his uniform had to be the cleanest and most immaculate and the whitest of all the dress of all the members—always.

Everything was designed to remind his followers of their lower station.

Abel did as the kings and clergies of old history did by making their followers kneel or stand below them when conversing, only he did it with clothing. He showed them who they were, which was nothing. And he was everything.

It was all about status.

Abel's dress and mannerisms and stature were to be held above all others.

He was their leader, their king, their savior.

Cleanliness is next to godliness. That was one motto he lived by. He exemplified it to them not just by making himself always appear cleaner than they were, but also by putting them to work every day so that their own clothes and bodies remained dirty and sweaty and beneath him.

"You serve the Lord, and the Lord will provide," he preached to them.

Abel's clothes were always clean. Theirs were not. It was that simple.

His laundry was done every single day. One of his wives made sure of that. It was her job to make sure that it was so. And she did a fine job. They all did fine jobs.

He would miss them—in a way—after the thing, he planned to happen did happen.

The discovery of the undercover agent ruined his plans in a way. He wanted to linger longer and enjoy his five wives, but that time had passed. The discovery of the undercover agent moved up the timetable. No big deal. He was ready. They were ready. It was time to act. The thing he planned to happen would happen soon, at least the first part.

His followers knew of the first part. They were part of the first part. They didn't know the exact plans of the second act. They thought both acts went together like a one-two punch. They didn't know that their sacrifice wasn't the main act. It was only the distraction, the announcement.

The second part would come in the form of a major terror attack on the real terrorists—members of the US government. The Deep State was his enemy. They were the real enemy of the people, as he saw it.

He promised his followers that the attack would send terror tremors across the United States and the world. It would echo through the halls of power. It would be worth their sacrifice.

Abel tracked behind Pretty Boy through a field of snow, with the tops of dead wheatgrass, half-leafless trees, and white-misted sky.

He slowed and stopped.

He knew it wasn't their final stop, but he had a flair for the theatrical, the drama of forcing the guy to walk to his own death, finding the right spot, and then pushing onward to a different stop, teasing him, taunting him—predator and prey.

It amused him, but this was nearing the end of the line for Pretty Boy.

Abel couldn't keep this up forever. Things needed to be done. Preparations needed to be made. And explosives needed to be checked and rechecked.

Plus, it was no fun anymore. Boredom had set in and displaced the joy he had enjoyed.

Pretty Boy lost all hope—mostly. Therefore, he lost his fear, and no fear meant acceptance, and acceptance meant no fun for Abel.

A man at the end of his rope was no fun to torment with the theatrics of hope or last moments of life because he has no last moments. He had nothing left to lose.

\* \* \*

Before the military, before Abel rose through the ranks in the Army to the title of general, before he was a revered cult leader, he had been a hunter.

He was a natural-born hunter. That was what he was good at.

Way back in the Tennessee woods, as a boy, he'd hunted with his father. That was back fifty-plus years by now.

For Abel, the fun in hunting wasn't about the ritual or the cycle of life or any of that nonsense. The fun came from the savoring, the relishing of the kill. That was what he loved.

Abel liked to hunt, and he liked to kill, and he liked to taunt—as simple as that.

He saw war the same way. That's what made him so good at it.

In war, you can't win by defeating the enemy. That's where Abel and ninety-nine percent of the military disagreed.

Simply winning never works, not in the long-term. Simply

winning doesn't work because enemies come back. They evolve.

Victories last only until the enemy's ranks replenish.

Abel often preached in his sermons about defeating the enemy.

Every Sunday, he preached to his followers from the grand, white steps of the compound's main building. He used to preach in the church that was off closer to the main driveway, but the population of his cult had grown too big.

Now, he did his preaching outside, and he did it almost every day at the same time.

Pretty Boy had witnessed one of these sermons. He remembered it.

Abel stood on the steps as usual and preached.

"You can't just defeat the enemy. You must do more. You must take the extra step. You can't just crush the enemy. You must crush the enemy's spirit. You must crush their hopes. You must dash all sense of who they are from the history books. You must beat them into unquestionable submission. That's the only true way to win a war."

As Abel finished this sermon, he stared down at the undercover agent. Chills ran down his spine as if Abel was threatening him directly. This was the sermon he had heard before they set a trap for him. He should've known. He should've escaped then, but he didn't.

Abel used to be in charge of a special Army unit. They were assigned to clean up the insurgents in Baghdad. They were good at it. They had been dubbed the Baghdad Cleaners by their peers. Abel and his crew got a reputation as "shoot first, ask questions later" types. They killed a lot of bad guys, which explained why the Army hadn't interfered with their unsavory methods.

Back then, Abel had a motto that he preached to his guys.

"Leave no enemy behind," a twist on "leave no man behind."

Abel believed this principle down to his core. It was the same as "win at all costs." That was why he was so good at war. At least, he thought so, and so did the Army apparently because they kept promoting him. They kept protecting him from allegations of war crimes. They kept burying the truth as long as it suited their goals.

He was good at his job. His team delivered results—no question. If they were given an Iraqi target to prosecute, they found him, and they killed him—period, point-blank.

During his tenure in Iraq, the Army gave him freedom of action. They called it all Black Ops and turned a blind eye while he and his crew did their thing.

Abel spent years in the US Special Forces, which let him do the things he loved to do—hunt and kill.

He hunted the enemy, he killed the enemy, and they paid him to do it.

As the war wound down, they couldn't look the other way anymore, not with journalists having more and more access to company units within the military. When the dust settled, people noticed things. Questions came up, too many for the Army to ignore.

They took away his job.

They had to put the muzzle back on him, but they didn't want to fire him. You don't fire your broadsword. You sheath it and hope for the best. In the end, they didn't fire him. They didn't demote him. They promoted him.

They made him a one-star general and gave him a medal and assigned him to his very own command. Essentially, they made him into a glorified desk jockey. They assigned him to one of the worst commands a general can get, a place with a bad reputation—bad because it was notoriously boring, which was spirit-crushing for a guy like Abel.

They'd sent him to Fort Polk in Louisiana, which was nicknamed Fort Puke by those who served there.

To other generals, there was no bad place to get a command, but that was because they were on a career path only, and Abel wasn't. He didn't join the army so he could advance his career and retire, not after having tasted what it was like to hunt and kill in the Middle East. Especially, not after it took him over a decade to meet like-minded soldiers and Marines and a couple of sailors.

By this time in his career, Abel had assembled a like-minded group, a group that would follow him to the ends of the earth—blindly.

He had found a core group of guys, of killers just like him. They all left their posts shortly after he did—all honorable discharges. Each of them waited out the remaining time on his contract. Then they left their respective military homes and joined up with him, becoming Athenians.

By the time Jargo, the most recent addition, joined him, Abel was already established as the leader of a cult, right there in South Carolina.

\*\*\*

Pretty Boy's real name wasn't Cain like in the Bible. His real name was officially ATF Agent Tommy Dorsch.

Abel knew his name. They all did. They knew everything about him that needed knowing. He couldn't keep secrets from them. They had ways of seeing to that.

Dorsch's hands hurt from the zip ties. His face hurt from the fists he had endured the night before. His body ached. His mind ached.

"Keep moving," Abel barked.

Abel shoved him with a quick left jab. He had grown tired of his prey, and Dorsch knew it.

Dorsch looked forward and to the right and saw old playground equipment covered by blankets of snow. Old metal pieces from a merry-go-round stuck up and out of the snow and dead grass. One end of a seesaw punched almost straight up and tilted a certain way as if it had been forever stuck in that position.

The cult had lived on the compound for so long by this point that the latest generation of children had been born there and raised there. All of them were young, under six years of age. Older children were brought in by members from the outside but were sent away, off to boarding schools.

Before six, they were trained and brainwashed into the ways of the Athenians so that when they went off to school, they would maintain their core beliefs and question everything else they were taught. But it was decided that they needed to be sent to boarding school every year for two reasons. The first was to meet the state's requirements for education for any child. The Athenians got tax breaks and all kinds of benefits for operating as a religion and church. And the second reason was that Abel wanted them to learn the evil ways of the outside world in order to cement the community's mistrust in it.

It all worked in tandem like he was setting up the perfect biosphere of people who lived and breathed as he saw fit.

In school, the kids would learn about evolution, but it was already instilled in them how false and fake the outside world was.

In the far distance, a train horn blasted for a long moment, breaking the silence, giving Dorsch a newfound, but brief hope. This was a reminder of the civilized world; he had almost forgotten the outside world existed.

Dorsch knew the train was far away because there were no sounds of singing tracks or train cars rushing by or a bell from street crossings.

Still, he listened raptly, feeling his blood rush through him with the fury of a river. His heart pounded in his chest as if his body was gearing up for one last attempt to save his own ass, but he did nothing. He didn't run. He didn't fight back. He didn't resist. Nothing changed.

The horn blared once more. Then it died away like an echo lost at sea. With the vanishing train horn, he was left with one image of the outside world. It vanished completely a long second later.

"Move," Abel barked again, not ultra-aggressively, not authoritatively, not forcefully, just low and calm and commanding, like a doctor soothing a sick patient. Only, a gleam of joy sparked across his face as if he enjoyed it, which he did.

He didn't hide it from Dorsch. He savored it right in front of him.

They walked on, continuing past the snow-buried playground equipment, past more leafless trees, far from the compound, far from the road, and far from the eyes of others in the community.

They walked beyond the center of Abel's farm-sized property, beyond more empty fields of snow, past more trees until they came to another open field—the last one.

They stood two-thirds of the way across the compound's entire property.

Now, there was no chance that anyone who Abel didn't want to see would see what was going to happen next. Unless they decided to shoot Dorsch, no one would hear anything either.

Dorsch felt the last remaining ounce of hope that he had left deflated from him like air from a balloon. He shouldn't have had any hope left anyway. He knew that because he was all alone.

The only people there were the people who lived on the property and him—the outsider.

His own people weren't coming for him. He knew that now. His backup wasn't coming. They were in the dark. They didn't know he was about to die.

His boss and friend, Agent Adonis, wasn't coming for him.

He wasn't going anywhere. He was Abel's prisoner till the day he died—today.

The sky above became overcast and turned gloomy and gray, like a painter's used-up mixing pallet.

South Carolina was in a polar vortex that swept across the nation, lasting a long time, turning the temperatures in the US down to record-low levels. Snow and violent winds bombarded states that normally never saw snow.

Abel was grateful for the momentary release in the weather. In a sick way, he believed the slowing of the snow was a sign from God. And he'd told this to his followers that very morning.

Since the train horn, the air around them filled with sounds of whooshing wind and distant noises of cracking branches and swaying trees and dead silence and nothing else.

Despite the hopelessness, despite the dead silence, Dorsch listened hard. He closed his eyes and slowed his walk to a shuffle.

At first, Abel thought Dorsch was praying. He couldn't fault the guy for doing that. He was, after all, a man of God, himself. So, he said nothing, but Dorsch wasn't praying. He was listening, trying to make out another sound that he thought he had heard.

He heard a distant buzzing sound breakthrough the rustling wind. It was far off and faint. It was somewhere in that realm of maybe it was there, or maybe his mind was playing tricks on him.

At first, he wasn't sure.

Dorsch ceased his forward shuffling and stopped and stared up at the sky, his eyes darting left, darting right, desperately searching. Frantic.

He needed to find what he was looking for. He needed to see it. He needed it to be the ATF's spy drone. He needed to know that they had sent it to find him—to save him. He needed to know that Adonis hadn't forsaken him, that his service to his country had meant something.

He needed these things to happen, to see it above them, but there was nothing. He saw nothing in the sky, no drone, no backup—nothing.

Abel stopped behind Dorsch and looked to the sky with him. He looked left, looked right, and mockingly followed Dorsch's gaze.

The six armed men who patrolled behind them also stopped, just like a group of highly trained bodyguards for a Middle Eastern dictator.

Each of the armed guards slowly scattered around Abel and Dorsch, forming a wide circle.

Abel asked, "What're you looking for?"

Dorsch stayed quiet.

"Are you looking for one of those drones?"

Dorsch stayed quiet.

"You think it's out there?"

Dorsch stared up at the sky.

"You think it can see you?"

Abel stepped forward, and with his free hand, he snatched Dorsch by the collar and spun him around so that they were face-to-face so that he could see into the agent's eyes.

Abel pulled in close and whispered to him.

"There's no drone. No one's coming for you. No one."

Abel breathed in and breathed out, slowly and jeeringly.

Dorsch could smell his breath.

"They wouldn't see us anyway. They'd have to send the drone down to see. Too much cloud cover, you see? Too much winter grey."

Dorsch breathed again.

Abel said, "Well, not unless they had infrared lenses strapped on it. Like we had in the Army, which they don't. Not for you. They're not going to waste that on you. I'm surprised they even bothered using a drone for you in the first place. Does the ATF even have infrared lenses on their drones?"

Dorsch stayed quiet.

"We did."

Abel breathed once more. Then he shoved Dorsch hard in the chest, forcing him to stumble backward, almost falling over, but he didn't.

Dorsch stayed standing and stayed quiet and stayed defeated.

Abel saw in Dorsch's eyes a single shred of hope, of resistance, possibly.

They hadn't broken him completely, not as Abel had thought, but enough was enough. He had things to do, things to prepare. He had an operation to oversee. He couldn't be out here all day, tormenting this guy, despite how much fun he was having.

They were surrounded by acres and acres of rolling,

snow-covered hills and dark trees. The sounds of stillness echoed across the sky, killing off any notion left in Dorsch's mind that he had heard a drone buzzing overhead.

In fact, the buzzing hadn't been there at all. It was his mind playing tricks on him, giving him a delusion of hope, like a mirage in the desert.

Abel breathed again, coldly, calmly like before. He could see his own breath. He could see Dorsch's breath. He could see the thick air around them.

Without a command from Abel, Dorsch assumed they were moving on; he turned and stumbled forward, again, weak, barely able to walk straight, partially from external bruises, partially from internal bruises and partially from sleep deprivation.

Blood was near-frozen on his face from being pummeled all night by six sets of hardened fists, fists that had pummeled a lot of people over the course of their existence. They were the kinds of fists that knew how to hold back and how not to. For him, they hadn't held back.

Dorsch had one black eye, and his nose was broken. Plus, he was pretty sure that he had at least two cracked ribs. Possibly, he had internal injuries other than cracked bones, but he wasn't sure of that. Most of the pain was merged into one overshadowing, continuously throbbing pain by this point.

The six armed men who surrounded him and Abel had the sets of fists that had pounded him into hopelessness the night before. He stopped stumbling and stood up as straight as he could and looked at them.

It was the first time that he noticed that they were no longer following behind him. Now, they were staying back, but flanking him and Abel in a wide circle. Then they all stopped and stood guard.

Dorsch took note of their weapons, again.

The six men were armed with serious weapons: assault rifles, a couple of shotguns, and one sniper rifle slung behind a guy's back by a shoulder strap as if it was the most important thing to him in the entire world.

They were all big guys, probably spent enough time in the gym between them to compete in all the Olympic Strong Man competitions and come away with the gold.

Two of them were above average height while three circled around six feet, and one was short and stocky.

The tallest one was a black guy armed with an M4 assault rifle. He stood a hair over six-foot-four.

The sniper was the next one down in height. He was over six feet tall. If he hadn't been that tall, the stock of the sniper rifle on his back would've been dragging behind him in the snow. It was a massive rifle.

Dorsch recognized it as a fifty-caliber, a very deadly rifle that fired a bullet that could punch a fist-sized hole through an engine block.

They were all former soldiers who used to swear their allegiance to their country, but now they swore it to Abel.

Dorsch looked at Abel. He saw the rock. He looked past it and saw a Glock was burrowed down in a holster on Abel's left hip, under the white winter coat. The holster stuck out like a sore thumb because it was the only thing he wore that wasn't all white.

Abel didn't brandish his weapon, not the Glock; instead, he squeezed his hand around the heavy stone, plucked from a rock quarry in the trees at the back end of the compound where a river zigzagged through the corner of the property.

He held the rock, gripping it tightly, keeping it down at his side, but visible. Every time Dorsch looked at Abel, he saw the rock, as if an unseen spotlight was trained on it.

Abel stood still. He watched Dorsch for a moment, studying him.

Abel had a look in his eyes, unlike any that Dorsch had ever seen before. In the academy, in his last five years working for the ATF, he took a lot of courses and read a lot of books and attended a lot of seminars about criminal psychosis and criminal behavior. A theme that always struck him in those courses was that criminals are often good people gone bad, as if there was some kind of redeeming quality about them, always lingering under the surface, as if they could be saved.

He saw none of that in Abel's eyes. There was no good left in him—no hope of redemption. There was pure evil.

Even though Dorsch had stopped moving, Abel barked an order at him.

"Stop right there."

Dorsch froze and stared at Abel. He looked down at the heavy rock again.

Abel said, "Face away."

Dorsch paused at first. Then he turned back to face away from Abel. He locked eyes with the tall black guy, who stared back and smiled, just a slow, demented grin, but its presence there was big and obvious.

"On your knees."

Dorsch didn't argue. He had no arguing left. He dropped to his knees. They slammed and sank down deep in the snow like two heavy cement blocks.

Abel saw Dorsch's breath again; only this time, it was heavy and frantic.

Abel stayed back for a moment, watching, enjoying, almost salivating. Then he spoke, asking a question that seemed way off in left field.

"Do you know your Bible?"

Dorsch stayed quiet at first, and then he nodded.

"That's not a very reassuring answer, but okay. It's not a sin to not know it. It's not one of the Ten Commandments to memorize the Bible."

Dorsch didn't answer.

"Do you know the story of Cain and Abel?"

"Of course."

His speech was a little battered, a little irregular, which happens when a trained, retired Special Forces operator slams the butt of an M4 into your jaw a couple of times, followed by his crew using their fists to pummel your face and torso.

Dorsch felt shame that he hadn't lasted longer through their beating him, but he was no soldier. He hadn't been trained by the military or ever seen any combat, not like these guys. What was he supposed to do? He was terrified for his life.

Abel saw the guy thinking. He didn't wait for him to finish his thought. Abel spoke anyway.

"Cain said unto Abel, 'Abel, let's go out into the fields.'"

Abel paused at the end and looked down at Dorsch.

"And Abel followed."

Dorsch stayed quiet. Fear overtook his face.

"We're out in the fields now. You can't tell because it's winter. Because of the polar vortex, we've got all this white snow. But we are. During the warm seasons, these fields grow things for us. We live off what God provides. You see?"

Abel looked around, waved his stoneless hand out in front of him, and brushed it over the vastness of hills and trees and snow and silence as if he were giving a sermon to a crowd of followers who weren't there.

"You hear that?"

Dorsch looked over the same vastness and listened.

"No. I hear nothing."

"Exactly. Nothing. No flapping helicopter blades. No

pitter-patter of SWAT boots on the ground. No ATF reinforcements. No FBI. No police. Not even a single drone. Where're your people now?"

Dorsch didn't answer.

"You've been forsaken, my son."

Dorsch stayed quiet.

"I'll tell you where they are. They're regrouping. They're huddled up someplace, planning, talking, scheming. You see, that's what people who work for your government do. They sit in their offices and make their career off your backs. They scheme. They're all about schemes and plans and asking permission. They don't live. They're not free. Not like us. Here."

Dorsch thought about his wife. He thought about the woman he loved. It wasn't her. He thought about his lover. He thought about how he wanted to leave his wife for her. Then he thought about guilt.

He looked over the horizon, past the trees and overcast sky. A dark object darted out in front of the clouds igniting his hope once again, like gasoline on a single flame. He thought, for one second, that it might be the drone after all, but it wasn't. It was a bird, just a blackbird, probably separated from its flock.

Abel saw Dorsch looking, once again. He glanced back fast and saw the same blackbird. He knew the thoughts that Dorsch was having. It was written across his face. There was another sudden burst of hope, which, like before, took a sudden nosedive into despair.

"Ah, a lost bird. A bird lost from its flock. Like you."

A fresh, single tear formed Dorsch's face. He said nothing.

Abel asked, "You know what that is?"

"A crow?"

"Know what they call a group of crows, don't ya?"

Dorsch didn't answer, but he knew. Everyone knew.

"They don't call it a flock. They call it a murder of crows. But that's a lone bird. He's not in a group."

Abel paused a beat and said, "That's a bird looking for a murder."

Suddenly, Dorsch burst into a pleading tantrum—uncontrollable and compulsory, which put a smile on Abel's face. They had broken him.

"Don't kill me! Please! They'll trade for me!"

"What'll they trade?"

"Your freedom! All of you! They'll negotiate! You can go free! Your people can go free!"

Silence.

Dorsch took a long breath. He spoke again in that battered voice.

"They'll come for me. They'll come to take you-all out if you kill me. People will die. Is that what you want? Your people are at risk. Don't you want them to live? They follow you. They trust in you. You can save them."

Abel held the heavy stone out in front of Dorsch. He raised it to his waist. Then he bent down and showed it to him. He clutched it in his boney hands like a pro ball pitcher clutches a baseball.

Dorsch said, "They'll come for me! Soon! They'll come with a hundred agents! They'll come with more firepower than you've got! Everyone will die!"

In a cold whisper, Abel said, "I'm counting on it."

With a sudden explosion of violence and force and power and rage and berserker, Abel leaped up on the balls of his feet, raised the heavy stone, one-handed, and thumped it down on top of Dorsch's head in the dead center of the agent's fair-haired swirls.

The stone cracked his skull.

Abel heard it. The men circling him heard it. Animals not hibernating in the trees around them heard it.

The murderless crow heard it.

The guy's skull *cracked* like cheap pottery versus a sledgehammer.

Blood splattered out and sprayed all over the white snow and covered the front of Abel's pristine, all-white garb that his wife had worked so hard to clean. And he thought nothing of it. He had other outfits in his wardrobe.

One fatal blow was all it took.

Dorsch slumped forward. Abel stepped back and watched the guy's body fall and hit the snow.

The guy's eyes stayed open—lifeless. His fingers twitched behind him.

Blood continued to percolate out of the huge crack in Dorsch's head and skull.

Abel stopped moving away. He crouched on his haunches to avoid getting more blood on his clothes or on his boots and stared closely at the Dorsch, watching him die.

Abel didn't hit him a second time, although the temptation was there. He just stared at the gouge in the top of the man's head. He watched the cherry red blood surge out like a slow-erupting volcano.

After a long minute, Abel stood up and dropped the rock. One side of it was soaked in blood; the other was clean. The rock thudded on the snowy ground.

He turned to his men and shot each of them a glance and a smile, one by one.

"They'll be coming."

"When?" one of them asked.

"By morning. We can count on it. He missed at least one radio check. Get to the tunnel. Make sure it's not compromised and double-check the van. The engine. The weapons. The bombs. All of it. No mistakes."

One of his other guys nodded because that meant him.

Another asked, "What about the body?"

"Leave it. They'll probably see him with one of those drones they've been flying around us. A visual confirmation that their inside agent is dead will speed things up. Or not. Won't make no difference."

Abel looked at his watch and noted the time.

"They'll be setting up around us by morning. Don't you boys worry. The federal government is punctual if nothing else."

All seven men walked away, back to the compound.

They left the dead ATF agent sprawled out on the snow in his own blood.

# THE JACK WIDOW BOOK CLUB

Building a relationship with my readers is the very best thing about writing. I occasionally send newsletters with details on new releases, special offers and other bits of news relating to the Jack Widow Series.

If you are new to the series, you can join the Jack Widow Book Club and get the starter kit.

Sign up for exclusive free stories, special offers, access to bonus content, and info on the latest releases, and coming soon Jack Widow novels. Sign up at www.scottblade.com.

## THE NOMADVELIST
NOMAD + NOVELIST = NOMADVELIST

Scott Blade is a Nomadvelist, a drifter and author of the breakout Jack Widow series. Scott travels the world, hitchhiking, drinking coffee, and writing.
Jack Widow has sold over a million copies.
Visit @: ScottBlade.com
Contact @: scott@scottblade.com
Follow @:
Facebook.com/ScottBladeAuthor
Bookbub.com/profile/scott-blade
Amazon.com/Scott-Blade/e/B00AU7ZRS8

Printed in Great Britain
by Amazon